MONTEZUMA'S MAN

Books by Jerome Charyn

MONTEZUMA'S MAN
BACK TO BATAAN
MARIA'S GIRLS
MARGOT IN BAD TOWN
(Illustrated by Massimo Frezzato)
BILLY BUDD, KGB
(Illustrated by François Boucq)
ELSINORE
THE GOOD POLICEMAN
MOVIELAND
THE MAGICIAN'S WIFE
(Illustrated by François Boucq)
PARADISE MAN
METROPOLIS
WAR CRIES OVER AVENUE C
PINOCCHIO'S NOSE
PANNA MARIA
DARLIN' BILL
THE CATFISH MAN
THE SEVENTH BABE
SECRET ISAAC
THE FRANKLIN SCARE
THE EDUCATION OF PATRICK SILVER
MARILYN THE WILD
BLUE EYES
THE TAR BABY
EISENHOWER, MY EISENHOWER
AMERICAN SCRAPBOOK
GOING TO JERUSALEM
THE MAN WHO GREW YOUNGER
ON THE DARKENING GREEN
ONCE UPON A DROSHKY

Edited by Jerome Charyn

THE NEW MYSTERY

MONTEZUMA'S MAN

■

JEROME CHARYN

THE MYSTERIOUS PRESS

Published by Warner Books

A Time Warner Company

Mysterious Press books are published by
Warner Books, Inc., 1271 Avenue of the Americas, New York, NY 10020

A Time Warner Company

The Mysterious Press name and logo are trademarks of Warner Books, Inc.
Printed in the United States of America

First printing: August 1993

10 9 8 7 6 5 4 3 2 1

Library of Congress Cataloging-in-Publication Data

Charyn, Jerome.
    Montezuma's man / Jerome Charyn.
        p.   cm.
    ISBN 0-89296-461-8
    1. Nez Percé Indians—Fiction.   I. Title.
PS3553.H33M65   1993
813'.54—dc20   92-50539
                                                        CIP

For Laura and Marco

Part One

1

He was descended from the Pierced Noses, or Nez Percé, a tribe that never mutilated prisoners or abandoned its own people. Its most celebrated warrior, Chief Joseph, guarded women, children, and old men during the Nez Percé uprising of 1877, after gold miners and speculators seized tribal lands in Idaho and Oregon. Joe Barbarossa was named after this noncombatant chief of the Nez Percé. He'd had five or six grandmas; his papa was a bigamist who kept losing wives.

One of the grandmas was the daughter of an Indian girl who fled into the mountains with Chief Joseph. But he couldn't remember her. He'd been shopped around as a kid, because of the many wives. Joe was Irish, Italian, Nez Percé, with a pinch of African blood.

He'd grown up in Oregon and California and the shanty towns of Illinois. He didn't have a native state. He was born in Oklahoma, but his papa was only passing through. He'd had a little brother, Lem, and a crop of half sisters. Lem drowned when he was nine. And one of the half sisters, Rosalind, had raised Joe. She'd never had a childhood, this Roz, and she was constantly trying to kill herself. All the other half sisters had disappeared on Joe. His blood mother, whom he'd hardly ever seen, was dead. His papa had abandoned Joe between his sixth or seventh marriage. Roz was the only kin he had.

It was Roz who got him through high school, who found his birth certificate when Joe decided to join the marines. She invented a past for him, a continuous line he couldn't have had without her. Joe went to Vietnam. It was 1972. He was assigned to the American Embassy in Saigon. He started to peddle drugs. He became familiar with the spooks working out of the Embassy's second floor. He played pingpong with them, supplied them with "pharmaceuticals." But there were rival gangs of dealers, soldiers like himself. He had to kill a couple, or get killed. He was one of the last Americans to leave Vietnam alive.

He became a cop in New York City, but he seemed to have little in common with other cops, or soldiers who'd served in Nam. He'd never seen "Charlie" in the bush. Saigon was like a mixture of Times Square and downtown El Paso. It was his own Little United States.

He tolerated Manhattan. He sold drugs. He was shot several times by dealers who were the same drug soldiers from Nam. But they didn't have a gold shield, like Joe. He captured muggers and bandits on the F train and was banging up people all over the place. But the PC, Isaac Sidel, banished him to squirrel land, the Central Park Precinct, because Joe was getting a little too careless, knocking off dealers who were close to the FBI.

Joe lived in the back room of a pingpong parlor on Columbus Avenue. That was his only address other than his sister's old apartment, which he used as a mail drop. Joe never slept there. All his clothes were at the pingpong parlor. It reminded him of the gambling clubs in Saigon. Joe used the pingpong parlor's last table as his desk. The table had been retired. Isaac's own blue-eyed boy, Manfred Coen, had been killed at this table, zapped by a Chinese-Cuban bandit. And Schiller, who owned the club on Columbus, had adored Coen, but he let Joe conduct his business from the table. He made no comparisons between Blue Eyes and Joe Barbarossa. Joe didn't have that crazy passion for pingpong.

He wore a white glove on his playing hand. He'd burned the hand while he was in Saigon. He'd fallen on a hot stove, fighting with a dealer. The hand never healed. The skin was always peeling and had a permanent gray color. And Joe would wear a fresh glove every day.

He was sitting behind the pingpong table, going over his accounts, when Schiller hollered to him from the spectators' gallery. "Phone call."

Barbarossa hollered back. "If it's police business, I'm not at home."

"It's your sister, Joey."

He picked up the wireless phone from its berth under the table and said, "Hello, Roz." His hand was shaking. He could hear the clack of balls from the other tables. But the club turned quiet. Players and kibitzers respected his privacy, and they didn't even know about his suicidal sister.

"I'm getting married, Joe."

"Where and when?"

"I'm not fooling. If I have a husband, he can sign me out of here."

"He wouldn't live long enough," Joe said.

"You're a fucking evil little prick . . . you lock me up because you can't stand the idea that I might be with a man. I hate you, Joe, with all my heart."

"Roz," he said, "I'll be right there."

He returned the phone to its crib. His ears were ringing. His hand twitched under the glove. All action had stopped at the other tables. There was a maddening burn in his eyes.

"Joey," Schiller shouted, "when will you be back?"

"Soon," he said. "Maybe never."

"If somebody calls, what should I tell them?"

"That I'm lost, out of commission. Say I'm dead."

"God forbid, Joey. God forbid."

He got into a cab outside the club. The driver didn't want to take him to Riverdale. "I'm going to Brooklyn, bub."

"No you're not. It's police business."

"Yeah," the driver said, "everybody's a cop."

Barbarossa shoved his gold badge into the driver's face.

"I eat badges," the driver said.

Barbarossa had to take out his Glock. It was an Austrian handgun with a plastic shell that made it look like a fancy toy.

"Fucking cap pistol," the driver said, and then he searched Barbarossa's eyes. "Riverdale. All right."

He drove west onto the highway, crossed the Henry Hudson Bridge, went up Kappock Avenue, and started to cry. Barbarossa looked at the name on his hack license: Leonard F. Furie.

"What's the matter, Leonard?"

"You're gonna kill me, aint you? You'll pick a deserted spot. And then you'll whack me. You're the Bronx Bandit."

"I'm a cop. I work out of Sherwood Forest . . . the precinct in Central Park."

"Sherwood Forest," said the driver, Leonard Furie, and almost crashed into a tree. "I can't go on. I'm too scared."

"Move over, Leonard. I'll drive."

And Barbarossa had to hop out of the car, climb into the front, and displace Leonard Furie. He bumped along Palisade Avenue, watching Leonard in the mirror. "If you try something stupid, I'll break your back."

They arrived at a walled mansion near the Hebrew Home for the Aged. The mansion had no letter box, not even a simple signpost. Barbarossa got out and handed Leonard two twenty-dollar bills, but Leonard wouldn't take them.

"You are the Bandit, aint you?"

"Yeah, Leonard. It's my passion. Killing cab drivers."

And Barbarossa marched through a tiny opening in the mansion's front wall. He'd entered the grounds of a sanitarium that was very discreet. It was called Macabee's. But you couldn't find it in the phone book. Macabee's never advertised itself. It cared for alcoholic senators and movie stars, manic-depressive millionaires, and suicidal sisters. Barbarossa wasn't part of the usual aristocracy. But he had a contact at the Justice Department, Frederic LeComte. And LeComte had gotten him through Macabee's door.

Barbarossa was a detective who earned fifty thousand a year. And he paid over a hundred thousand to the sanitarium. He sold drugs. But he was almost as poor as Isaac Sidel. He had to buy clothes for Roz, pay for all the champagne she drank at Macabee's.

He went upstairs to her room, knocked twice. "Roz, it's me."

"Wait," she said. "I'm not ready for you, Joe."

His hand was twitching again under the glove. "Come in," she said.

And his heart made a crazy hop when he saw her sitting in bed, her blond hair turning white at the roots. Roz was forty-one, but she looked like a little aging girl who was shut inside Macabee's walls.

"Joey, I shouldn't have made a fuss. I'm not marrying anybody. Who would marry me? I live in a jail without jailers . . . I'd like to get a job, Joe."

"What would you do?"

"Attack people. Scratch out their eyes."

He had to hold his gloved hand to keep it from twitching. She smiled at him. "I could be your accomplice, Joe."

"Roz," he said, "whose eyes have I scratched lately?"

"It was just an idea. When I tell the other patients that my brother is a policeman, they scream, 'That's impossible, dear. Macabee's is much too expensive.'"

"I moonlight a little," he said.

She laughed. "Would you kill for me, Joey?"

"If I had to."

"I wasn't a very good mother," she said.

"You're not my mother. You took care of me, Sis. You didn't have a choice."

"I could have stuck your head in the bathtub and drowned my baby brother."

"You never even spanked me, Sis."

"But I did think of drowning you. Only what kind of freedom would I have had? I was attractive. Lots of men wanted to give me money if I'd live with them . . . I could have drowned you, Joey."

"Yeah," he said. "And I could have played pingpong with the man in the moon . . . or become the emperor of Saigon."

"You were the emperor. You sold hashish to the ambassador's wife."

"I did not," he said.

"You're still dealing, Joe. They'll kill you like a dog one day. They'll shoot you down and I'll have to bury you. I don't want to bury my brother."

"I'm still here, Sis."

"How many times have you been wounded?"

"It's not the same as being dead."

"Of course. A bullet in the shoulder. A bullet under the heart. It adds up. I won't be your widow, Joey. I've worked too hard."

She started to scratch her own palm, which was already scarred from previous scratchings.

"Sis, I'll get you out of Macabee's. We'll live together."

"You have your own little cave in a pingpong hotel. I'm a burden, Joey. I belong here."

He grabbed her palm with his gloved hand so she couldn't scratch. She fell asleep on his shoulder. He rocked her and stroked the roots of her hair. He placed her head on the pillow, sat with her, and watched the tiny wet motions of her lip.

He went downstairs. He knew there were nurses around.

They kept sharp objects out of Roz's reach and wouldn't even let her have shoelaces. They seemed to float out of the woodwork in times of crisis. But he couldn't find a doctor or a nurse. No one ever bothered him about the bills. He would knock on the bursar's door once a month and pay her in cash. He never asked for a receipt.

There was a cab waiting for him outside the walls. Macabee's could anticipate all his gestures, all his moves. Barbarossa got into the cab. Christ. It was the same fucking driver.

"I was cruising the neighborhood," Leonard Furie said. "I got the call on my radio. It's a nursing home. Macabee's. It caters to the best people . . . I'm sorry. I shouldn't have freaked. You're not the Bronx Bandit."

"And what if I am?" Joe asked, thinking of Roz in her jail without jailers.

And Leonard F. Furie started to laugh.

2

He couldn't stop thinking of the Nez Percé. Chief Joseph had died on a reservation, a teepee Indian who sat for days and wouldn't utter a word. Joe was partial to the same long silences. Schiller left him alone. The kibitzers didn't intrude upon his territories. Schiller's back room had become his mattress. He had a few mementos from the years he'd spent with Roz. An ancient beebee gun. A hunting knife. A stamp album with pages devoted to big and little countries. But he'd been a poor collector. He had stamps from Costa Rica, but not Portugal or Argentina or Poland and Japan. He'd had no sense of the world. His world had been Roz.

He was inside the Sheraton Centre, with a mask in his pocket, waiting to rip off a dealer called Frannie, who'd been an MP in Saigon, who'd shot Barbarossa twice, who'd carved his own kingdom out of midtown hotels, cashing in on conventions and trade fairs. Frannie kept a mistress at the Sheraton Centre, a fashion model who also put out for strangers and carried drugs. Her name was Charlotta. Joe was sleeping with her, and he'd learned Frannie's schedule from Charlotta. And Frannie's secrets. Frannie couldn't make love unless Charlotta told him stories about all the men she'd ever had. Charlotta was his personal Scheherazade.

Joe couldn't afford to kill Frannie right now. Frannie was working underground for the FBI, and his death would fall back on Joe. They'd been feuding for years. Joe's burnt hand was a present from Frannie. He had two bullet holes. And Frannie had lost a piece of his ear.

It was Charlotta who let Joe into her suite. She wanted to frighten Frannie, who'd acquired another mistress and was keeping her at the Pierre.

"Shhh, Joe. He's in bed."

"No bodyguards?"

"He wouldn't dare. I don't like those drug babies of his. He knows it. He has a couple hundred thou in his coat."

Frannie used his coat as a cash register. He had pockets all over the place.

"The coat's yours, Charlotta."

"You have to take it, or he'll smell something fishy. Where's your mask?"

"In my pocket."

"Put it on," she whispered, but Charlotta's whispers were as loud as a horse. She was all coked up. But Barbarossa had to depend on her.

He put on the mask. Charlotta walked across the carpets in her dressing gown. Barbarossa couldn't get excited. He wasn't jealous of Frannie, and he didn't covet Scheherazade. He looked at himself in the mirror. He was menacing enough in his mask. It was a black stocking with eye holes. He didn't bother changing cannons, because most bandidos loved the Glock. It was lightweight, but had the wallop of an iron fist.

He could hear Charlotta from the next room. "Fran," she purred. And she started to tell her story.

"It was last year. At the Mark Hopkins."

"You were in Frisco, since when?"

"You took me, you dope. It was the cement salesmen's convention. And I met this old man with an eye patch."

"How old?"

"Fifty, at least. And he had nothing downstairs, just a little wienie. It was like a belly button with a knot at the end."

"And what did you do?"

"I gave him a bath, I scrubbed his thing and it started to grow."

"You scrubbed him like that, without fixing a price?"

"Come on. I never made it with a man who wore an eye patch. It excited me."

"I bring you to Frisco and you betray me with the first eye-patch man you meet?"

There was a pause. "It wasn't the first," Charlotta said. "I lied." Barbarossa could hear a slap. He barged into the bedroom. Frannie was lying in a silk gown. He covered his genitals when he saw the mask. His anger shot up to his eyes. He'd been a farm boy until Vietnam. Now he owned half the Bronx as a civilian drug soldier.

He started to rock on the bed.

Barbarossa discovered a huge tear on Frannie's face. He didn't like it.

"Don't shoot," Frannie said. "Are you with the Purple Gang?"

The Purples operated out of Harlem and Detroit and the broken cantons of the Bronx. They didn't have a single white soldier.

Barbarossa didn't like it at all. Charlotta had set him up. He'd been worrying about Roz, and Frannie's whore had shoved steel wool into his eyes. But why would Frannie make himself vulnerable to Joe, listen to Scheherazade with his prick out, and let Barbarossa come waltzing into the room? Barbarossa didn't have a choice. He had to go along with the game, or risk ruining his own cover.

He locked Frannie and Charlotta in the closet and seized the money coat. He didn't examine the pockets. He walked out of the suite and into the arms of two fucking Mormons, FBI men. It was LeComte's show.

The Mormons took the money coat. They marched Barbarossa into a room at the far end of the hall. Frederic LeComte was sitting on a couch, dressed in blue like he always was, the cultural commissar and little boy blue of the Justice Department, who had his pick of FBI agents. LeComte wouldn't roost in D.C. He'd pounced on Manhattan with his own narrow chest. He was on a crusade against the Mafia. He'd involved himself in the war between Sal Rubino and Jerry DiAngelis for control of the Rubino family. He'd taken Sal's side. But Sal was in a wheelchair and Jerry DiAngelis walked the street.

"You're a bad boy, Joe."

"Yeah, you didn't have to suck me into this hotel."

"But how else could I have found you? You break all our appointments."

"Leave a message for me at Schiller's club."

"I left sixteen messages. You didn't answer one . . . you belong to us, Joe."

"I never took a dime from the Bureau. I'm not a fucking paid informant."

"Dimes aren't everything."

Barbarossa had killed an undercover agent in a dumb duel. LeComte got the Feds off Joe's back, and now Joe had to do him little favors from time to time.

"Isaac's in trouble."

"Frederic, why the fuck should you care?"

"Because he's going to be the next mayor of this town, and a dead mayor does me no good."

"You could be wrong. He might not run for mayor."

"He'll run," said the blue boy of Justice. "But Jerry DiAngelis wants to waste him."

"He loves Jerry. Isaac's a Mafia man, a member of the tribe."

"Not anymore."

"Frederic, what can I do?"

"Stick close to him, become his shadow."

"He'll sniff me a mile away. He knows I'm your fucking scout. He'd never trust me."

"Try."

"There's an easier way. Just indict Jerry."

"I'm working on it, Joe. But even if I sit him down in jail for a while, he'll still have his shooters out on the street."

"Then get Margaret Tolstoy to babysit for Isaac."

"I can't," LeComte said. "She's minding Sal Rubino's wheelchair."

Margaret was one of LeComte's undercover girls. She'd had a long history with Sidel. They'd met in junior high school, when she was a Roumanian refugee. And the Commish was crazy about her ever since. LeComte was using her as a nurse for Sal Rubino.

"Margaret's your answer. Margaret can sleep with all of Jerry's shooters. They'll forget about Isaac."

"Margaret's occupied. I'm counting on you, Joe. You killed a Drug Enforcement agent."

"The guy was the biggest dealer in town."

"But a dealer who belonged to the DEA. They're possessive people. I had to dance around them, Joe, pull a lot of strings. I put out for you. Don't leave me with an empty basket. Get close to Isaac. I don't care how you do it, but get close."

"I'll become his pingpong instructor," Joe said.

"He doesn't do pingpong. It reminds him of Manfred Coen. I hear you inherited his table."

"I'm not Coen."

The same two Mormons ushered Joe out of the room. LeComte called to him. "Joe, if you have it in your head to hit on Frannie, forget about it. I need him in the Bronx."

Frannie had closed the north Bronx to DiAngelis' people. He was LeComte's little soldier. He sold crack to schoolchildren.

He had an army of twelve-year-olds with machine pistols and Glocks. They were Frannie's elite guard. They couldn't be prosecuted in open court. They were a little too young. But they could maim each other and kill rival cadres of twelve-year-olds. Barbarossa couldn't get back to Charlotta's suite. The Mormons stuck to him. But he'd damage Frannie one day soon. And LeComte could go fly a kite.

3

He returned to Schiller's. He wasn't Blue Eyes, even if he lived at Blue Eyes' table. He was Barbarossa, the great-grandson of the Nez Percé. He couldn't connect with a woman. He had a small society of whores. He'd visit them and run away, like some wild Indian. He had no real hours at Sherwood Forest, he had nothing to do. Isaac had left him in a kind of limbo, had avoided him for months. Barbarossa would play pingpong at the precinct, wander around in his white glove. He didn't like to play at Schiller's. He wasn't Manfred Coen. He could balance his checkbook, but he was already overdrawn. He couldn't get to Isaac unless he grew some wings.

"Joey," Schiller shouted, "phone call."

"Schiller, I never take a call while I'm meditating. You know that."

"It's the police."

Some sergeant-secretary was summoning him to the fourteenth floor at One PP.

He rode downtown to City Hall, walked under the arcade of the Municipal Building, and entered Police Plaza. He'd never been comfortable here. It reminded him of some red bunker in Saigon. It was an enormous anthill where all the good policemen pretended to run the City of New York. It was like playing pingpong with a bunch of spooks. You'd hit the ball over the net and it would land in an impossible country.

Joe arrived on the fourteenth floor. Malik, the trials commissioner, could barely bring himself to say hello. Malik would have loved to capture Joe inside his court. But Internal Affairs couldn't get near Barbarossa. He had a fucking angel on his shoulder, Frederic LeComte.

He didn't have to wait for Isaac. He was let into the PC's office, with its plants that climbed the wall. Isaac was near the window, looking gaunt. His sideburns had swallowed half his face. He was glocked last winter by some phantom who turned out to be Lucas White, Barbarossa's own captain at Sherwood Forest. The Cap had been half crazy. He took money from the Maf to hit Isaac under the Williamsburg Bridge. Isaac lay in a coma for two months, and the Cap killed himself.

Isaac mourned Captain White, he mourned Blue Eyes, he mourned every fucking child in the City who couldn't spell. He was the hairiest PC the town had ever had.

"My chauffeur has died on me."

"Malone is dead?" Barbarossa asked. "Since when?"

"He's not a corpse, Joey. He's in the hospital, with a bleeding ulcer. He can't drive. And his doctors keep telling him that I'm the one who made him sick. He's loyal, Malone is. He'd like to come back. But I'd rather not ruin the man. I need a chauffeur."

Barbarossa's gray hand started to pulse. "I'm not a hackie, Isaac."

"Well, I'm making you one. You get free meals when you drive the Commish. I'm like a gravy train."

"And if I refuse? You'll bounce me back to the Police Academy. You'll put me in a kennel with all the bomb-sniffing dogs."

"I could do a lot worse. Your hours are my hours, Joey. Day and night. You'll have to wear a beeper. You won't be able to go to the toilet without dreaming of the Commish."

"Isaac, you could have a thousand other candidates. Why me?"

"I trust you, Joe."

"Am I supposed to laugh, Isaac, or cry? LeComte has me on a fucking string. I belong to the little boy blue."

"You can report our conversations word for word. I have no secrets from LeComte."

"He traps me in a room at the Sheraton Centre. He says, 'Get close to Isaac. Isaac's gonna be the next mayor.' "

"I never said I'd run."

"That's what I told LeComte. But he still worries. He thinks Jerry DiAngelis wants to pull your plug."

"It's a temporary crisis. It'll pass."

"Isaac, I can't keep up with all your wars. You kill Sal Rubino, but he doesn't stay dead. Sal hires the Cap to hit you. He whacks you six times."

"Five," Isaac said. "Only five."

"You go into a coma. Sal sits in a wheelchair with a fucking manufactured face. He gets his clan back from Jerry, has Jerry on the run. You come out of the coma, kidnap Sal, break the Rubinos' backs. So why is Jerry after you?"

"Because I wouldn't let him murder Sal.

"You murdered him once."

"It's not the same thing."

"Ah," Barbarossa said, "I'll inherit Malone's ulcer if I listen anymore . . . I'll be your chauffeur. Boss, when do I start?"

"Today, tomorrow. I don't care."

And Joe Barbarossa walked out of One PP with a two-hundred-dollar pager hooked to his belt. It had a clock radio that could sing him to sleep and a tiny window that could read whatever borough Isaac was in. Barbarassa felt trapped. How could he make his drug scores while he was married to Sidel? But it was LeComte who bothered him, not Isaac.

He wandered through Manhattan, seeking out LeComte's little cribs. The first four were unoccupied. Barbarossa had his usual skeleton keys and picks. He broke into the fifth crib, fumbled in the dark. He heard a strange noise, like the bark of a wounded animal. He put on the light, saw a whirling mass of hair, and couldn't tell if he was being attacked by an orange dog or what. The dog knocked Barbarossa on his ass. But he'd never met an orange dog that could clutch a pistol in its paws. He was angry and confused and frightened until the orange hair materialized into Margaret Tolstoy.

"Can I stand up, Margaret, or are you gonna waste me?"

"Barbarossa, what are you doing here?"

"I'm Barbarossa now, huh?"

He'd slept with Margaret, made love to her in one of LeComte's cribs, because he had no cribs of his own, and neither did Margaret. But all their kissing had been professional, a way of feeling each other out, like dogs sniffing new territory. But she hadn't worn an orange wig on that occasion. He was guilty. He'd slept with Isaac's fiancée. But how could Barbarossa respect all the nuances of a forty-year romance? And he was turned on by the bitch.

"You were always Barbarossa," Margaret said. "Why are you here?"

"I'm looking for that little shit LeComte."

"To ambush him or kiss his ass?"

"Both," Barbarossa said.

And she laughed with her almond-colored eyes. She was centuries older than Barbarossa, Isaac's age, but he could understand how half the Mafia chieftains in America had fallen for Margaret Tolstoy. She seduced mobsters for the FBI. She'd lived with Sal Rubino, spied on him, until Sal tried to wax her in New

Orleans, where she'd gone to flirt with his cousins, Martin and Emile. It was the Pink Commish who'd saved her life. He'd come down to Bayou St. John with Jerry DiAngelis and shot Sal, who liked to play Lazarus.

"I'm also looking for LeComte. But I didn't expect you, Joe. You shouldn't sneak up on a lady in the dark."

"You're not a lady," Barbarossa said. "You're a walking arsenal, a human torch."

"That's not what you told me in bed."

"I lied. I thought if we kissed, you might have a sentimental attachment to me."

"I don't have sentimental attachments."

"But you're in love with Sidel."

The almond eyes delivered cold sparks. "That's none of your business, Barbarossa."

"I'm Joey," he said. And LeComte walked through the door with a pigskin attaché case. He stared at Barbarossa.

"I have an appointment with Margaret, Joe. This isn't one of your safe houses."

"I had to get in touch."

"Then you signal, you write me a letter."

"I didn't feel like doing one of our post-office tricks."

"What's so urgent that you had to come here?"

"I don't like it when you and the Bureau pull my prong. You set me up at the Sheraton, you put on the pressure, tell me to babysit for Isaac, and the next thing I know, I get a call from the fourteenth floor, and Isaac, who hates my guts, asks me to become his chauffeur."

"That's perfect," LeComte said. "Even better than I could have imagined."

"Then your imagination stinks. I'm tainted. I could go down any minute."

"You're the most decorated cop in New York. Two medals of honor."

"Three." Barbarossa said. "But everybody knows I do drugs."

"So what?"

"Either Isaac bugged your little office at the Sheraton, or he's playing some kind of three-dimensional chess that's beyond me, you, and Einstein."

"Einstein didn't play chess. He couldn't memorize the moves."

"Frederic, tell me what's going on, or I walk."

"The man's getting lonely for Blue Eyes."

"Fuck yourself. I'm not Manfred Coen."

"It's a coincidence. Or part of some chaos theory. Isaac believes in all that crap. He couldn't have bugged my office. I'm untappable. Margaret, isn't that right?"

She had all the chaos a man could ever want in her almond eyes. She was worth twenty LeComtes.

"Maybe it's the kid who's right," she said.

"What does that mean, Margaret?"

"We want to guard Isaac without him ever knowing it, and he hires Barbarossa. He's on to you, Frederic."

"On to all of us," LeComte said. "But the fact is we have Joey behind the wheel."

"And Isaac has you by the balls," she said. "He lets Barbarossa drive him where you expect him to go. He could have ten other drivers."

"Joey will be able to tell."

"How's Sal?" Barbarossa asked.

"Behaving," Margaret said. "He's in love with me, but I can handle it."

"Loves you so much that he wanted to kill you."

"Men are like that. They can't make up their minds."

"I never wanted to kill you," Barbarossa said.

"But you're not in love with me, kid."

And Barbarossa marched out the door.

4

He got the keys to Isaac's black Dodge from the caverns under Police Plaza. The Commish had his own tiny garage. And Joe stopped caring if Isaac was manipulating him, using him as the propeller of some prescribed, public life. He soon realized that the PC had no other existence. That's all there was. Barbarossa drove him everywhere. He was putting in sixteen-hour days. But he didn't declare any overtime. His own little business was shot. He had to deal while Isaac was at the office or in bed. And the PC's bedtime was unpredictable. He could wake in the middle of the night and ask Joe to drive him across the Brooklyn Bridge. Isaac would sit up front with Joe, wrapped in a blanket, because he was always cold, and he would watch the streaks of moonlight in the water. Then they'd go into some secret diner in one of Brooklyn's black belts and sit with a bunch of Rastafarians and ask for mocha ice cream. Several of the Rastas saluted Isaac. They must have lived with him inside the house of detention at Riker's. The Commish had been to the clink, accused of conspiring with Jerry DiAngelis and his father-in-law, and now Jerry wanted him dead.

They returned to the car, rode out to Gowanus, and passed a social club near Owls Head Park. The club belonged to Jerry's people. It was on Senator Street.

"Joey, do you have a mask for me and you?"

"Mask?" Barbarossa said in his own mechanical way.

"Come on. The black stockings you wear during your drug capers."

Barbarossa handed Isaac one of his stocking masks. Isaac put it on backwards, and the eye holes revealed two patches of gray-black hair. Joe had to twist the stocking around, or Isaac would have stayed blind.

"Boss, what are we gonna do with our masks?"

"Rob that social club."

"Jerry aint gonna like it. He'll see blood when he hears about two masked men knocking over one of his sanctuaries."

"That's the point. I want him to see blood."

"It won't heal your feud with him."

"Joe, would you rather talk or make some pocket money?"

And they both leapt out of the car with their Glocks and black masks. It was five in the morning. They looked like a pair of harlequins under the harsh light of the lamp posts, local bad-asses who'd had too much to drink. The club's door wasn't locked. Isaac turned the knob and entered with Joe Barbarossa. The club was packed with old men who spent their nights playing cards because they couldn't sleep. They weren't alarmed by the masks. Joe collected three hundred and eighteen dollars in cash, one old pistol, and two blackjacks. He prayed to his ancestors, the Nez Percé, that he could avoid a shooting war. He wouldn't have known what to do with these old men.

Isaac tore the telephone wires, smashed the coffee machine, and ran out of the club with Joe. He was smiling under his mask. Barbarossa carried him away from Senator Street in Isaac's black Dodge. They took off their masks.

"Boss, what if we'd had to whack a couple of old guys?"

"Don't complain. You have your pocket money . . . Joey, I wouldn't have hurt a bunch of old geezers."

"War is war. You could have had a shotgun in your eyes."

"Not on Senator Street. Desperadoes never come to Gowanus . . . I'm rich. I can afford a pair of spectacular shin guards and a first-class catcher's mitt."

Isaac managed a baseball team, the Delancey Giants, for the Police Athletic League. He was always short of cash. He would scrounge nickels and dimes from every cop on the fourteenth floor. Barbarossa had already contributed twice. Isaac was obsessed with his Giants. He had baseball on the brain.

They knocked off two more social clubs. Barbarossa brought Isaac to his flat on Rivington Street, went uptown in the Dodge, and parked outside Schiller's. He slept in the back room, distressed about the cash in his pocket. He didn't know anything about Isaac's chaos theories. But he couldn't go on hitting clubs like that without bumping into a little chaos. And if Joe had to whack someone, he hoped it wouldn't be an old man.

He was earning an extra thousand a week with the mask and becoming famous as one of the Black Stocking Twins. The social clubs never reported a crime. That's how the Maf did business. But a legend was already growing around the Twins. And during their fifth week together, as Joe was pulling out of the caverns under One PP, a fucking black giant stood in his way. It was Sweets, Isaac's first deputy commissioner, who had to manage the Department while Isaac was on his escapades with Joe. He looked like a refugee from the Harlem Globetrotters, with a cat's glowing eyes in the damp, dark tunnels of the garage. The most distinguished law firms were trying to woo him away from Police Plaza, but he wouldn't abandon Isaac.

He climbed into the back seat of the Dodge. His knees were almost as high as Isaac's chin.

"I'll kill you motherfuckers. Show me your masks."

"Sweets," Isaac said.

"You shut up." He turned to Joe. "Mr. Barbarossa, do you realize you're riding with a maniac?"

"He's the boss," Barbarossa said.

"And you're the big innocent, aren't you? I'll bust your hump, Barbarossa. Are you hearing me? It's time to retire. No more team of stick-up artists."

"Who told you about us?" Isaac asked.

"The FBIs. They have microphones in all the Mafia clubs. I won't tolerate a private war between Jerry DiAngelis and the Commish. I'll arrest you, Isaac. I'll bag both Black Stocking Twins."

"Joe's untouchable," Isaac said. "He's LeComte's baby."

"LeComte deals his babies when he has to. I can embarrass Justice's little commissar."

"Jerry started the war. I have to finish it."

"Then do it with a search warrant."

"LeComte's indicted him four times. He couldn't make any of his charges stick. Jerry's like a diva in the courtroom. He can mesmerize a jury. The don who looks like a movie star."

"You were blood brothers once."

"Not anymore."

"End your new career, Isaac, or I'll end it for you."

And Sweets climbed out of the car.

"Boss," Barbarossa said. "He's not fooling around."

"He works for me," Isaac said. "He's my First Dep. I'm the Commish."

"He can still bust us."

"I've been to Riker's. I've sat in jail. We have to go on stinging Jerry. We're the Black Stocking Twins."

But Isaac didn't steer him to a social club. They went to Ratner's, a dairy restaurant on Delancey, where an elegant old man sat in a silk scarf. He was Izzy Wasser, the melamed, Jerry's father-in-law and the brains of the clan. He'd suffered a stroke, but he was sharper than the Twins.

"My favorite holdupniks," he said. "Isaac, you're prospering at our expense."

"Call it a contribution to the Delancey Giants."

"I have my own charities," the melamed said. They sat around a table, while Barbarossa discovered dish after dish. Hot mashed carrots with prunes in the middle. Salmon cutlets. A cold potato pie.

"Isaac, the nonsense has to stop. I can't be responsible for Jerry. You have a daughter, Isaac. Don't forget."

The color had gone out of Isaac's eyes. He could have been a vampire. "Kill him, Joey."

"I can't. He's the melamed."

"Kill him."

"Isaac, it's lunchtime. You'll have two hundred witnesses. We're in a cafeteria."

"Then I'll kill him," Isaac said. "I'll tear off his face."

"Ah, you don't mean it," Barbarossa said.

"He threatens my daughter . . . he doesn't leave Ratner's alive."

The melamed pulled on his silk scarf and swallowed a baked apple. "I didn't threaten. I'm trying to tell you that Jerry is rash."

"I know all about it, Iz. He tried to waste me and Margaret at Chinaman's Chance."

"He wanted Rubino, not you or Margaret. Margaret happened to be there."

The Chinaman's was a bottle club in Spanish Harlem where a certain Delia St. John loved to dance. Joe had been her protector once. She was a "child" model who'd worked for Sal Rubino's pornography mill. She'd slept with all the honchos of Manhattan, including Martin Malik. Delia married Papa Cassidy, a rat-bastard billionaire, and retired from the club. But she was giving a command performance for Sal when Jerry arrived with the melamed and his shooters. Jerry wasn't quick enough. Isaac appeared like a magician, with his own squad of detectives, wearing bulletproof vests and waiting in the shadows. Barbarossa hadn't been invited to this showdown at Chinaman's Chance, but it was already part of the folklore at One PP.

"Iz, I'm not lying down for Jerry or you . . . Jerry can go to his shooters, but I'll cripple your organization. I don't have to finagle with masks."

"Isaac, you're a hothead. Just like Jerry. Sal has been meddling in our business. He has to go."

"He lives in a wheelchair. How much can he meddle?"

"The man has a monopoly on cement. He's been bribing our best contractors and our captains."

"He's Sal Rubino. Half your captains used to be his."

"Mule," the melamed said. "You won't listen."

"I listened. I saved your Family from extinction. I made my bones with you, Iz. I was your Family. And you tossed me out."

"You're the police commissioner. You went on the road for the FBI."

"I never betrayed you, Iz."

"You will."

Isaac walked out of Ratner's with Barbarossa and dialed his daughter from the telephone in his car. Marilyn the Wild lived in Seattle with her ninth or tenth husband. No one could keep count, not even Marilyn. Isaac talked to her latest husband, a Legal Aid lawyer.

"Mark, what happened?"

He stared at the ceiling and started to groan. Then he turned silent. It was Barbarossa who had to hang up the phone and tuck him into his blanket. He sat like a teepee Indian, Chief Joseph of One Police Plaza.

"She's flown the coop again. Gone. She falls in love and marries the man, but she's like her father. We weren't made for marriages."

"Where is she, boss?"

"That's the problem. You can't tell with Marilyn. She could be crisscrossing the United States. My daughter likes long bus rides."

"She'll surface, boss."

"I'm not so sure. She could hide forever under a new married name."

They crossed into Brooklyn. Isaac stood on the esplanade in Brooklyn Heights, looking out at the lost horizons of lower Manhattan, crazy castles of stone and glass. People asked him for his autograph.

"Your Honor," they said, imagining Isaac as their mayor-king.

"I haven't declared," he had to say. "I'm not a candidate."

"Our children are dying, Commissioner Sidel. The schools aren't safe. Our old have to sit in the dark by themselves. Do you know how much it costs to hire a nurse?"

"I'm a policeman," Isaac said. "I can't solve all the riddles of New York."

"Your Honor, this is Brooklyn, not New York."

He began to shiver. Barbarossa had to bring him back to the car. He sat up front in his blanket. "I'm restless, Joe. I have to hit one of Jerry's clubs. It's the only thing that will calm me down."

"It's risky, boss. Sweets is on to us. So are Jerry's people. There'll be shooters at all the clubs."

"All right, all right, but I'm not retiring the Twins."

Part Two

5

He was losing his marbles, one by one. He couldn't remember the names of his adjutants. He was struggling against some swollen thing that swallowed up his past. I'm Isaac Sidel, he had to tell himself. I'm the PC. My daughter's name is Marilyn. My mother used to be Sophie Sidel. My dad is a portrait painter in Paris. He panicked. He couldn't recall his brother's name. Leo, he said. Like Count Leo Tolstoy, the father of *War and Peace*. But Leo Sidel wasn't a count. His wife had rid herself of him. His children ran from Leo. He was in and out of alimony jail until Isaac settled a small allowance on him. Leo couldn't seem to hold a job even while his brother was the Commish, a guy suffering from selective amnesia. What the hell was the name of Leo's two kids? A boy and a girl. He could conjure up their faces, hear them call him "Uncle Isaac."

He'd forgotten to shave this morning. His shoes weren't tied. He had a Band-Aid on his finger. He was a detective who couldn't find his daughter or follow the clues of his own fucking life. Homicides were up in Manhattan. Handguns were everywhere. Hospitals were closing. There were crazies out on the street. The north woods of Central Park had become a private crib for crack babies. But he was the first Alexander Hamilton Fellow. He'd gone around the U.S. lecturing on crime. Justice and Frederic LeComte had sponsored Sidel, the Hebraic police commissioner who'd drawn Latinos and blacks into his Department, who had a Turkish chief judge, Chinese deputies, a Rastafarian lawyer. But he couldn't remember most of their names.

He was up on the fourteenth floor, where he could dream of crimes he might commit, with or without a black mask. The phone started to buzz. Barbarossa was waiting for him. Isaac went into the bowels of One PP and rode out of the commissioner's berth, with Barbarossa behind the wheel. Barbarossa was a vagabond who lived at the same pingpong club where Manfred Coen had died, and it was the ritual of pingpong that bound him to Isaac. Barbarossa was also LeComte's little spy, but Isaac couldn't have cared less. He enjoyed Barbarossa's company. It was like riding with Blue Eyes' ghost.

"That actress," Isaac growled, "what the hell was her name? She was a calendar girl. She married DiMaggio."

Barbarossa didn't even prick up his ears. "Marilyn. Like your daughter . . . Marilyn Monroe. What's the matter, boss?"

"My fucking mind is going. I can't remember the names of my nephew and niece."

"You don't have a niece. You have two nephews. Davey and Michael. We visited them last month."

"That's impossible. I know I have a niece. I can picture her face."

"That's Caroline. Davey's girlfriend."

"Girlfriend? The kid's in kneepants."

"He's going to college, boss."

"I'm telling you, Joe. Time is fucking with my head. I wake up and I can't remember who I am."

"You're the PC. Your ass is always on the line. Somebody suffers, you suffer with them. It's hard to pull back . . . boss, a call came in while you were coming down. It's your brother."

"Brother?" Isaac said.

"Yeah, he was caught shoplifting. They're holding him in a dinky lockup at a department store. The store dick won't release him."

"Does that department store know who he is?"

"Yeah, boss. But the detective is a ballbreaker. He won't release Leo until you come for him."

"What's his name?"

"The dispatcher didn't say."

"And the store?"

"It's a big shoebox on Fordham Road. Fashion Town."

"Never heard of it."

"No one shops there."

"Except my brother Leo . . . what's my schedule like?"

"You have a three o'clock with Cardinal Jim on Gun Hill Road. Should I cancel?"

"No," Isaac said. "Let Leo sit. It will do him some good. The cardinal doesn't like cancellations. We'll go to him first. Then we'll collect fucking Leo."

Jim O'Bannon, the cardinal archbishop of New York, liked to rendezvous with Isaac in distant streets where he wouldn't be noticed. Isaac enjoyed these little cabals. And it gave him a chance to ride through the City like a random voyager. Joe would pick the most "scenic" route, where Isaac could observe one wasteland after the other.

They crossed into the Bronx, rode up the Grand Concourse, the borough's own blasted Champs Élysées, with broken courtyards, blighted trees, Art Deco palaces with ghostly, crumbling roofs. Isaac must have found some of his marbles. His mind started to flash. He had an image of Leo in short pants. The image was forty years old. Isaac had been a bandit long before he became police commissioner. He robbed ration stamps in the middle of World War II. Leo was his courier, little Leo, who could run across lines of policemen with contraband in the pock-

ets of his short pants so Isaac could buy silk stockings for his
sweetheart, Anastasia, better known as Margaret Tolstoy. Leo
had been the fuel of Isaac's romance . . .

They got to Gun Hill Road. The cardinal stood outside his big
black Lincoln in an ancient shirt. He loved old clothes. He took
a walk with Isaac, tore at the cigarette in his hand and toyed
with the tobacco. But Isaac was spooked by that picture of Leo
in short pants.

"There's a bit of a crisis, love."

"Tell me about it, Jim."

"I have a problem priest. He's been undressing little boys.
And now we're being blackmailed."

"Who's the blackmailer?"

"One of your lads."

"A cop?" Isaac said. "I can't believe it."

"I didn't say 'cop,' did I? A lab technician. Broderick Swirl.
He's one of your Crime Scene boys."

"I'll cripple him."

"Aint that easy. I met the lad. Mentioned your name. He
didn't blink. He'd like a monthly stipend from the Church. He
has photographs, Isaac."

"Is he Catholic?"

"Indeed. A former friend of my priest. Our lawyers are against
any sort of scandal. They've set up a discretionary fund. We
wouldn't be involved. And we can always pounce on him at a
later date."

"Don't," Isaac said. "Once you pay him, that's it. Lemme have
a go at him."

"He's a devil. He won't scare."

"I'll run over to Crime Scene and nail him to a door."

"The lad's convalescing. He broke his leg. He lives right
around the corner. That's why I brought you up here. Shall we
visit him together? Sort of good cop, bad cop, eh? I could bash
him around the ears."

"I'd have to arrest you for aggravated assault."

"You're a bloody civilian, like me."

"But I wear a badge with five gold stars. Good-bye, Jim."

The cardinal scribbled Swirl's address and the name and parish of the problem priest. Isaac hugged the old man. "Jim," he said, adopting his policeman's brogue, "I'll expect a bit of compensation."

The cardinal smiled. "Ah, now I have two blackmailers. What is it, Isaac?"

"I'm short a third baseman. I'd like to borrow one of yours."

Both of them managed teams for the PAL.

"That's robbery," the cardinal said. But he loved to barter with Isaac. "I'll see what I can do."

The cardinal left and Isaac rode around the corner.

"Joe, gimme my mask."

"Does Jerry have a club on the Grand Concourse? I wouldn't mess with his black captains, boss."

"I'm not." Isaac pointed to a private house. "I'm going in there. Just sit where you are."

"What about your brother Leo?"

"Leo will have to wait."

He should have gone through the files at Crime Scene and kidnapped Swirl's folder, but he was feeling reckless, like the Black Stocking Kid. He stepped out of the car, pranced onto a lawn, put on the mask, climbed a crooked porch, knocked on the door, and entered Broderick's house.

The blackmailer was waiting for him in a miserable armchair. His right leg was in a cast. He looked about thirty years old. He was wearing a gold chain around his neck. His eyes didn't seem to startle at the sight of the mask. Where did a lousy lab technician get such a big pair of balls?

"Fuck it," Isaac said, and he tore off the mask.

"That's better," Broderick said. "That's much, much better. I work for you. Are you gonna waste me, chief?"

"No. Not right now."

"I'm a pretty good photographer. Did the cardinal show you my snaps of Father Tom?"

Ah, Father Tom of St. Anne's parish. He'd already forgotten the name of the priest on Jim's slip of paper.

"You have a pension, Mr. Swirl. I can bring Internal Affairs right down on your back. Have you ever met Martin Malik? He's my trials commissioner. He'll tear your heart out. He's a Turk."

"I'm not a cop. You can fuck me or fire me, but you can't give me a departmental trial."

"Sonny, I can turn every one of your days into a living hell."

"I've already been there, Commissioner Isaac."

He had a cat's crazy grin.

Isaac heard an echo behind him. Barbarossa had come into the house with his white glove. The grin disappeared from Swirl's face.

"You know each other?"

"Sure, boss," Barbarossa said. "Brod's one of my customers. He buys dope from me. I recognized his fucking bungalow. I've been here before . . . right, Brod?"

The blackmailer shook his head like a little boy.

"And what happens to people who cross Uncle Joe?"

"They get lost," the blackmailer said. "I swear, Joey. I didn't know you were with the Commish."

"Haven't you heard of the Black Stocking Twins?" Barbarossa said, dangling his mask.

"I've been sick," the blackmailer said. "I haven't been out of the house."

"You're entitled to a mistake, Brod. But only one . . . don't worry, boss. He likes to do a little blackmail on the side. He's got a thing about priests. But it's all finished. Just go outside for a minute."

Isaac was like a drugged man. He walked out and stood on

the porch. Barbarossa appeared with a thick envelope. "It's his whole inventory."

"Tear up the pictures. I don't want to look."

He sulked in the car. His own driver had more sway in the City of New York. He'd have to retire to an old people's home. He was fifty-six. But he was still a fox. He'd have a new third baseman for the Delancey Giants. And Cardinal Jim would have to hide his problem priest.

He started to dream. He'd become a priest, Father Isaac. And his parish was a baseball field with broken red grass. The bleachers were filled with boys and girls. The girls all looked like Isaac, the boys like Margaret Tolstoy. He couldn't tell what position he was meant to play. He was lost in that sea of red grass.

"Boss?"

Barbarossa had his hand on Isaac's shoulder. "Boss, we're here."

Isaac couldn't rouse himself from his own murderous sleep. *Margaret.* "Here?" he said.

"At the shoebox on Fordham Road."

"Why'd you wake me?"

"Boss, we have to get Leo."

It was a shoebox, like Barbarossa said. A bargain basement three floors high. Fashion Town. The clothier of Leo Sidel. The dummies in the window had a maddening, sunburnt look. Bronzed men who could have been white, black, Latino, or Native American. Their nostrils, their eyes and ears looked like the holes of a mask. But the dummies were draped in shirts and vests that mocked Isaac, who had his own bargain basements on Orchard Street. Isaac loved to wear Orchard Street's best.

"Come with me, Joe."

"Boss, you'll get embarrassed about your brother. And you'll hate it if I see you cry."

"I won't cry," Isaac said. "I promise."

Barbarossa had become his noble savage, Friday with a pink face and a black stocking mask. He moved in mysterious rings around Isaac, repairing his life.

The store was a bombed-out zone with racks of clothing that seemed to extend for half a mile, like Isaac's red grass. He asked for the security department and had to travel into the heart of the store with Joe Barbarossa. They went down a flight of stairs into the darkness. A light was switched on. And Isaac saw his brother Leo inside a cage with six black men. With them was the warden, wearing handcuffs around his belt and carrying a policeman's billy. He was an enormous man, this warden, like a thick, prehistoric creature that was beyond any of Isaac's baseball dreams.

"I'm Kronenberg," he said. "You must be the Commish. And your chum?"

"Detective Barbarossa," Isaac said.

Kronenberg laughed. "Your bodyguard and your babysitter."

"Yeah, something like that," Isaac said. "Barbarossa's my twin." He was going to beat Kronenberg's brains out. But he hadn't said hello to his brother, who sulked behind the warden. "Kronenberg, how come you're in that cage with all these men?"

"It's discipline," Kronenberg said. "They'd be biting their fingernails without me . . . and robbing each other."

Kronenberg came out of the cage. He had to duck under the narrow door. He was half a head taller than Isaac. He didn't even bother to lock the cage. Isaac had a much better view of Leo now. Leo had been stripped down to his underpants. Isaac shivered. Leo couldn't seem to shake his short pants.

"Kronenberg, I don't like it when my kid brother is obliged to stand half naked in the dark."

"He's a thief," Kronenberg said. "And he's not naked."

"A thief?" Isaac said. "Have you read him his rights?"

"I have him on tape, Sidel. He stole three pairs of pants and a shirt. And I don't have to read him his rights. I interrogated him. That's my privilege. I'm a licensed security man. I can't keep going back and forth to the precinct all day. I collect the trash in this box and then I make a run to the precinct. It's strictly legal."

"Is it legal to let men live in the dark?"

"I'm saving electricity, that's all, and teaching them a lesson. They're all trash, including your brother. I checked him with our credit agency. He's a chronic shoplifter. You can't waltz him out of my jail, Sidel."

"I don't intend to waltz him anywhere. You're going to set him free."

"Not a chance."

Isaac peeked inside the cage, saw those seven unfortunate, masklike faces, and started to cry. He was thinking of Leo and the six black men cooped up in the cellar of a crazy department store. And he was thinking of Isaac, who'd sent his brother out on missions to protect his own supply of ration stamps.

The warden began to gloat. "Go on. Get out of here."

Isaac socked him on the side of the head. The warden crashed into the cage and Isaac socked him again, grabbed the warden's billy, dug it into the skin under his throat, and turned to Barbarossa. "Sorry, Joe. I didn't mean to cry."

"Boss, lemme talk to the clown."

Barbarossa stooped over Kronenberg. The warden was blubbering now. "I have friends. I can get to the mayor."

"Mr. Kronenberg, the mayor is Isaac's biggest fan."

"Then I'll shoot the Commish."

"With what? He can tear up your gun permit, revoke your license. Do yourself a favor. Sign a release form for Leo Sidel."

"And the other six," Isaac said. "I'm not leaving without them."

"Boss, you don't even know what they did. They could have swallowed a couple of babies."

"I don't care. Joe, I'll kill this fat fuck."

Barbarossa helped the warden to his feet, found the release forms, guided Kronenberg's hand, and helped him sign the forms. The six black men walked out of the cage, said good-bye to Leo, and left.

Barbarossa found Leo's clothes. He walked Leo out of the department store, with Isaac behind him, bewildered in that long, long corridor of clothes.

Isaac sat with Leo in back of the sedan while Barbarossa drove across the ruins of the Grand Concourse and out to Indian Road, where Leo lived, at the very edge of Manhattan.

"Isaac," he said, "there's a cop outside my building."

"I put him there. I have enemies, Leo. I wouldn't want them to get any ideas."

"But all my neighbors see that cop, and they start expecting things."

"That's not my fault . . . have you heard from Marilyn?"

Leo said nothing.

"Dammit, Marilyn leaves her husband and I'm the last to learn about it. Where is she, Leo?"

"I'm not allowed to tell."

"Does she have money? Is she safe?"

"Yes, Isaac. She's safe."

"Will you give her a message from me?"

"No messages."

"All right," Isaac said. "Leo, you promised me you wouldn't steal."

"I can't help myself," Leo said. He seemed destined to sit or stand in tiny jails.

"Don't I pay your fucking bills? You want clothes, I'll buy them for you."

"I couldn't wear them," Leo said. "I need my own clothes. I'm fifty-two."

"You're crazy," Isaac said. "You're a fucking kid." He was crying again. "Leo, I shouldn't have made you my mule."

"I'm nobody's mule."

"But you carried my ration stamps . . . during the war."

"I don't remember."

"You walked in front of policemen with my stamps in your pockets. I couldn't have done it."

"Big deal," Leo said. "But at least I had a brother then, not some shit who plays God and punches people. Stop crying."

"Kill me, I'm a crier. Didn't I get you out of that closet? . . . Next time I might not be able to save your ass."

"I know," Leo said, and disappeared into his apartment house on Indian Road.

Isaac's face went dark.

"What can I do, boss?"

"Find me one of Jerry's clubs."

"Boss, it's fucking dangerous."

"I don't care. We won't do Brooklyn. Jerry's expecting us. We'll do the Bronx."

"He's expecting us in the Bronx."

"I'm frustrated, Joe. I need some fun."

He didn't want to drift back into dreams of Margaret Tolstoy.

Barbarossa brought him to Belmont, an Italian enclave in the Bronx that hadn't changed since World War II. It was its own small "Repubblica Italiana," with live chickens staring out of cages, one eye closed, and little octopuses swimming in sea tanks. But Isaac hadn't come here to shop for octopus meat. He and Joey put on their masks and entered Gerusalemme, a social club that was attached to a chicken market on Arthur Avenue.

Barbarossa didn't like it. Belmont was much too lively. And a little house of chicken feathers was always rotten luck. But he'd sworn himself to Sidel. Gerusalemme had the usual flock of old men, card players who drank peach brandy.

"Little grandfathers," Isaac said, "sit where you are. We came for your money, not your blood."

These same little grandfathers smiled at the Black Stocking Twins. We're fucked, Barbarossa told himself. Three of Jerry's shooters rose up from behind the club's coffee counter with shotguns cradled in their arms. Barbarossa recognized Rinaldo Reese, a former detective who'd joined Jerry and became his captain in the Bronx.

"Glad you could make it. Gentlemen, gimme your Glocks. Nice and easy. No funny stuff . . . how are you, Joe?"

Barbarossa could feel that mad fire coming from the eye holes in Isaac's mask. "Boss, we'll have a massacre. You'll hit the old men."

The Twins handed their Glocks to Rinaldo and took off their masks.

"That's beautiful," Rinaldo said. "It's like a dream. Now come into my office."

They went through a door behind the counter and into the back room of the chicken market. Barbarossa saw cage after cage of birds. The floor was matted with feathers and dried yellow droppings. Barbarossa wasn't scared. If he had to live around such a stink, he'd rather not live at all.

The birds were slaughtered in this room, and it had a constant aroma of blood, feathers, and shit. Barbarossa grew dizzy. He had to blink. His nostrils burned.

Rinaldo laughed. "Enjoy yourselves. We'll give you a first-class burial . . . Don Isacco, would you like to leave a couple of lines to the melamed? He's fond of you. You shouldn't have broke with Jerry. You were a terrific war counselor."

"And you were a crooked cop."

"Not like Joe. I didn't have the Department behind me. And I didn't have the FBI to bring me into the best killing fields . . .

sing, Isaac, sing for your last supper. How's Sal Rubino? Are you greasing his wheelchair?"

"All the time," Isaac said.

"You shouldn't have sided with Sal."

The cages exploded around Isaac. Birds flew into the air. Barbarossa sneezed and clutched his heart. The Commish hadn't gone down. But Rinaldo lay in all the feathers and shit with the other shooters.

Frannie poked through a wall of dust. He was with his coca babies. Isaac was bewildered. He'd seen twelve-year-old hitmen, but not like these brats. They had a professional pride and camaraderie that was beyond Isaac's comprehension.

"Isaac," Barbarossa said, "meet Frannie Meyers. He's LeComte's troubleshooter in the Bronx."

Isaac looked at his belt. The coca babies had returned his Glock.

"This is my borough," Frannie said. "Jerry D. has to pay a tax if he's planning to kill the Commish."

Isaac couldn't take his eyes off the coca babies. He'd have to go back to public school, climb up the kiddie ladder. But he shouldn't have been philosophizing so hard. The babies disappeared.

Joey sat him down in the back seat of the Dodge. But he wasn't all alone. Margaret Tolstoy, *his* Margaret, was on the cushions with a mop of orange hair.

"Isaac," she said, "Sal would like to see you."

6

Barbarossa wasn't in command of the car, Margaret was. A back-seat driver. He had two bosses now. Isaac and the bitch. He took his directions from her. He drove Isaac's big black cradle into Manhattan and parked in a garage near the East River, while Margaret wiped the chicken feathers from Isaac's eyes and hair. Margaret treated him like a baby.

They rode upstairs to Sal Rubino's penthouse. She kissed Isaac before she got off the elevator. Barbarossa started to understand the habits of forty years. She was crazy about the Commish, only she was Sal Rubino's nurse, and the kissing would have to stop once she marched through Sal's door.

Rubino didn't have regular soldiers. He had a pair of Mormons with field radios and closed-circuit television. He was the Bureau's greatest resource in LeComte's war against Jerry DiAngelis. Nothing could get built in the five boroughs without Sal Rubino and his little empire of cement.

He wheeled himself into the parlor, wearing white gloves. Barbarossa couldn't bear to look at him. Sal had lost his face. One of his eyes was closed, like the chickens of Arthur Avenue. And whatever skin he had was a forest of plucked feathers. He had one narrow curling line for a mouth. His chin receded into some featherless void. It was LeComte who'd found him in the bayous, who'd created this new fucking Sal, an adopted son of the FBI. He'd been a jeweler long before he was a don. He liked to make wedding rings for Margaret. He loved her, hated her, and had her as his nurse. She was a gift from LeComte. Sal was jealous of Isaac *and* Barbarossa.

"He's a loyal boy," Sal said, talking about Barbarossa. "I never cared for that Captain White. A cop who can't live without his rosary. It figures he'd have to kill himself. Isaac, I wanted Joey to shoot out your lights. I offered him a bundle, huh Joe?"

"Yeah," Barbarossa said.

"Joey has scruples," Isaac said. "He'd never shoot me for hard cash."

"Boss, I almost did."

"You're saying that just to be nice to Sal."

"Boss, I had bills to pay. I would have glocked you . . . if the Cap hadn't interfered."

"You'd have stood in the dark, under the bridge, like a spook?"

"No. I would have done you face to face."

"I don't believe it. You couldn't have looked me in the eye and pulled the trigger."

"I've done worse, boss, much worse, to pay my bills."

Isaac could feel a knot under his heart where his tapeworm had once been. The tapeworm hadn't recovered from Isaac's coma. It died under the Williamsburg Bridge.

"Isaac," Sal said, "would you like a chair? Now I'm happy, I really am. Darling," he said to Margaret. "Will you get Isaac an aperitif?"

"I'm not your darling."

"Yes you are," Sal said. "You rub my back, you sleep in my bed."

"Sal, stuff your aperitif. Why'd you bring me here?" Isaac asked.

"You're valuable property, you and Joe. The Black Stocking Twins. I couldn't give you to Jerry's people. Margaret would cry. She's in love with you, Isaac. But Margaret belongs to me . . . and you ought to know the truth about my quarrel with Jerry."

"I know the truth. Jerry and you can't exist in the same tribe."

"He was one of my captains, right? But how many captains have the melamed behind them? He's nothing without that old man. And the old man wants my dolls."

"Dolls?" Isaac said.

Rubino wheeled himself to one of his closets, opened the door, and removed an enormous, clanking figure with a long spike in the middle of its head. It was a doll with a helmet and green hair, black eyes, red lips, and a full suit of armor under a gold skirt. The doll was holding a sword in its right hand. The sword was large enough to have pierced Isaac Sidel. "Who is it?" he said.

"Giuseppina the Brigandess."

Giuseppina was lovely and ferocious, like Margaret Tolstoy.

"Sal, when did you become a puppeteer?"

Rubino let Isaac have the doll. It weighed twenty pounds and was three feet tall, without the metal spike. Giuseppina's shield was made of hammered gold. She had golden kneecaps, which could bend like any man's.

"All right, she's incredible. But I wouldn't kill for a doll."

"Yes you would."

"Does she have gold under her armor, Sal?"

"She's strictly wood, and the armor isn't worth much. But she belongs to the greatest set of dolls on the planet. Isaac, didn't your father ever take you to the Sicilian puppet theater?"

"I haven't been to Sicily, Sal."

"Come on. The puppets played New York. I went with my uncles a million times."

"I guess we didn't belong to the same circle."

"Don't insult me. You're with my Family now."

"Sal, didn't the melamed tell you? I've been drummed out of the Maf."

"You're with my Family," Sal said. "That's why you're here. You saved my life at Chinaman's Chance."

"You're a little senile. Or did you just happen to forget New Orleans?"

"I didn't forget. You killed me, and I put you in a coma. That's the way of the world. Or I wouldn't be telling you Family secrets."

"What secrets?"

"The dolls, you dummy. There are fifty of them, and they're worth a fortune."

"Who would buy a battalion of dolls?"

"About ten private collectors, six museums, and five Swiss banks. And that doesn't include a couple of holding companies in Monaco and Ireland, and whoever else is fronting for the private collectors . . . too complicated for you, Isaac?"

"I collect baseball cards," Isaac muttered. "But that's different. I mean, a quality card creates its own market. It survives fifty, sixty years . . . a piece of colored cardboard with some print. It's ephemeral. It's not supposed to last. But I have a Joe DiMaggio in mint condition. I have a Mel Ott."

"I piss on Mel Ott. We're talking dolls, not pinup pictures of men in flannel pants . . . you and your baseball. I grew up with the puppets. I went to every performance of the pupi palermitiani, right on Mulberry Street. I followed the dialects. I learned how to hate from those dolls, and how to caress your enemy with a little smile . . . those dolls were much more ephemeral than a stinking baseball card. They had to perform night after night. The armor broke. The heads fell off. No Sicilian doll ever lasted more than three years."

"What about your brigandess?" Isaac asked, stroking Guiseppina's green hair.

"That's the angle I'm getting at. My little girl comes from a different line of dolls. She's an aristocrat. Her puparo was the greatest of them all."

"Joey," Isaac said, "tell the don not to be so technical. Ask him what a puparo is."

"Isaac, ask him yourself," said his own brigandess with the orange hair.

"He's the maestro," Sal said, "the maker of dolls. He was called Peppinninu. But nobody knows his regular name. He put aside fifty dolls for his own fucking pleasure. But he didn't have a workshop, like the other pupari. He was always on the run. He had to hide his dolls in different towns."

"And his own collection got scattered."

"That's right. A couple landed in Cairo. Nine or ten got to New York."

"And you and Jerry have been competing for the fifty dolls."

"There are so many buyers, Isaac, I can name my own price. I was asking a million for every doll. I got a million. But now I've decided to sit. I'm not in the mood to sell Giuseppina."

"That's what this crazy war is about? A miserable doll hunt? How long has it been going on?"

"Five years."

"And all this time the melamed leaves me in the dark."

"He's a son of a bitch. But you're my Family now."

"Let's do a little arithmetic," Isaac said. "How many dolls have been recaptured? How many are in the collectors' hands?"

"Forty, so far."

"That leaves Giuseppina and nine missing dolls. And you want the fucking Police Department to find those dolls."

"Not the Department. The Black Stocking Twins."

"Grand," Isaac said. "Joey and I join the hunt. Do we run off to Cairo?"

"Not Cairo," Sal said.

"Where then?"

"Manhattan . . . maybe Palermo, maybe Brooklyn, maybe the Bronx. Isaac, the maestros were secretive men. They hid the dolls in cellars. A cellar is very deep."

"So you offer me a pretty bundle. My heart's desire, huh? You'll finance the whole Police Athletic League. You'll build another St. Patrick's Cathedral. All we have to do is bag the missing dolls."

"Correct."

Isaac dropped Giuseppina into Sal's arms.

"I'll think about it," he said.

He stared at Margaret Tolstoy. She must have been privy to the hunt for Peppinninu's dolls. Was she Sal's silent partner? Isaac saw blood. There was betrayal behind every doll. He didn't believe in puppet makers without a past. Peppinninu was a profitable fairy tale. The whole story stank. He'd have heard about these dolls from the melamed. But could Isaac be sure? The melamed had used him again and again.

Margaret accompanied Isaac and Joe to the elevator. She kissed the Pink Commish, her tongue focusing brutally in his mouth, like a brigandess. She wouldn't say a word about the dolls. He climbed into the elevator with Barbarossa.

The door closed, and Isaac saw the last pinch of her orange hair.

7

He couldn't stop dreaming of Margaret Tolstoy. She was Anastasia the brigandess when she arrived at Isaac's school.

It was 1944, and there was a shortage of sugar on every shelf. Isaac was standing under the Williamsburg Bridge with a small nation of thieves. He planned to retire from school. He was fourteen. Little Leo was with him. Leo carried Isaac's ration stamps.

The thieves barked at Isaac. "Sidel, Sidel."

"What?" he said, clutching bags of sugar in the different pockets of his coat.

"I have mousetraps. I have beebee guns. I have prophylactics. Lambskin, Isaac, the best in the world. Made for a king."

"I'll sit on my sugar," he said.

"We'll kidnap Lana Turner. We'll lend her to you, Isaac."

"Keep your Lana Turners."

"We have you six to one," the thieves said. "We could take your sugar, Sidel. And your little brother."

Leo started to cry. Pee trickled from his pants.

Isaac pulled a hammer out of one pocket.

The thieves disappeared from their trading post under the

bridge. Isaac had to station Leo near an open steam pipe until the pants dried. Then he marched back to school with little Leo. He'd signed up for French because it was the language of philosophers, and Isaac wanted to learn from all the little fathers of the French Revolution. But he couldn't get past the heartache of grammar.

He was preparing to fall asleep when a girl walked into his French class. She had large, almond-colored eyes. Her body had a fullness, a texture, that had nothing to do with growing pains or the ripeness that was natural to daughters of the Lower East Side.

She was thirteen and she spoke in rapid-fire French.

Anastasia was a refugee. She'd been to Hilter's Paris. She'd studied the ballet. She'd starved in Odessa. Now she was a foster child who lived with a collection of aunts.

He'd walk her home from school, his pockets bulging and Leo right behind him in pissy pants. He had to beat up all his rivals, who would have also liked to walk her home.

She kept watching him. "Why you wear coat in class?"

"I'm a businessman. I move sugar. I steal it, buy it, collect it."

"And him?" she said, pointing to little Leo.

"He's also a businessman. He carries my ration stamps."

She invited Isaac and Leo to meet her aunts. They were stingy women who sat over a samovar. They bullied Anastasia and scowled at the two businessmen until Isaac cracked open a sugar bag, poured some sugar into a big jar, and gave that jar to the aunts.

They were much kinder to Anastasia with Isaac around, these ersatz aunts.

He went under the bridge with little Leo and returned with a pair of silk stockings and a gold ring. He had to give up most of his ration stamps, because silk was scarce. All the silk in America went into producing life preservers and parachutes.

Anastasia's eyes exploded when she saw the silk.

She kissed him suddenly in the street. Isaac's knees began to knock. Her mouth was moist. Her tongue was like a salamander's tail. It flicked and then it was gone.

She entered her aunts' building with Isaac and Leo, brought them into an alcove under the stairs, and put on the silk stockings over her tattered white socks.

"I know a couple of whiskey priests," Isaac said. "They'd marry anyone for a bag of sugar . . . but we'll have to keep it a secret until I'm seventeen."

He walked home with little Leo.

"Isaac, can I marry her too?"

"Keep quiet," Isaac said. But Anastasia vanished from the Lower East Side. He visited her aunts with his crop of sugar. They already had another niece, a cross-eyed girl who polished the samovar.

"Where's my fiancée?"

"The government has her. Men in big hats."

He used whatever influence he had to find Anastasia. He paid a retired policeman who'd joined the black market of sugar dealers.

"It wasn't the immigration dicks. I searched the records. No one named Anastasia entered the port of New York. She could have been an illegal alien. But I doubt it. It's some hanky-panky, Sidel. A child-labor scam."

"But she was in Odessa last year."

"Odessa? Did she hopscotch across half of Europe?"

"But she knows French. She lived in Paris."

"During the Occupation? Is she Goering's mistress?"

"She's thirteen."

"I hear Goering wouldn't touch a girl over twelve."

Isaac punched the policeman, who landed on his ass, then coughed into a handkerchief. "You have courage, kid. I could

crack your skull. I've done it before. I've hurt people real bad
for less than you're paying me. Forget about her."

But he couldn't. The kiss had marked Sidel. He was still like
that boy with bags of sugar in his pockets. Only the sugar had
turned to dust, and instead of a tapeworm he had that constant
image of Leo trundling behind him in short pants.

His lawyer, Marlon Fitzhugh, arrived at Police Plaza. Deputy
commissioners shuddered at the sight of his dreadlocks. But
Sidel liked to have a Rasta in the house. He would have hired
Fitzhugh as the Department's own chief counsel, but Marlon
preferred to stay on the far side of the police. Most of his clients
were militant churchmen, tax dodgers, and roustabouts who
plunged into the depths of Brooklyn and rarely came out. Isaac
was his only white client. Fitzhugh adored that essential anarchy
of Isaac.

"I may have to go back to Riker's, Marlon. I was up in Belmont
with Joe Barbarossa."

"As the PC and his chauffeur or the Black Stocking Twins?"

"We hit one of Jerry's clubs, and three of his soldiers got
killed. We didn't glock them, Marlon, I swear. It was another
guy. Frannie Meyers and his moon children."

"The badass who sells drugs to black kids. It's lucky he keeps
to the Bronx. He's been sentenced to death in Brooklyn."

"But that won't save me with my own First Dep. Sweets knows
all about the Twins. He's put me on notice."

"You could fire the man."

"I couldn't fire Sweets. He's the best First Dep I ever had."

"He can't touch you, Isaac."

"But he could go to Internal Affairs, or sit with the Bronx D.A.
It's Riker's, Marlon, I'm telling you. The Black Stocking Twins.
Three dead soldiers in the Bronx."

"Isaac, you're paying me by the minute, so listen, please. The man can't touch you. The Twins can glock all the soldiers they want."

"Who says?"

"LeComte."

"Frederic got to Sweets?"

"He doesn't have to get to Sweets. Your budget is tight. Le-Comte pays for all the frills. You couldn't even have a crime lab without the FBIs."

Fitzhugh pressed a button on the time clock he carried with him to all his clients. The clock had once belonged to Bobby Fischer, chess champion of the world, who fled into his own obscurity without the clock. Isaac didn't like this closing down of the timer. It meant that Fitzhugh was no longer charging him. The Rasta wanted something from Isaac.

"I have a message from some of my people. They want you to run for mayor."

"Marlon, the Rastas never vote."

"They'd vote for you. I'm offering myself as your precinct captain in Crown Heights. And the time I give, Isaac, all of it, is off the clock."

"I'd have to go up against the Democratic machine."

"We are the machine."

"Becky Karp isn't going to lie down for us. She's the mayor, Marlon. She owns City Hall."

"The woman can't even step into Brooklyn. You'll whip her ass in the primary. She's a lost soul."

"But I'd have to behave myself. I couldn't wear a mask."

"You can hit Jerry DiAngelis' clubs for the rest of your life."

"Marlon, I can't declare myself right now. My daughter is missing. And . . ."

"Decide, Isaac. Brooklyn can't wait too long. The borough's lying in a mountain of shit." Fitzhugh raised the button on his timer. "Commissioner, you're back on the clock. What else can I do for you?"

"Did you ever hear about a bunch of Sicilian dolls made by a guy called Peppinninu?"

"Isaac, all the voodoo dolls I know never got to Sicily."

"But they're worth millions."

"So am I. Or I would be if I had more paying clients like yourself."

Fitzhugh retrieved his clock and walked out on Isaac, who sat brooding behind his desk. He was the police commissioner and former Hamilton Fellow. He had a whole city of experts at his disposal. He could get curators and librarians and professors of Italian history on the phone. But none of them knew about the pupi palermitiani. He did uncover one source, an assistant curator at the Museum of Natural History who had a passion for puppet theater. Isaac made an appointment with her at a café across from the museum.

Barbarossa brought him uptown. Isaac was already discouraged.

"It's a lot of crap. Million-dollar dolls with green hair. Sal's trying to bend my whistle. It's an FBI caper. LeComte's the puppet master. He pulls all the strings."

"The Bureau is collecting dolls?"

"It's pocket money. LeComte likes to turn a profit . . . do we have a man at Port Authority, Joe?"

"I put him there myself."

"Does he have Marilyn's photograph?"

"Boss, I wouldn't let him go in blind."

"What about that computer jockey at One PP?"

"Nelson Chan? He isn't at Police Plaza. He's with the property clerk."

"I hope he's a terrific thief. I want him to tap into VISA and American Express. If Marilyn's been using her plastic, we might be able to track her down."

"Boss, forgive me, but your daughter has nine or ten married names."

"Tell him I want a printout on every single Marilyn there is."

"Nelson's not that much of a genius. It could take him a year. And the FBIs will arrest him long before that."

"He has diplomatic immunity when he works for the Commish."

Isaac stepped out of the car and entered the Green Hut Café. The curator recognized him and called Isaac to her table. Her name was Monica Bradstreet. She was half Isaac's age.

"Thank you, Dr. Bradstreet, for taking the time. Aren't you a little young to have an interest in the dolls of Sicily? I mean, it's not like Pinocchio. It's esoteric stuff."

"Don't patronize me, Commissioner Sidel."

"I'm sorry," he said. "But have you been to any of the puppet theaters in Palermo?"

"They're all tourist traps. The greatest pupari have disappeared. They're dead."

She had a doll's face, Monica Bradstreet, with lips that were as red as Giuseppina's. And she had a greenish tint to her hair.

"And you haven't been to a single performance?"

"No."

"Not even in New York? How can you help me?"

"Commissioner, there are nine journals devoted to puppet theater. I've read every single article written on your Sicilian dolls. So please don't test my seriousness. What is it you'd like to know?"

"Background. Anything. I don't have the least little handle."

"It was popular theater, theater for the poor. It flourished at the end of the last century. The pupari would hire a barn or a cellar or a tiny stall in the back alleys of Palermo. They had an inventory of dolls, wooden skeletons they would dress in armor and colored skirts. But it wasn't their variety that interested the poor. It was the narratives, Commissioner, tales about Moorish kings and Christian knights, about brigands and clowns. They were always stories of rebellion, with blood and blindness. The tales would expand into enormous narrative cycles, sometimes for a year and a half, until the population got bored. The best pupari would assume all the voices, men's, women's, children's. They would stand behind the curtain, above the stage, and manipulate the dolls with strings and iron rods. It was the rods that made the dolls spectacular, because their movements were violent and unpredictable. A sword fight could last for twenty minutes. Both contestants might lose an arm, a leg, even an ear."

"The dolls didn't have much of a future then."

"They weren't made to have a future. The puparo was often an outlaw, with the carabinieri at his heels. He hid behind the puppet screens and told the most incendiary tales. He incited rebellion in his own way, rebellion against the mainland, against the king and his tax collectors."

"Each puparo had a code, huh?"

"More than a code. He sang out some collective will."

"The will to destroy, like the dolls were destroyed . . . but I'm interested in one particular master, Peppinninu."

Monica laughed. "Peppinninu was the name of a clown in the puppet theater. He had huge testicles. His knight would beat him all the time. So a puparo could wear that name like a mask. I told you. He belonged to a society of outlaws."

"But in all those articles you read, did you hear about fifty dolls that were put aside and never used?"

"Commissioner, no puparo could afford that kind of luxury. Even the most successful ones were a week or two from starvation. It would have been idiotic. They had to use up their inventory, before they themselves were used up."

"But there could have been one crazy dreamer."

"Perhaps. But outlaws are very pragmatic people. Where would they store these mercurial dolls? In their own britches?"

"But if the fifty dolls did exist, how much would they be worth?"

"More than I could pay. But I've never seen them advertised. It's a hoax, Commissioner Sidel."

"Ah, but I held one in my hands. Giuseppina the Brigandess."

"And you think she's part of some fabulous collection. Shame on you, Commissioner, looking for the Maltese Falcon, like Sam Spade. Well, there were falcons in the puppet theater. With snakes and devils on a string. Mermaids and flying fish."

"I'm not Spade," Isaac said. "I'm only the PC." He wasn't involved with mythical birds and flying fish. He wanted Peppinninu.

He got up and shook hands with Monica. She searched his eyes with her doll's face. "Call me again if you have any other questions."

Isaac strode out into the street. Someone had gotten to the lady. She protested a little too much. He climbed into the car, wrapped himself in his blanket.

"What now?" Barbarossa asked.

"We're going to the masks."

8

They rode out to the middle of Mafia country, Brooklyn's Bath Beach. The Commish was fond of suicide patrols. Bath Beach had a crime rate of zero. It was the one community that always policed itself. The Families allowed no internal wars. Opposing dons lived side by side with their mistresses, their wives, their cats, their dogs. And Isaac intended to introduce the Black Stocking Twins into the fucking normal, easy flow of Bath Beach.

Barbarossa parked the car on Bath Avenue, next to a precinct that could have been a Sicilian dollhouse made of bricks. The Commish had no shame. He and Joey went to their masks. But they didn't seek out a social club. They ran up the steps of a private house and knocked on a door near the roof. A blond beauty opened the door. Joey recognized the bitch. It was Alicia, the love of Jerry DiAngelis' life. She was his comare, which was as much of a sweetheart as any man could have when he already had a wife.

"Don't be scared," Isaac said under his mask and thrust himself through the door. "I came for Raoul."

The blond beauty began to cry.

"Alicia, I won't hurt him. I'm renting him for a while."

Barbarossa could see that little boy behind the beauty. Raoul, who must have been eleven. He didn't have those killer eyes of Frannie's coca babies. Raoul was like a startled young deer, Bambi of Bath Beach.

"Please," Alicia said, brushing up against Isaac. "Don't take him. I'll give you money, anything."

"No bribes, Alicia. Raoul will be all right."

"Who are you?"

"The Black Stocking Twins."

"You must be crazy. Do you know whose child this is? He belongs to Jerry DiAngelis . . ."

"Mama," the boy said, "listen to the man."

But Alicia wouldn't listen. She hurled a lamp at Isaac, who ducked but couldn't get out of her way. She kicked Isaac, clawed at his mask.

"Help me, will ya, Joey?"

"Ma'am, don't struggle," Barbarossa said. "You'll make it worse for the boy."

His voice must have calmed Alicia, who stopped trying to scratch Sidel. Raoul took Barbarossa's hand.

"Joey," Isaac said, starting to panic. "Should we pack something? A little suitcase with shirts and underpants?"

"No, boss. Let's get out of here . . . ma'am, I wouldn't scream, because we might get nervous and take it out on Raoul."

"I won't scream," Alicia said.

Her sad eyes were a fucking heartbreaker. Barbarossa wanted to touch her hair. "Boss, let's go."

He clomped down the stairs with Raoul, who was wearing a polo shirt. Isaac was behind them, like a ragged boy in a black stocking. The Twins got into the car with Raoul and took off their masks.

"I'm Isaac," Isaac said. "Remember me? We met at a party once."

"I remember."

"We can stop for some candy . . . but not in this neighborhood."

"Boss, don't sweet-talk him. Leave the kid alone."

The three of them sat up front in Isaac's black Dodge.

"Boss, you shouldn't have kidnapped the fucking kid."

"Don't curse in front of Raoul."

"I'm not cursing. Jerry's gonna shit a red-hot brick."

"I want him to."

"Your daughter's out there in the dark. Your brother's sitting up on Indian Road. They're easy targets."

"Jerry wouldn't touch them. He's not like that."

"But he'll let you have Raoul, huh?"

"He knows my limits."

"Yeah, your limits. You steal a kid, you frighten his mother."

"I have to flush out Jerry, get him to the table. Raoul's the only card I have."

"Isaac Sidel, champion of all the kids, crabbing about schools when you're a kidnapper. I'm voting for Rebecca Karp, not you. Boss, you're the Devil."

"All right, I'm the Devil. But at least I'll learn from Jerry what this dance of the dolls is about."

"Where do we go now?" Barbarossa asked.

"I dunno. I thought Raoul could stay with you."

"At the pingpong club?"

"Why not? You could teach him the game."

"Boss, I'm not Blue Eyes."

"It has nothing to do with Coen," Isaac said.

"Well, I'm not dying at Coen's table."

"Die?" Isaac muttered, his face a mottled color.

"What if Jerry comes to the club with his shooters?"

"Then you give him back Raoul."

He didn't even have time to rip off any Colombian dealers. He was saddled with the kid. And Barbarossa had bills to pay. He didn't want Rosalind thrown out of Riverdale. He sold his last kilo to a young wizard on Wall Street. The wizard was twenty-one years old. He could predict the rise and fall of companies by staring into a screen.

"I'm hungry. I need more blow," the wizard said.

"You'll have to wait."

"I could try another snowman," the wizard said.

"I'm bonded," Barbarossa said. "As reliable as the American eagle. I never disappointed a customer in my life. Don't blame me if you run around the corner and get yourself killed."

"Joey," the wizard said. "I can't wait too long."

But Barbarossa couldn't get back into the business. He cleared off the envelopes and files from Coen's table and started to play pingpong with Raoul. He had to wear his holster, because he couldn't be sure who might sneak up on him at Schiller's club.

"Would you like to call your mother, Raoul?"

"After the game."

The entire spectators' gallery had fallen in love with Raoul. "A refined boy," they said. "Who's his father?" But Schiller seemed to know. He had the natural telepathy of a man who lived all day under artificial light.

"Sidel got you into this," Schiller said to Joe. "Raoul is Jerry DiAngelis' secret son, isn't he?"

"Not so loud," Barbarossa said.

"Why do you follow the whims of that gangster Sidel?"

"Isaac's the PC," Barbarossa said.

"He's still a gangster. He always was."

"I work for him, Schiller. I'm his man."

"That's no excuse," Schiller said, and he boiled string beans and cabbage for Raoul on his private burner at the rear of the gallery, while Barbarossa gave lessons to the kid, taught him the rudiments of pingpong.

The club was very quiet. There were no calls from One PP asking Joe to drive Sidel to the borders of Brooklyn and the Bronx. It was Schiller who discovered the boy's interest in science. Raoul was a fanatic about space travel. He understood how you could get lost in a black hole and never come out, how you could grow younger all the time if you traveled far enough and fast enough in one direction.

"Raoul," Barbarossa said, "what if you got to the end of the line, the fucking edge of the cosmos?"

"There is no edge," Raoul told him, as if he were talking to a child.

"You wouldn't bump into a wall of gas?"

"Gases don't have walls," Raoul said. "They have vapors which sometimes seem like a wall."

"Ah, so here we are, living in a cradle that never ends."

"It will end," Raoul recited to Joe. "The universe will stop growing and everyone who's alive will be squeezed to death."

"A sad story," Barbarossa said.

He was at the table, hitting a pingpong ball with Raoul, when a woman walked into the club. She looked strange and not so strange, like the business of matter and antimatter that Raoul had told him about. Everything in the universe had its own fucking twin, according to Raoul. The woman had frizzy hair. It was Isaac's lost girl, Marilyn the Wild.

She looked at Barbarossa with his holster and pingpong paddle. "Blue Eyes?" she said.

Barbarossa put down his paddle. "I'm not Coen."

"I'm sorry," she said. "I must have been delirious . . . a boy I once knew died at that table. And I was on some kind of pilgrimage."

"You mean this table is like a shrine."

"Yes," she said. "Exactly. And he wore a holster while he played."

"But not a white glove."

She approached the table. "I'm Marilyn Daggers."

"Mrs. Daggers, I know who you are. I work for your dad."

"Oh, God," she said. "Then I wasn't wrong. You are Manfred Coen." And she started shouting at Raoul. "Is he a detective too?"

She ran from the table.

Joe beat her to the door. "Wait," he said. "I'm Barbarossa."

"Well, Mr. Barbarossa, I'll tell you right now. I'm never going to mourn another one of my father's men."

"Don't go," Barbarossa said, but he didn't have the slightest idea what to do with Marilyn Daggers Sidel.

9

Isaac waited for the shit to fly. He had Raoul. He'd broken the little world of Jerry DiAngelis, boss of the Rubinos, who liked to move about Manhattan in his mythical white coat. Jerry had grabbed the Rubinos from Sal. He was the new lord of the Maf, with silver streaks in his black hair. He created fields of danger wherever he walked. He had a ferocious temper. He began punching people when he was twelve, and he'd never stopped. He shied away from interviews. He wasn't like Sidel. He couldn't afford to discuss his own poetics of crime. He let his father-in-law, the melamed, do most of his talking. Jerry didn't theorize. He loved Raoul.

And so Isaac waited. But there was a terrific silence in Mafia land. Didn't have a single threat on the phone. But the shit would have to fly. Isaac was certain of that.

He'd been hungry ever since he woke out of his coma. The Commish couldn't stop eating. And while he sat in his favorite Newyorican restaurant, he noticed someone beside him. Le-Comte was sitting at the next table in his habitual colors: blue on blue.

"That was brilliant," he said. "Swiping Jerry's bastard."

"Don't talk that way about Raoul."

"Pardon me. Isaac, would you like a holy war in the streets?"

"Who's Peppinninu?"

The cultural commissar rolled his eyes. "Is that what this is all about?"

"Who's Peppinninu?"

"An exercise in evasion, like everything in Sicily."

"Sicily," Isaac said. "The FBI is also Sicily. Your whole fucking life is an evasion. Where does Margaret fit in?"

"Isaac, you can't blame me because she happened to show up at your junior high school during the war. How could I have bothered you then? I wasn't born."

"You were a schemer long before you were born. Your molecules were all over the place."

"But that has nothing to do with Margaret. She's Sal Rubino's nurse."

"And she collects me outside the Gerusalemme social club, with three corpses sitting inside, and brings me to Sal."

"She saved your life."

"She and Frannie Meyers, with his children's army. That's some confederates you have in the Bronx. Kids in diapers who sell cocaine and carry Glocks."

"I have to fight Jerry DiAngelis however I can."

"But you're the one who encouraged Sal to tell me about the dolls, and don't deny it."

"Yes, I encouraged Sal."

"Why me?"

"You can retrieve the dolls. I can't."

"And what's your cut?"

"Let's just say I'm Sal's partner in the enterprise."

"Silent partner, huh? Is Justice going into venture capitalism?"

"We have to borrow, Isaac, same as everybody. And I have to finance certain operations."

"Then talk to me, LeComte. Who's Peppinninu?"

"Does it matter? The dolls exist. I have museums in five countries competing for them. There's nothing like those dolls. You saw Sal's brigandess. She's unique. She has whole histories behind her."

"Then raise your millions. Sell Giuseppina."

"That's the catch. The museums aren't interested in singletons. They want the fifty dolls."

"And you can provide the fifty?"

"Not on my own. You're our stalker. You're the Commish."

"And what about Jerry DiAngelis?"

"Jerry's out of the race. He's auctioned the dolls he had to our associates. He's sorry now. He'd like to get his hands on Giuseppina. But he can't have the little lady."

"Give me one reason why I should help you and Sal?"

"If we make the sale, Isaac, I can finance your campaign."

"I'm not running."

"You have to run. Rebecca can't win."

"You should be glad. You'll have a Republican at City Hall."

"I'd rather have my Hamilton Fellow."

"So that's it. I run for mayor and redeem Frederic LeComte."

"Isaac, your own trials commissioner, Malik, will get the Republican nod."

"Good. He'll be the first Moslem mayor we've ever had."

"He can't govern the City."

"LeComte, I'll tell you a secret. Nobody can."

The cultural commissar got up from the table. "Return Raoul. It's not the right time for a civil war."

LeComte walked out of the restaurant. Isaac had his second serving of Moros y Cristianos. Black beans and white rice.

There was a sedan outside the restaurant. Isaac smiled.

"Hello, Iz."

"Foolish man, get inside."

Isaac climbed into the sedan. There weren't any soldiers around. The melamed sat alone.

"Isaac, prepare an obituary, please."

"Jerry has to talk to me first."

"Don't you know him and his pride? He'll never talk while you have Raoul."

"I wouldn't have snatched the kid if you hadn't given me the idea."

The melamed closed his eyes. His skin looked like brittle paper. "What could I have said that brought you to such a conclusion?"

"Didn't you sit in Ratner's and tell me to watch out for my daughter?"

"I told you that Jerry was rash."

"And I'm supposed to be the cautious one. The don wants me dead."

"He wants a lot of things. But your daughter's alive and so are you."

"Don't discuss Marilyn," Isaac said. "She's not part of the negotiations."

"Are we negotiating, Isaac?"

"Yes."

The melamed opened his eyes again. His skin seemed to burst with its own peculiar light. He could have been ten years old or a hundred and ten.

"Iz, you should have told me about Sal's dolls when I was with the Family."

"Dolls?"

"Don't," Isaac said. "You're not an actor, Iz. Neither am I."

"Sal's puppet theater? A small detail."

"You've been fighting over those dolls for five years."

"It's Jerry's project. I don't meddle in all the Sicilian stuff. You'll have to ask him."

"That's what I'm trying to do."

"But you've damaged your standing, Isaac. How can Jerry look into the eyes of his soldiers when he's lost his son?"

"I rented Raoul. There's no danger in that. Jerry knows."

"You've questioned his honor. Now he'll really have to kill you."

"Not until we talk," Isaac said.

"Talk? He'll rip out your tonsils."

"Come with me, Iz. I'll take you to Raoul."

"God forbid. I can't have a part in it. Bring Raoul back to his mother, Isaac. Then Jerry's captains will swear it was a mistake. Two idiots took the wrong boy."

Part Three

10

She'd gone on a pilgrimage and hadn't meant to stay. She only wanted to peek at Coen's table. But she realized the little sin of her life. She couldn't really live with a man. Blue Eyes had haunted her all through her marriages. She'd married to get away from Coen. And the marriages were like stations of a particular cross. That cross was Coen. And here he was, like a risen Christ, with a pingpong paddle and a white glove. Barbarossa. He wasn't blond, but he did have blue eyes.

And Marilyn had to laugh. Because after ten or twenty minutes, she thought of marrying him. She met Schiller, the impresario of that cluttered place. And she met the boy, Raoul, who was a hostage in one of her father's campaigns.

She couldn't seem to hide very much from Isaac's new man. He noticed the scars on her wrist.

"It's nothing," she said. "I was desperate . . . it must have been between marriages. I was living in San Francisco, I think."

But Joe's heart was pounding underneath his holster. It was almost as if a second Roz had drifted into the club, a suicidal sister. He had so much fucking tenderness, he could have cried. He wanted to take care of Marilyn, shelter her in Schiller's back room. But it was like a stinking cage where he slept and squirreled tiny portions of dope. He was a dealer who couldn't deal. He had no product and no chance of robbing some coca merchant. He couldn't keep up with the Colombian trade while he drove Isaac and guarded a little boy.

"I have a sister. Rosalind. She raised me. Roz never married. She has depressions. They're irresistible, like the pull of the moon. I have to keep her locked away in a house, a home for chronic patients."

"And I remind you of her."

"A little," Joe said. "I love Roz, Mrs. Daggers."

"Forget the Daggers part. I'm Marilyn."

Marilyn didn't have a tapeworm like her dad; she had a different radar. *I'm Barbarossa.* It was the start of a romance. She could have taken off her clothes. She wouldn't have been ashamed, not even in front of Schiller and the boy and that circle of kibitzers. But would she lie down with Barbarossa and mourn Manfred Coen? How could she tell in advance?

She looked up and saw the brown eyes of her dad. She'd loved him while he lay in his coma. But he'd survived all his bullet wounds.

"Joey," he said, "you're taking Raoul back to his mother. And no mask. You walk upstairs like a gentleman and deliver the kid."

"Boss, it's Bath Beach."

"There won't be a problem. Jerry's expecting you."

Barbarossa left with the boy. Isaac didn't care about Schiller's dirty looks. Schiller could go piss in a bottle. Isaac was the PC. He could shut down this rathole whenever he liked and end the myth of Coen's pingpong table.

"I was worried. You run from Mark and you don't say a word. I thought you'd be happy with a Legal Aid lawyer. He's your kind of man."

"Isaac, I slapped you once. I'll do it again."

"You're camping out with Leo, aren't you? On Indian Road. My brother tells me nothing. All I'm good for is getting him out of jail."

"I asked him not to tell you."

"Were you going to avoid me, huh?"

"No, Isaac. I needed a rest, time to get ready."

"Ready for what?"

"This. But I didn't expect to meet you in the middle of a crime scene . . . isn't that what they call the place where someone gets killed? The cops rope it off and make chalk marks around the body."

"Marilyn . . ."

"Don't bother rehearsing that old story about Coen. I hope your new angel is a little less devoted to you."

"I don't have an angel. I never did. Keep away from Joe. He's a murderer and a thief."

"Good for him. If he's mean enough he might stay alive . . . good-bye, Isaac."

"Where are you going?"

"To Indian Road. I like to watch the moon with Uncle Leo."

"During the day? That's quite an accomplishment."

"Oh, you can always conjure up the moon, Isaac. All you need is a little imagination."

"When will I see you?"

"That depends."

"On what?"

"If you're nice to Joe."

He was like a duck with a wet ass. He realized it when he turned the corner of Cropsey and Bay Thirteenth in Isaac's Dodge. All of Bath Beach had arrived for Raoul's homecoming party. People hissed at Joe. Sicilian grandmas made the Devil's sign, wiggling their thumbs in preparation to scoop out his eyes. Grandpas shook their backsides and pretended to break wind. Jerry's soldiers spat on the Dodge.

Barbarossa could have been on Nguyen Hue Street in downtown Saigon, with its population of spitters. Bath Beach looked a little like the low buildings along Ben Nghe Canal, where the Mafia was mostly Chinese and the drug lords were marines like himself, men of privilege who sold ounces of every kind of shit on earth. But Barbarossa could never seem to get rich. Wherever he was, he had bills to pay.

He got out of the car with Raoul. All the spitting stopped. The soldiers bowed to Raoul, their own little prince. His ambiguous birth gave him a special aura in their eyes. Raoul didn't live with Jerry. He lived with them in Bath Beach. He and Jerry's comare belonged to Brooklyn. Alicia was the uncrowned queen of Bath Avenue. No merchant would allow her to pay for any of their products. And none of the local stregas put a curse on Jerry's Jewish wife. Bath Beach might lose Alicia and the little prince if Eileen happened to die.

Raoul held Barbarossa's hand, and that qualified him as some holy personage, at least for a little while.

"Don Raoul," the soldiers said, bowing to their prince. Barbarossa grasped the fortune he might have made off the kid. But he wouldn't have taken advantage of Raoul. He was learning the laws of science. And one day he would disappear into his own private black hole.

Up the stairs he went with Raoul to the apartment near the roof. He didn't have to knock. Alicia was waiting at the door. The little prince seemed embarrassed when his mama hugged him. He let go of Barbarossa's hand.

"Thank you," Alicia said to Joe, with the maddening eyes of a blond queen.

"Don't thank him," said a rough voice from inside the door. It belonged to the don of dons, Jerry DiAngelis. No one called him padrino. He was too young, too glamorous in the white coat he had around his shoulders. He was Jerry, that's all. And whatever other Jerrys there might have been in the Maf simply lost their own name. It was "Jerry wants," or "Jerry says," or "talk to Jerry." The melamed was the brains, the manipulator of Jerry's war machine, but Izzy Wasser was always at the edge of things. The captains never had an audience with him. They offered presents to the little prince and made their appointments with Jerry DiAngelis, lord of the Rubino clan.

Barbarossa entered the apartment after Alicia and Raoul. Jerry stood inside without a bodyguard. He was close to fifty, but there were no signs of aging in his silver hair. He was shorter than Joe, but not even a possible descendant of the Nez Percé could compete with a don's white coat, worn in every season of the year, as if Jerry's coat could make the seasons.

Raoul ran out of his mother's arms and into the lizardlike wings of Jerry's coat. The don didn't hide his happiness from Isaac's Twin, the robber policeman who collected medals while he sold drugs. Jerry gathered up Raoul inside the coat, cradled him, swung him around, and dropped him gently on his feet.

"Mr. Black Stocking," he said to Joe. "I don't have a quarrel with you. You work for that stronzo, Isaac. But if you ever put on a mask again in one of my clubs, I'll kill you with my own hands."

"Ah," Barbarossa said. "It's Raoul's homecoming party. You shouldn't make threats."

"It's not a threat, Joey. It's a little fact of life."

"I'm a soldier," Barbarossa said. "I do what Isaac says."

"You're a fucking cop."

"And how many cops do you have on your payroll?"

"I despise every one of them."

"Isaac too?"

"That stronzo was never on my payroll."

"He was once your war chief."

"But he didn't take a dime."

"That makes him dumb."

"And dangerous. You can never tell where the stronzo will turn. Only a crazy man would kidnap Raoul."

"The boss is like a baby. He wouldn't harm Raoul."

"But he comes into Bath Beach with his masks, frightens Alicia. The longer you stay with Isaac, the faster you'll go down. I'll see to that."

"Ah," Barbarossa said, "you'd disappoint the kid. I'm studying science with him. And I haven't finished the course."

He went downstairs to Isaac's Dodge. The car had been caked with mud, the windows marked with children's crayons. Barbarossa couldn't read all the hieroglyphics. Were they calling him "kidnapper" in some Bath Beach dialect, with borrowings from Sicily? He drove to Cropsey Avenue and got the car cleaned.

The men at the car wash winked. They read the hieroglyphics. And they knew that the little prince was fond of this robber policeman.

He went up to Riverdale, rode along Palisade Avenue to his sister's nursery, the walled mansion that wouldn't give out its name. He'd promised to take Roz on a little shopping spree. There weren't any rules at Macabee's. The sanitarium entertained Roz and kept her alive.

Barbarossa met an odd couple on the road. Two octogenarians in bathrobes, a husband and wife. They were trying to escape from the Hebrew Home for the Aged, which was one hill beyond Macabee's. They were treading on the road with such determination that Barbarossa didn't have the heart to capture them.

"Can I give you a lift?"

"Never mind," the woman said. "We're running away."

The Hebrew Home was like a privileged colony with hundreds of celebrated guests: retired musicians, opera singers, actors, professors, and impresarios. The waiting list was immense.

"What's wrong?" Barbarossa asked.

The man kept marching, but the woman turned to Joe.

"The food stinks."

Barbarossa tried to reason with them. "It's an institution. What do you expect?"

"They put us in separate rooms," the man said, without looking back at Joe. "I didn't live this long to become a bachelor. I want to share a room with my wife."

"Ah, it's the bureaucracy," Barbarossa said, driving as slow as he could. "They'll sort it out."

"We have to walk half a mile a day to the dining room. And sometimes we never meet."

Barbarossa was in a hurry to get to Roz, but he couldn't desert this couple. He followed them for a quarter of a mile. They stopped abruptly on the road and wept in each other's arms.

"We're lost," the man said.

Barbarossa returned them to the Hebrew Home. And then he collected Roz. She wouldn't leave Macabee's without adding some color to her face. It troubled him to watch her, because he could remember Roz and her mirror when she was preparing for a date, marking her eyes with a black pencil.

"Sis, it's not the king's breakfast. We're going to Fordham."

"I wouldn't want to embarrass you, Joey. I don't look like your sister. I could be your maiden aunt."

"Ah, you're a knockout."

She started to cry. "You never used to flatter me. That's why I loved you so much. You told the truth, even when you were five."

"I'm a policeman," he said. "I have to lie a little."

She laughed, and all the grayness of a shut-in seemed to go out of Roz. It's a fucking miracle, Barbarossa thought. Smiling. It cures the face.

They walked out of Macabee's holding hands. A dope-dealing cop who had to squire his big sister to Fordham Road, where

Leo Sidel had lived for half a day in the belly of a department store.

"You look different," Roz said.

"Ah, I met a girl . . . just for an hour. Nothing happened. We stood in front of a pingpong table and talked."

"That's not very romantic."

"Sis, it's more romantic than you think. Her boyfriend died at that table maybe nine years ago. That's why we met. She was making a pilgrimage to the table."

"I'm wrong. It is romantic . . . what's her name?"

"Marilyn Daggers . . . don't giggle. Daggers was the name of her last husband."

"How many husbands has she had?"

"Nine or ten."

"Is she Mrs. Bluebeard?"

"Ah, the husbands don't count. She was in love with Manfred Coen . . . the cop who died at the pingpong table."

"And now she's in love with you."

"I never said that. She's the boss's daughter. She belongs to Isaac."

"Poor Joey," Roz said. "If there's anyone Marilyn Daggers doesn't belong to it's her dad."

Barbarossa parked on Fordham Road, with the PC's card in the window. Not even Her Honor, Becky Karp, would have dared tow Isaac's Dodge away. He walked into Alexander's with Roz. It was the Macy's of Fordham Road. Roz went from counter to counter. She tried on dresses, sniffed perfumes, chatted with sales clerks, reminisced with a clerk she might have recalled from a previous outing. The sadness seemed to depart from her body. She had a rhythm at Alexander's, a melodic move that was like dancing. Joe would become a crybaby if he watched her much longer. That's what she lived for. A stroll in Alexander's.

She wouldn't let him buy her anything but the simplest garments she might need at Macabee's.

"Clothes have one language, Joey. Seduction. And who am I going to seduce?"

"Ah, that's just a speech. You love colors. You'll feel good, Roz, in a purple dress."

"I'm driving you into the ground. I know how expensive Macabee's is . . ."

His pager began to sing. It was like an alarm clock. He was waking up all of Alexander's. He saw Schiller's telephone number in the tiny blue screen. He showed his badge to a sales clerk and dialed the pingpong club from her telephone.

Barbarossa heard a familiar growl. "Sidel here. Who is this?"

"Barbarossa."

"Get your ass over to the club. Schiller's hurt."

"Is he at the hospital?"

"No. I'm feeding him soup. He had a visit from Jerry's people. They totaled the place. It looks like an atomic bomb."

11

He had to bring Roz home to Macabee's and try not to alarm her. His hand was twitching under the glove.

"Tell me, Joey."

"Ah, some big don wrecked Schiller's club."

"He must have had a reason. What did you do?"

"Borrow his son."

It took Joe half an hour to soothe his sister and another twenty minutes to bump through traffic and arrive at Schiller's.

The pingpong tables had been reduced to firewood. The nets were all gone. The gate of Schiller's gallery had been sprung from its moorings and hurled across the room. Coen's table, which Barbarossa grew to love in spite of a history that could pain him, was a pile of green splinters.

Schiller's was swollen with dust. Barbarossa had to search for Isaac and the old man. Detectives from Isaac's own elite squad were all over the place. They wore black leather coats and carried shotguns under their arms. Their faces seemed to float across that dust bowl.

Schiller was lying on a blanket in the broken remains of his back room. Isaac leaned over Schiller, fed him with a spoon.

"He hates me, this old man."

"I don't hate you," Schiller said. "You're a murderer, that's all."

"Joey's a murderer too."

"But he doesn't kill his own kind."

Barbarossa couldn't even see Schiller's wounds in all the dust.

"Isaac, Schiller's a vegetarian. He wouldn't step on an ant. Why would Jerry's people touch him?"

"Because I wanted to protect Coen's table, that's why. I'm attached to it. The gangsters gave me a push. It's nothing."

"Nothing? The boss is right. They turned the club into a black storm."

"But they were polite. They allowed all the kibitzers to leave."

"Isaac, we have to go to the masks," Barbarossa said.

"Shhh," Isaac told him. "Not in front of the old man."

"You think I'm an ignorant?" Schiller said. "The Black Stocking Twins. You stole the boy from his father, brought him to my club, kept him a prisoner, and you have to bear the responsibility."

"The Department will pay for all the damages," Isaac said.

"I'm not talking about damages, Mr. Sidel."

Barbarossa heard a brouhaha in the front room. Isaac's detectives were bumping into each other. "Where is he, where is he? Where's the son of a bitch?"

A white package walked through the dust. It was Jerry D., with Raoul inside the skirts of his coat.

"Mr. Schiller, I have to apologize for my men. They're animals. They weren't acting on orders from me. They found out that Raoul had been hiding here, and one of my captains got ambitious. I've already punished him. But I make no excuses. The entire club will be restored, piece by piece. Raoul would like to say something."

The little prince's head emerged from inside the coat.

"Schiller, when will the world end?"

"On a Tuesday," Schiller said from his blanket. "Because it's the one day when all the planets tilt too far. And that's when they're likely to collide."

"Jerry," Isaac said.

"Stronzo, I'm here to pay my respects. I'll deal with you another time."

"But I'll tell my detectives to let you out of the club."

"I don't need permission from your detectives."

"But they're trigger-happy. And there's so much dust. They might bother the boy."

"Stronzo, they'll never bother Raoul."

Jerry D. gathered in the skirts of his coat, hugged Raoul to his chest, and walked back into the dust.

"What's a stronzo?" Schiller asked.

"A piece of shit," Isaac said.

"A long, unlucky piece of shit," said Barbarossa.

Schiller closed his eyes and waited for the dust to disappear.

Part Four

12

Strange firemen arrived with a huge vacuum cleaner that was like a pregnant python. It took six men to maneuver the machine. The mouth of the python sucked up all the dust. Schiller moaned when he saw the entire field of destruction. Nothing in the club had been spared. The lockers, his private burner, the benches, pictures on the wall, the walls themselves, which looked like cotton candy. This was no ordinary gambit in one of Isaac's wars. it was like the horrifying aftermath of Coen's death that had been building, building for years, the final piece of chaos in Isaac's calendar of chaos.

Schiller decided to sell the club, or rather, the ruins of it. He couldn't bear this address without Coen's table. But Schiller had visits from several foremen of the building trades, personal friends of Jerry D. They took no measurements. They kibitzed with Schiller, smoking black cigars and strong cigarettes. And while Schiller met with landlords who were ready to pounce on his lease and turn the club into a supermarket, painters and carpenters showed up, an entire company of men, who camped out in the ruins. No one ordered them about. They didn't seem to have a master plan. But they had their own cassettes. They listened to Caruso while they hammered and sawed.

Schiller wasn't impressed. He was preparing to sign with one of the landlords when he noticed a pingpong table in the far corner. It had a familiar tilt. The legs were wobbly, as they should have been. The green surface was chipped, and the entire top of the table was like a small, scratchy ocean.

Schiller started to shake. He muttered to himself. "Coen's table." He was a vegetarian who didn't believe in visions. He decided not to sell his club. He badgered the chief carpenter.

"Who taught you how to build that table?"

"Ah," the carpenter said, with Caruso in his eyes. "It was Jerry."

"What Jerry?" Schiller asked.

"Jerry," the carpenter said. "Jerry D."

"The Mafia king with his white coat? He gave you the measurements?"

"He didn't have to measure. He had a drawing. I learnt it by heart."

"Impossible," Schiller said.

"Hey," the carpenter said. "We do quality work."

He and his company finished in less than a week. Schiller had his four tables, his spectators' gallery, his burner, his back room. The club stank of fresh paint. The floors didn't have their old gravelly look. The burner was brand new. But he did have Coen's table, or some marvelous rebirth. It wasn't a forgery. Schiller was very sensitive to fakes.

The kibitzers couldn't contain their own wonder. They all flocked back to the club. "It's Manfred's ghost," they said. "He supervised the building of the table."

"Shush," Schiller said. "Coen was a good boy. He wouldn't haunt us like that."

"But you told us yourself. Sometimes you could see him at night . . . near the table. With his short pants and his badge."

"Only when I'm tired," Schiller said. "Then I start to dream. And dreams don't build tables."

"Look," the kibitzers said. "That's Spinoza talking. The philosopher with a rope around his belly. He raises vegetables with the wax inside his ears."

Barbarossa walked into the club. He'd been living at the Prince Regent Hotel. All his check stubs had been lost in the ruins, all his memorabilia, his pingpong paddles, his handcuffs, his extra shirts, his off-duty gun, his extra gloves. He gravitated toward Coen's table. He'd have to off a couple of dealers pretty soon. He was behind in his sister's rent. He'd have to visit the bursar at Macabee's, do a little dance.

"That's Coen's table," Schiller said.

"I'm not blind."

"That's Coen's table."

"Aint it a bitch," Barbarossa said.

"Joey, how did it get there? It was destroyed. You saw it yourself."

"You're the logical one. You tell me."

"The Mafia king hired a carpenter and had it rebuilt."

"Jerry's no pingpong magician. He was never in your club, not until it was totaled."

"Joey, Joey," Schiller said. "A Mafia king can do whatever he wants."

And he walked away from Barbarossa, who hadn't been with Isaac in a week.

The Pink Commish had hurled himself into some sort of exile. He wouldn't page Barbarossa. He watered his plants. Barbarossa didn't like all this silence. He was Isaac's chauffeur, or else he wasn't. He went to One PP and drifted into Isaac's office. The begonia had climbed up the windows and was strangling the walls. Isaac had the look of a jungle creature. His sideburns had begun to grow into a beard.

"I can't get to Jerry. He won't give me a meet."

"You shouldn't have kidnapped Raoul."

"I called the melamed. He swears Jerry's sitting on the moon . . . I had to grab the kid. There was no other way."

"You can't get close to Jerry, with or without Raoul."

"He'll budge. You'll see."

"Boss, I'm not trying to get familiar, but if you ask me, you have your own dick in your hand."

"I'm not asking you, and you are too familiar," Isaac said. "Keep away from my daughter."

"I met her once."

"That's almost half a history with Marilyn the Wild."

"I like her," Barbarossa said. "I won't lie."

"She's a married woman. Keep away."

"Boss, nine husbands aren't much of a marriage."

"Her marriages have nothing to do with Joe Barbarossa. I don't want you near Indian Road."

"What if she comes to Schiller's again?"

"That's no problem. Schiller's doesn't exist."

"You're wrong. Schiller got his club back, with Coen's table. It's risen out of the black dust."

"I'm glad," Isaac said. "If Marilyn comes through the door, you hide from her."

"Can't," Barbarossa said. "You'll have to kill me, boss."

He walked out of Isaac's office, hopped into the Dodge, and raced up to Indian Road.

Leo Sidel was much sturdier outside the tombs of a department store. Barbarossa had to wonder if he was wearing stolen pants and a stolen shirt. But he didn't have that feckless feel of Isaac's delinquent brother. Indian Road had once been a privileged address, the home of aristocrats who preferred the calm of upper Manhattan, with Inwood Hill and Spuyten Duyvil Creek. But most of the aristocrats had left. And Leo was part of some lost tribe that was sliding down from gentility. He couldn't have afforded the rent without Isaac.

"I was looking for Marilyn," Barbarossa said.

"Come inside, Mr. Policeman."

"I'm Barbarossa."

"I know who you are . . . my rescuer. Marilyn mentioned you. It's a pity. She just left. She likes to shop. We both have a weakness for bargain basements . . . you look like a youngster."

"I'm thirty-seven."

"And a very notorious cop. Medals follow you around, I hear, and a couple of corpses."

"Did Marilyn tell you that?"

"Mr. Barbarossa, you have a reputation. You escort the police commissioner. You fight his battles. You wear a mask sometimes. The news starts to travel."

Barbarossa sat with Leo in a window seat that looked out upon the heights of Riverdale, where his sister lived.

"I keep getting calls from the biggest Democrats. They offered me a bounty if I can persuade Isaac to run. Becky Karp is sinking. She had a terrific dive in the last opinion poll. But I couldn't recommend my brother. On top of being a bandit, he's a real shit."

Leo served coffee from a silver pot. Barbarossa's cup had a golden rim. "My mother's china," Leo said. "She was kicked to death by a gang of young hoodlums . . . am I wrong about Isaac, Mr. Barbarossa? I was his accomplice when I was a kid, a tremendous thief."

"I came for Marilyn, Mr. Sidel. I can't judge Isaac. He doesn't want me to visit your niece."

"Of course not. He found her second husband, did you know that? And then sabotaged the marriage. He's like that. You can't fight him. He feints, he counterattacks. You have to lose. He had a girlfriend once. I was in love with her. A Roumanian princess. She disappeared. I still have dreams about her, Mr. Barbarossa."

"You shouldn't. She's surfaced, Mr. Sidel. She kills people for the FBI . . . I have to go. Could you please tell Marilyn I'll try again."

"Does she know where to reach you?"

"Yeah. Manfred Coen's pingpong table."

Barbarossa went down into the street. Indian Road. But this wasn't the land of the Nez Percé. *Chief Joseph*. Barbarossa would have to lead his own children's march against the U.S. cavalry. He couldn't stop thinking of Riverdale. He rode up to Macabee's. His sister was asleep. He knocked on the bursar's door. There was a tiny cluttering noise, and then the door opened. The bursar's face peered out of the darkness, like a bloodless valentine.

"Joe Barbarossa," he said. "My sister is on the second floor . . . I'm a little behind in my rent bills."

"You aren't behind at all," the bursar said. "In fact, your payments are a year in advance."

"I'm lost," Barbarossa said. "I haven't been slipping cash under your door."

"But that was rectified this week."

"Who paid my bills?"

"We received a lump sum."

"Was there a name attached to the money?"

"Yes," the bursar told him. "The name was Raoul."

Barbarossa left the sanitarium, his hand twitching under the white glove.

13

He didn't care if the universe collapsed in upon itself, or if the arrow of time was hiding under Isaac's Dodge. He took his own rocket to the moon and arrived in Bath Beach. He got into a shoving war with Jerry's bodyguards, who were stationed outside Alicia's building on Bath Avenue.

"Hey, stupid, you can't come here. It's off limits. The street belongs to Jerry."

"Raoul's my teacher, and I came for a lesson."

"Don't joke about the little prince."

Two of the bodyguards had him by the hair, but Barbarossa held his Glock between their throats. A window opened under the roof. Jerry stood against the sill, wrapped in his white coat, and called down to his bodyguards.

"He's harmless. A pingpong player. Let him up."

Barbarossa climbed the stairs to Alicia, Jerry, and Raoul. He felt like a moron, wagging his finger in Jerry's face.

"Mr. DiAngelis, no one, no one pays my bills."

"Ah, sit down. Have a bite. Raoul loves you."

"But I'm not one of your warriors."

"Come on. You were kind to the kid."

"The Maf can't meddle in my sister's affairs."

"I wasn't meddling. It's a gift. No strings."

"There are always strings," Barbarossa said.

Jerry rolled his eyes. "Raoul, will you calm this crazy cop?"

"Mr. Joe," the boy said, with all the directness of a little prince. "Sit down and eat."

Barbarossa sat down at the table. Alicia smiled. He couldn't get over how beautiful she was. He'd never had a comare . . . or a wife. He was Barbarossa, the robber policeman and remote relative of an Indian chief. He'd have to remain Roz's little half brother for life.

He had a thick soup made with corn and pimentos. He had pies filled with spicy meat. Jerry's comare had been raised in Argentina. She had a drop of Castilian blood. She could have married a playboy or a diplomat. But she loved Jerry D., and she lived among the Sicilians of Bath Beach, accepted the confines of a hidden marriage. She had Raoul.

Barbarossa stuffed his mouth with meat pies. He started to sweat.

"What's the matter, Mr. Joe?"

"It's nothing," Barbarossa said. "A mild case of malaria."

"Were you in the jungle?" Raoul asked.

"No. I caught it in Saigon . . . there were tremendous mosquitoes during the rainy season."

"And the mosquitoes bit Barbarossa's ass," Jerry said.

"Papa," said the little prince. "Malaria's not a joke."

Jerry D. had dark splotches on his cheeks. "Didn't I tell you, Joey? Raoul loves you."

"Is that why you have bodyguards in the street?"

The splotches disappeared from Jerry's face. "You work for Isaac, and you ask me that? People get ideas. They learn from the police commissioner. He comes into the house with a mask, he runs off with my boy, and I'm supposed to welcome the news? LeComte is a copycat. He could let one of his Mormons put on a mask . . . I'm not giving any second chances."

Barbarossa apologized. "Now tell me how your carpenters resurrected Manfred Coen's pingpong table."

"It was easy . . . Raoul. The kid has a photographic mind. He kept crying, 'Coen, Coen.' I trust Raoul's instincts. He made a thousand sketches of the club."

"Papa, don't exaggerate."

"Joey, they're works of art. I got me the best builders in town and I said, 'Follow every fucking detail.' Didn't I, Raoul?"

"It's nothing special," Raoul said. The little prince was forlorn. His only friends were adults, and he had to endure their odd behavior. They liked to scream and show off. Mr. Joe had a little more sense. He didn't scream so much.

"Son of a bitch," Barbarossa said.

"Don't disappoint Raoul," Jerry said. "I told him how you were losing money driving Isaac around, how you had to support your own big sister, and he said, 'Papa, we have to help Mr. Joe.' Honest to God. No strings."

"Where'd you learn about Rosalind?"

"From LeComte . . . or one of his spies. He doesn't own the street. I do."

"Then do me a favor. The boss is dying up on the fourteenth floor. He has puppets in his head. And some mysterious mother called Peppinninu. Will you meet with Isaac before he melts away?"

"He's a stronzo. Worse than any stranger."

"Then you'll have another PC on your hands, because Isaac won't last. Sit with him."

"Ah," Jerry said, looking at Alicia and Raoul. "I'll think about it."

Barbarossa was like the pingpong ball between a pair of strategists. Isaac and Jerry D. were knocking him around over the net. Barbarossa couldn't even have one simple secret about his

suicidal sister. Isaac owned him, and what about Jerry and Le-
Comte and Raoul? He was the perfect puppet . . . and pingpong
ball. No one had the right to separate him from his sister. He
could have pulled Rosalind, found her another sanitarium. But
he'd begun to feel like a man on the run. And what excuse could
he give to Roz?

He had to hunt down Sidel. The boss wasn't at Police Plaza
or his flat or his Newyorican restaurant. Barbarossa discovered
him on Delancey Street. The boss was wandering like a bum.
He loved to live in the dark under some bridge. And this was
our next mayor. The champion of schoolchildren. The great
detective. The guy who'd been glocked. Barbarossa had to get
out of the car and escort Isaac to his usual front seat.

"Joey, what's happening? Have you been guarding my calendar?"

"You don't have a calendar, boss."

"Where you been? With my daughter up on Indian Road?"

"I missed her by half an hour."

"Joey, remind me to break your leg."

"I was with Jerry D."

Isaac emerged from the collar of his shabby coat. He had a
brittle smile. He was clutching his Glock, digging its plastic nose
against Barbarossa. "I was listening to LeComte's stoolies on
tape. There was talk about my chauffeur grabbing money from
the Maf."

"I'm not your chauffeur, boss."

"What would you call yourself?"

"The Black Stocking Boy. I run a kindergarten class."

"But Jerry D. is still paying for your sister's room up in Riverdale."

"Not Jerry, boss. Raoul."

"That kid must have a terrific allowance."

"I didn't like it, boss. And I went to Bath Beach. I ate some
of Alicia's gaucho pies."

"They welcomed you, huh?"

"Raoul adopted me. Jerry's spies learned from LeComte's spies that I was behind in my bills. So Raoul adopted me."

"It's a classic situation."

"Go on, glock me, boss. You can believe it or not."

Isaac put his plastic gun back inside his pants.

"I have to believe you, Joey. Do I have a choice? Raoul adopted you. We'll leave it at that."

"There are benefits, boss."

"Like what?"

"Jerry agreed to a powwow. You'll have your meet."

"Now I am suspicious," Isaac said, wriggling inside his bum's coat.

The PC's just another homeless person, like I am, Joe figured to himself. But Joe had Blue Eyes' pingpong table. And yet he didn't. It had turned into a table according to Raoul. And Barbarossa couldn't tell who the real author was. Raoul or Manfred's ghost.

"Joey, where's the meet?"

"At the Baron di Napoli social club."

"That's some meet," Isaac said. "We go into Jerry's main headquarters without our masks?"

"Boss, what can I tell you? Take it or leave it."

14

Isaac took the meet. It was either sit with Jerry or go to hell. He couldn't get that puppet master out of his rotten skull. Peppinninu. He didn't care about the rude economics of fifty dolls. The "merchandise" could have a billion backers and buyers. Isaac wasn't an entrepreneur. He needed all the folly of a mad quest. But first he had to solve his war with the don.

He arrived at the Baron di Napoli with one lonely knight. Barbarossa. And Jerry had his captains, who sat with rifles in their laps, since the Baron di Napoli was also a rifle club. These captains mocked Isaac, who'd been chased out of the Family. They squinted into their telescopic sights, aiming at Isaac and clicking their teeth.

"Cut it out," Jerry said. He wasn't wearing his white coat. His red blazer had bone-colored buttons that seemed to match his silver hair.

Isaac pointed to the ceiling.

"Stronzo," Jerry said, "I'm not scared of LeComte's microphones."

"Good. Then I'll be blunt. You wanted to kill me at Chinaman's Chance. You started the war."

"I came to the Chinaman's for Sal Rubino. You shouldn't have been there."

"I'm a cop. I go where I have to go."

"You killed my baby brother."

Isaac groaned. "Is that the source of it, Jerry? Is that where the wound begins? Nose followed me to a baseball diamond. He would have whacked the cardinal and a lot of innocent kids. He was unwired . . . I didn't pull the trigger."

"I know. Your detectives shot him, Barbarossa and that pretty boy, Caroll Brent. But I can't blame Joe. He did his job. You were the triggerman without a trigger."

"Jerry, he was LeComte's rat."

"That doesn't absolve you. He was a dopey kid. He got confused."

"He was knocking off your captains."

"He got confused, I said . . . LeComte, are you listening? I fuck you where you breathe. You and your stronzo sweetheart, Isaac Sidel."

"Joey, let's get out of here. I can't have a conversation with this mutt."

"You'll stay," Jerry said. "I haven't finished."

"I beg your pardon, Jerry dear . . . Joey, are you coming or not?"

"Boss," Barbarossa said, "listen to the man."

"I get it," Isaac said. "Raoul turned Joey around. You can have him. He's your soldier."

Jerry's captains wagged their heads at the former Don Isacco, who looked like he belonged in a hospital for bums.

"Stronzo, my kid doesn't train soldiers for me."

"Then he's a charmer," Isaac said, marching to the door.

"I should have whacked you, Isaac, and I will."

Isaac turned to face the don and his cavaliers, captains with telescopic sights. "I'm ready," he muttered.

"Steal my kid, you cocksucker. That's a capital offense."

"How else could I get your attention, huh?"

"Attention? Isaac, you're marked for life."

"Don't complain. Didn't Raoul have the best chaperone in the world? Barbarossa."

"That's a trick of fate. It means nothing."

"Good-bye, Jerry. Good-bye, Joe. I'm leaving."

"Boss," Barbarossa said, "this was supposed to be a truce."

"A truce with him?" Isaac said, pointing to Jerry D. "He has his shooters. I have mine. I can live without you, Joey. I'll create a thousand Black Stockings. I'll bomb all his clubs."

"Jesus, Jerry," Barbarossa said. "Talk to him about Peppinninu."

"I aint in the mood."

"Ah," Isaac said. "The dummy sold all his dolls. I got that from the horse's mouth."

"Some fucking horse," Jerry said, and started fumbling with a lock. He opened a closet behind the Baron di Napoli's coffee bar. The closet had a steel door. Isaac peeked inside. His head started to swim. His knees sank a little. On a wall, at the rear of the closet, hung five dolls, with the fury of combat on their faces. They were knights of their own particular realm, with painted cheeks, enormous wooden mustaches, big dark eyes, and jeweled skirts. The metal rods rising out of their helmets were attached to hooks in the ceiling that held the dolls in place. Each warrior had a slightly crooked sword in one hand and a shield in the other, and a green or red or violet mop trailing from his helmet, like another head of hair.

"Mr. Sidel, meet my paladins, the dolls of Sicily."

"Do they have names?" Isaac asked, grabbing his own pathetic knees.

"Ah, call them whatever you like."

"But do they have names?"

"Certainly. There's Orlando, Rinaldo, Ruggiero, Gano the traitor, and Charlemagne the king."

"Which one is Charlemagne?"

"I'm not sure . . . Isaac, you can take your pick. Gano's the one with the longest mustache."

"But LeComte said you sold your dolls."

"Yeah. Sold them to myself. I set up a couple of phony collectors, my own middlemen. Why should I give my moves away?"

"So Sal has his brigandess and you have your five bachelors."

"More than five," Jerry said. "I wouldn't keep my whole treasure in one closet."

"And you've been fighting with him over the dolls . . . both of you are trying to catch the biggest fish. A museum? A billionaire?"

"Isaac, all you ever think about is money. I wanted to make a killing. But it got complicated. Experts would get down on their knees and look inside the closet. They quoted prices. They started to sing about this renegade puppeteer who ran down from Naples with his dolls and his guapperia, his stories of outlaws and kings. The carabinieri chased him from town to town. He learned all the Sicilian dialects. His own dolls were a little too clumsy. So he copied from the Sicilian masters. He made smaller dolls, dolls he could carry on his fucking back, like a peddler. But he was no Neapolitan jerk. He had royal blood in him, this puppeteer."

"The baron di Napoli."

"I never said he was a baron."

"He called himself Peppinninu. It intrigued you. And you started collecting the dolls."

"The dolls were in the Family, you dope. I had them since I was a boy. They belonged to my old man."

"He was a doll maker?"

"Stop kidding. He was a grocery clerk. He didn't have a pot to piss in. I had to go out and punch people when I was twelve or we would have starved. The old man would get one wormy wheel of cheese for Christmas. But I had the dolls. I kept them.

JEROME CHARYN

And then this curator comes along. A German. From Cologne.
He starts offering me big dollars. Well, I was a Rubino captain.
I had to tell my don."

"You told Sal?"

"Not that little shit. His uncle Paolo. The don says he'll investigate things. But he wasn't interested in any dolls. He'd already
made plans to have me killed. Sal had poisoned Don Paolo's
mind, said I wanted the whole Family. I had to fight back. It
was the don and his brother Vincent who got killed."

"What about that curator from Cologne?"

"I'm not finished. I was gonna sell. But I get a knock on my
door. It's Roberto DiAngelis. The cousin of a cousin. Another
grocery clerk. He sold cheese with my old man until he retired.
He came to me because now I was his don. He fed me a story
about the dolls. The five paladins had been his. He gave them
to my father to hold. He buried the rest."

"And he was Peppinninu in disguise."

"Keep quiet. He'd inherited the dolls. Peppinninu had been
his master."

"This Roberto was also a puppeteer?"

"One of the best. But he couldn't make a living on Mulberry
Street with a part-time puppet theater. And he wouldn't sell his
Peppinninus. They were sacred to him. Isaac, how could I check?
My old man was dead. 'Don Roberto,' I told him, 'any moron
can pretend to be a puppeteer.' He took me to his cellar and
started pulling on his dolls behind a little stage. He did a whole
saga in forty minutes. About Orlando and his mad fits. I cried like
a baby girl. How could I not believe him? He was a DiAngelis, a
cousin. I swore to him that I'd protect the dolls. I don't fuck
with Family honor."

"But what is Don Roberto doing with his dolls?"

"It's not my business, Isaac. He won't sell. And that crazy old
master of his must have been an anarchist. He didn't want any
of his dolls in a museum."

"Sounds fishy," Isaac said.

"Stronzo, are you calling me a liar?"

"Where is Peppinninu's disciple?"

"On Mulberry Street."

"Take me to him, Jerry. I've never seen a Sicilian puppet show."

"He's retired. I told you. You could get a hernia lifting a doll that's almost half a man. And I can't betray his secrets."

"I'm not moving, Jerry, until you promise me a show."

Jerry glared at Isaac. "Stronzo," he said.

15

They crossed the street, Isaac, Joe, and the don, Jerry Di-
Angelis. They entered another social club, one that had no
guests, and they climbed down into the darkness. Jerry snapped
on a light. And Isaac had a lesson in enchantment. He discovered
the stage of a Sicilian puppet master, with its curtains, its frame,
its back cloths, all registering images of knights and brigands in
terrific battle. There were hundreds of warriors, fighting in field
after field. It was a tiny universe of blood and armor, with mag-
nificent ladies watching from various hills. There were bridges
and castles in the distance, castles that seemed to float right off
the cloth.

Isaac recognized Charlemagne, the isolated king. He battled
no one. He stood with a crown on top of his helmet, contemplat-
ing all the blood.

"Hey," Jerry shouted. "Don Roberto?"

An old man popped up, his head above the curtain. He must
have been standing on a scaffold behind the stage. He was holding a gun.

"You brought the Commish?"

"Didn't I promise?"

Another head appeared. It belonged to young Robert, the child of Don Roberto's old age. He was a lethargic boy in his twenties, this assistant puppet master. Isaac had never seen such an odd coupling of father and son. He had to hop on his toes and reach above the roof of the stage to shake young Robert's hand. The boy had an iron grip to go with his lazy eyes and the spikes in his hair. Don Roberto was still holding his gun.

"Who's the sweetheart?" he asked, waving the gun at Barbarossa.

"That's Joe. He drives the Commish."

"I don't trust him."

"He plays with Raoul."

"That's different," Don Roberto said from his little roof and began to berate his son. "Hey, this isn't a picnic."

Young Robert pulled on his spiky hair. "You're rushing me, and I don't like it."

Both of them sank behind the roof of the stage, like divers into some sunken sea. Isaac could hear a rumble. Then the curtain opened and he saw three tremendous dolls sway with a loud, lyrical pull. Isaac was touched by their metallic dance. They had all the awkwardness of wooden skeletons with armored skin. They seemed more alive to Isaac than Isaac was to himself. The dolls raged in a Sicilian he couldn't understand. But it was still like Shakespeare. He could sense their music.

A woman was on the stage, with two men. Marietta, the warrior queen, with Rinaldo, her liege man, and Moro, the Saracen giant and knight. Moro's head poked around the roof. He had a turban and terrible whiskers. His mouth was completely red. He wore trousers instead of a skirt. His hand was bigger than Isaac's, bigger than the queen's head. He roared at Rinaldo.

It was a love triangle, and Isaac shivered with the fascination of a little boy. The two knights, Rinaldo and the giant, cluttered and clanked around Marietta in a war dance. They sang and spat and menaced one another with their crooked swords. Then the action stopped, and Isaac was heartsore. The dolls had lost their mobility. They stood like dead people.

"Commish," Don Roberto croaked from behind the stage. "I could interpret for you."

"I don't need interpretations."

"I could throw in a little English."

"I prefer the Sicilian way."

"You could trip and get strangled in the melodrama."

"Please," Isaac said.

"What about the sweetheart?"

"Please don't stop the show."

The metal and wood jerked back into motion. Rinaldo and the giant dueled for a solid hour. Sword fell upon shield. Pieces of armor dropped off Rinaldo. He lost his shoulder guards, his neck plate, his iron shoes. He was nothing but raw wood, with eyes and a few other articles. He had to withdraw.

Moro the giant stood alone with Marietta and serenaded her. The queen wouldn't answer him. She raised her sword. And now there was another battle. She was much too swift for the giant. He wouldn't parry her blows. He didn't have the passion to fight Marietta. He was lovesick, that's all. Isaac thought of Anastasia, his own warrior queen.

The curtain came down suddenly, in the thick of battle. It appealed to Isaac, who didn't like ordinary endings.

Ah, he was Moro, the whiskered one, who could defeat knight after knight but never win his queen.

There wasn't any room for Roberto and his son to come out from behind the wings. They had to climb off the scaffolding, cross the stage on their hands and knees, and crawl out from under the curtain, like prisoners of their own establishment.

The maestro wore a gold scarf. He was in his seventies. He'd dyed his hair black and colored his cheeks, like Isaac's own dad, Joel Sidel, the Cézanne of Paris, who was still alive. Young Robert had no affectations. He swam inside his pants. The colors had faded from his shirt. But he had the incredible forearms of a man who had to maneuver enormous dolls and navigate their exits and entrances.

He also had a syrupy voice, and Isaac realized that young Robert did the spoken parts, sang Marietta and Rinaldo and the giant.

They marched upstairs to the vacant social club. Young Robert began to twitch. His father shouted at him.

"He's a hyena. He can't handle the dolls."

"I do my best."

"It's like working with a piece of cardboard. He's so stiff. I have to crouch like a hunchback, and my own boy is asleep."

"Don Roberto," Isaac said, "the sword fights were wonderful."

"They stink."

"Ah, he's never satisfied," Jerry said.

"Leave me alone . . . I was on a stage ladder since I was ten. You had to have three hands. Two aren't enough." He sat down on a stool and started to drink from a silver flask. He offered the flask to Isaac.

Isaac took a gulp. The PC could have been drinking whiskey with worms in it. He offered the flask to young Robert.

"He don't deserve none," Don Roberto said, and swiped the flask out of young Robert's hand. "Let the sweetheart drink," he said, smiling at Barbarossa.

"Careful," Jerry said. "Joe could smash your face."

"I'd love a good wallop," Don Roberto said, sucking on his flask.

Isaac was in awe of the old master. "Maestro, who taught you your craft?"

"I taught myself. No doll maker ever gives his tricks away. I had to educate my elbows and my teeth. It's no Punch and Judy business. A Sicilian doll can break his leg running across a stage. And what if you have a partner who's asleep? You have to do it all yourself."

"And Peppinninu?"

"A mean and miserable guy."

"From Naples."

"So he said. I was nine when I met him. Palermo was a snake pit. I was starving in the streets. The carabinieri were the biggest bandits. They chewed on your bones."

"What about the Sicilian Maf?"

"Ah, Il Figli. The Society of Sons. They were lovable boys. Shot each other's heads off with their 'piccolos,' the little shotguns they carried under their coats."

"Did Peppinninu have a piccolo too?"

"He didn't have much more than his own pants. I felt sorry for him. He couldn't learn any of the dialects. He would louse up all the stories about Charlemagne. And he'd get dizzy going up and down the ladder. But he could carve like nobody could. And he didn't give a crap about tradition. He never copied from another doll. *His* dolls were dreamers. They had trouble in their eyes, like 'Ninu. Took him a month to finish a doll's hand, a whole week for an eyelash."

"How did he ever last long enough to do fifty dolls?"

"Fifty? He did a baker's dozen. I was there. I guarded his treasure. Thirteen dolls."

"But that's not the treasure Sal Rubino talked about. He said fifty dolls."

The maestro started to laugh. He had green and black teeth that looked like the borders of a terrible trough. "Sal's insane. I performed for him when he was a kid. Did you know that? He'd sit with his uncles, Paulo and Vincent. The two dons. He never missed a show. Not like Jerry here."

"Roberto," Jerry said, "I didn't have time for recreation."

"Recreation? The dolls are our past. That's all we have."

"Terrific. I have enough problems running the Family. Sal's been digging up half the cellars in Manhattan, looking for Peppinninus. Right, Roberto?"

"Right . . . my own son hates me, because we have to live like rats in a shoebox."

"You don't have to be a submariner," Isaac said. "Sell Sal all the dolls you have."

The maestro revealed his rotting teeth. "You're Sal's agent. You and the sweetheart. The Black Stocking Twins. You've been going into the cellars . . . for Sal."

He took the pistol out of his pocket. "I'll finish the sweetheart first."

"Ah, gimme the gun," Jerry said.

"No. The sweetheart is mine."

"Gimme the gun."

The old man started to whimper. Jerry took the pistol out of his hand. "You'll hurt yourself. You can't blame Isaac. He has to practice his logic. That's what he's paid for. He's the Commish."

"I couldn't sell," said the maestro. "Not to Sal. Not to the museums. 'Ninu was my master. I had dinner with him every night for seven years, when we could afford to eat. He couldn't attract a crowd. The only independence he had was the dolls. He wasn't kind. He cheated me. But he was my master. And when he died, I buried some of the dolls, bundled up the rest, and brought them to America, the fucking promised land, the land what made me a two-bit clerk along with Jerry's dad."

"And those dolls are still buried in Palermo?"

"Nah. The other pupari were jealous of 'Ninu. They were jackals. They would have dug up every doll. I went back and forth to Sicily. I brought over the dolls two at a time. They were like my children, Mr. Isaac. They were my children."

"And I'm your beautiful doll," young Robert said.

"They don't answer back. They don't give you heartburn and hiccups."

"How did Sal get his hands on Giuseppina?"

"Because I was a fool. And desperate. And my second wife was sick . . . the mother of this hyena. She was in the hospital with a damaged heart. Jerry was in jail. I had to go to Sal. I borrowed money. I gave him Giuseppina as collateral. I never liked her. Her hands are too big."

"And she's the only doll he has?"

"Swear to Christ," the old man said.

"Then where do the collectors come in? How did they discover Peppinninu if you had most of the merchandise?"

"Dunno. He was already a myth. He'd killed a dozen carabinieri on his way to dying."

"Jerry, what happens now?"

"Nothing. Roberto stays in the cellar until I get Sal."

"Sal is LeComte's baby. And even with your five paladins in the closet, you can't battle the FBI and all the other people LeComte has inside his cuffs."

"I'll manage," Jerry said.

"Not without me and Barbarossa."

Isaac shook hands with the maestro and his son with the spiky hair. He would have hugged Jerry, but they'd lost that old comfort between them. They were reluctant allies, involved in a grab bag of ambiguous dolls.

Isaac marched into the street with Barbarossa.

"I want a tail on that cellar, Joey."

"That's impossible, boss. Jerry will spot our sound trucks. This is his country, not ours."

"Then we'll borrow an FBI truck. Let him think it's LeComte. I love the dolls but not mythical doll-makers. Peppinninu is nothing but a fancy cover."

"You can never tell, boss."

"Yeah, Sal says fifty dolls. Roberto says thirteen. It's a fucking shell game. I don't like it."

And both of them climbed into the Dodge like a pair of Peppinninus.

16

He turned to pingpong. Barbarossa had been the champion of Saigon, but he was reluctant to establish his sovereignty at Schiller's. He would play after midnight, when the usual sharks had earned their supper money and would leave him alone. He didn't wear a headband or short pants. But the kibitzers were mesmerized. "He has Manfred's strokes."

And Barbarossa would have to hurl his paddle into the spectators' gallery to break their mad concentration. "I'm not Coen."

He wouldn't bet on a game. He'd hit the ball with Schiller, or some wizard who wanted to relax at the last pingpong club in Manhattan. Barbarossa's customers would come by and pester him.

"I don't have any product," he'd say between strokes. And all his customers disappeared. He planned robberies. He dreamt of drug lords and traficantes. But he played pingpong. He began to understand why Blue Eyes had retreated here. His table was an outpost of tranquillity until Isaac brought his own dirt into the club and got Coen killed.

It was 2:00 A.M., and Joe was hitting with Schiller. The old man had never really recovered from Coen. He was agile in his straw shoes, but he was still Coen's orphan. And Barbarossa drifted into his own dream with every slap of the ball. He wanted to free his head of dolls, those enormous children with helmets and plumes of hair. And then a doll whisked in front of him. He couldn't tell how much armor she was wearing. It was Marilyn the Wild.

"Can't sleep, Joe. Mind if I watch?"

"Ah," he said, "I'm sick of playing," which wasn't true. Schiller never compared him to Coen, but Marilyn could. She'd confuse him with that dead angel of Isaac's. But Barbarossa didn't intend to die.

Schiller returned to the kibitzers, who'd forgotten how to sleep. And Barbarossa was a little bothered. He couldn't take Marilyn into the back room. It was like a warehouse with a bed. He didn't even have a radio. He wouldn't entertain Isaac's daughter in a barren closet.

"I have to confess something, Joe. I dreamt about you before we ever met."

"Marilyn, the man is supposed to say that, not the lady . . . stuff about a dream girl. But I have a hard time remembering my dreams."

"I don't. I dream and dream. Are you embarrassed, Joe?"

"Embarrassed? About landing in your dreams? Yeah, I'm embarrassed."

She touched his hand, not to tease him, but to give him comfort. And he almost cried. "My sister," he said. "She has a place . . . we could go there."

"Joe, whatever you like."

They walked past the spectators' gallery and out of Schiller's. He drove her down in Isaac's Dodge. They never kissed, not once in the car, but Barbarossa could feel all the static. He wanted to rock this skinny girl in his arms. No one would have to kill him. He'd die of tenderness.

He parked on Thirty-fifth and Second. Roz's place was on

Tunnel Exit Street. What kind of address was that? She'd lived over the Midtown Tunnel, in a mountain of fumes. Your face would get black from standing near the window. But Joe had kept the apartment. All of Roz's belongings were here, closets of clothes. And it was the first time Barbarossa had brought a guest.

Marilyn didn't complain. She ran her finger along the soot on the windowsill. She watched the cars come shooting out of the tunnel like shiny ghosts. The landscape appealed to her, and she wouldn't let Joe pull down the blinds. It was like living in a concrete yard.

Joe was on a dream walk. His body touched Marilyn's and the two of them made love on Roz's bed, drowning in sheets that Joe had bought his sister, to prepare for some homecoming that would never happen. He couldn't even feel his own maleness. He didn't have any desire to bite Marilyn, or imprison her. He'd had girlfriends, mistresses, and "matinees," sweethearts for an afternoon. He couldn't spend the night, not with any of them, and here he was falling asleep with Marilyn the Wild in his sister's apartment on Tunnel Exit Street.

He was Barbarossa, the man who never smiled. It was peculiar, because he couldn't bear another body sleeping next to him, and now Barbarossa and Marilyn cuddled like a pair of dolls in a baby carriage . . .

He woke to the smell of coffee and the usual tunnel roars. Marilyn had composed some kind of breakfast. She was wearing one of Rosalind's robes. There was marmalade but no milk, almonds and an old apple that had been lying in the fridge.

"You were playing pingpong in my dream," she said.

"I'm not Coen," Barbarossa said, starting to shake.

"It wasn't Manfred . . . that's the whole point. But I couldn't recognize you until we met."

"Anyone can play pingpong."

"It was you, Joe. Can't you accept the responsibility for it?"

"I'll try."

They had their breakfast, Barbarossa savoring the coffee Marilyn had brewed for him, while he was surrounded by his sister's things.

"I have my own secret," he said. "I held on to the apartment, but it wasn't only for Roz. It was for me and you. It wasn't conscious. It was inside my head."

"Did my father talk about me? *Marilyn the Wild*."

"I wasn't thinking Marilyn. But it was you. I could feel it the minute you walked into the club that first time."

"It was like a click."

"Not a click. A small explosion."

"You think we'll ever get married? I'm not pressuring you, Joe. I was wondering, that's all."

"My sister will have to come to the wedding. I couldn't get married without Roz."

"Isaac will kill us."

"Who cares? Let him kill us."

"Where will we live?"

"In Roz's apartment," Joe said. "She wouldn't want us to live anywhere else."

"Couldn't we make a compromise? I mean, move your sister's clothes to another apartment, one that we picked?"

"But we'd have to keep a room for Roz. She'll cry. She used to say, 'Joey, get married. You shouldn't live alone.' And I'd say, 'Roz, what do I want a wife when I have you?' And now she'll be as happy as hell."

"What if she doesn't like me?"

"Ah, she'll like you."

"But what if she doesn't, Joe?"

"Don't say that. Roz has to like you. If she doesn't, it's on account of her craziness. And I wouldn't let her craziness spoil our marriage."

She'd seen Barbarossa's raw gray hand without the white

glove. He'd stroked her with the hand, which had all the texture of an emery board with chicken pox, and she hadn't said a word.

He put on the glove. "We should go for a walk."

"Where, Joe? Into the tunnel?"

"Tudor City," he said. "It's on a hill. We can look down over the United Nations."

"And pick out all the diplomats."

He laughed. "You can't see a diplomat from the top of the hill. But it's quiet. It has its own garden. It's not like being in New York."

"Good," she said. "I've never been to Tudor City . . . could we afford an apartment, Joe? I have a little trust fund from my mother. She's very rich."

"Marilyn, I have to tell you something. I used to be a drug dealer when I had the time."

"It figures. Isaac called you a murderer and a thief."

"That son of a bitch," Barbarossa said.

Marilyn couldn't stop laughing. Both of them got dressed. They kissed in front of Roz's mirror, each one looking at the other's eyes.

"You're kind of beautiful for a combat veteran," Joe said.

"What veteran?"

"Nine marriages."

"Oh, my God," Marilyn said, cupping a hand to her mouth. "I forgot. I can't marry you right away. I have to get a divorce from Mark. He's my husband."

"Your father told me. A Legal Aid lawyer."

"He's kind, but I don't love him. I shouldn't have married Mark."

There were bits of static in Barbarossa's blue eyes. "I could turn out to be another Mark."

"I never had any clicks with Mark. Not even the smallest explosion."

"I'd hate it if he started to haunt our marriage."

He clipped on his gun and his handcuffs and went into the street with Marilyn. The sidewalk shivered with that constant tread of cars.

They walked up to Second Avenue and away from the tunnel. Joe had a big surprise. There was a boy sitting in the back of Isaac's Dodge. Raoul.

"Jesus, kid, how did you get here? This is my future wife, Mrs. Daggers."

Raoul shook Marilyn's hand. "My father brought me . . . so you wouldn't be alarmed."

"Alarmed about what?"

"I'm not sure, Mr. Joe."

The don himself stepped into the car, Jerry D., wearing his white coat like a king's mantle. "Glad to meet you, Mrs. Daggers."

"We're engaged," Barbarossa said.

"Then I'd like a ticket to the wedding, if there is a wedding."

"Jerry, you shouldn't threaten me like that."

"Well, there's been an accident. Don Roberto was kicked to death."

Joe's blue eyes didn't register the slightest sign. "Let Marilyn out of this."

"I can't, Joey. That's why I brought my kid. She might run to a pay phone and call the Commish. She's Isaac's girl, aint she? . . . I won't harm Mrs. Daggers. But she'll have to come with us."

"Where?"

"To the fucking remains of Don Roberto's puppet theater."

17

The boy wasn't allowed into the cellar. He sat upstairs in the deserted social club across the street from the Baron di Napoli. He had two bodyguards. Jerry and Marilyn and Joe descended into the cellar. The don wasn't even wearing a gun. He didn't make eyes at Marilyn or menace Barbarossa.

Don Roberto was lying on the cellar floor, wrapped in his own curtain, with images of Saracen and Christian knights. His entire face was covered with swollen blue marks. Joe could barely recognize Don Roberto. His ears and nose and mouth were in the wrong place. His eyes were pits in his head, with a lot of jelly.

"Mrs. Daggers doesn't have to see this. She's not the coroner, Jerry. And she has no interest in the dolls."

Marilyn squeezed Joe's hand. "I want to stay."

"Jerry . . ."

"No. I want to stay."

The puppet theater had been torn to pieces. The stage had collapsed. Only the scaffolding stood, and Joe could imagine how Don Roberto had manipulated the dolls. It was like a very low ladder, with a robust upper step that served as a platform. The maestro would have had to live in a permanent crouch as he pulled the rods and strings of a doll.

"Where's young Robert?"

"Dunno."

"You found the old man like this?"

"I didn't find him. My soldiers did. They were bringing Roberto his lunch."

"And you figure it has all the signs of the Black Stocking Twins."

"You and Isaac were the last to see him alive."

"You were there, Jerry. You were also a witness."

"But I didn't kill him. I bring you to the maestro. He does a performance and he's dead."

"So Isaac and me are the bad guys."

"Roberto was a cautious mother. He wouldn't have let strangers into the house. He'd have had to recognize his own killer."

"And what was our motive?"

"Dolls, Joey, dolls. All the Peppinninus he'd buried are gone."

"Okay. We whack the maestro and force young Robert to dig up his dolls. Is that the picture? But why would I need the money? Raoul is paying my bills. And Isaac gives whatever he has to the Delancey Giants. He's like a monk."

"A monk who's running for mayor."

"He hasn't declared himself, has he?"

"There's no one else but Isaac. And he'll need a treasure chest."

"So we take the dolls and turn them into liquid. Who's our broker?"

"Papa Cassidy."

"Jesus, that son of a bitch hates Isaac."

"But he'd put out for the next mayor of New York."

"Look at me, Jerry. Did I kill this old man?"

"You've killed for much less of a reason."

"Did I kill Roberto and roll him inside the curtain?"

The don began to waver. He couldn't seem to say yes or no. And then a masked man came charging down the stairs. He had a Glock in his hand.

"Boss, will you take off that fucking mask. We're having an innocent conversation."

Isaac twisted the stocking off his head. "Jerry, you shouldn't have got my daughter involved in this."

"I came with Joe," Marilyn said.

Isaac peeked at the maestro lying in his own tapestry of knights while the don shoved his chest into Isaac's gun. "Where's Raoul?"

"Upstairs. His two babysitters are a little unconscious, that's all."

"Isaac, did you bring an army into my streets?"

"I'm not that stupid," Isaac said.

"How'd you make us? We just got here."

"I have a microphone in the back seat of the Dodge."

"You bugged your own fucking car?"

"Jerry, lemme bring my lab men down here. They'll solve this caper. They're geniuses."

"No cops. I don't want this shit in the papers. The Feds will start climbing on my ass."

"Then I'll just have a look," Isaac muttered, seeking clues with each turn of his head. It wasn't the Maf. The Maf wouldn't have wrapped Roberto inside a funeral flag. The marks on Roberto's face had come from a different company.

"Isaac, you're not welcome to look."

Isaac would have persisted, but Barbarossa squeezed one of his eyes. They'd developed this telepathic language between them. Isaac didn't have to dance around a corpse. Barbarossa had "read" the riddle of the puppet master's death.

"All right, Jerry. I surrender."

Isaac walked upstairs with Marilyn, Jerry, and Joe. Raoul's babysitters were lying on the floor, with handkerchiefs stuffed into their mouths. Six of Isaac's detectives, wearing black leather coats, were performing magic tricks for Raoul, who sat on the coffee bar with his legs crossed.

"Jesus," Jerry said, "you did bring your troops."

"My daughter was in the cellar. I couldn't take any chances."

"And if they had to hurt my kid?"

"Come on. Did Raoul complain once? They're teaching him tricks."

Jerry hurled himself at the six detectives, who squinted at Isaac, shrugged, gathered up their magic material, and fled the social club without saying good-bye to Raoul.

"Isaac, get off my streets."

"Ah, Jerry," Isaac said, with Marilyn and Barbarossa at his elbows.

"Mr. Joe," Raoul said, "you have a beautiful wife."

"She's not my wife."

"But she will be," Raoul said, and Isaac began to wonder if Jerry's little bastard was a wizard with brutal insights.

He walked out with Marilyn and Barbarossa into a street filled with cops. There were fifty of them, with the same long leather coats. Barbarossa despised them.

"Boss, you shouldn't have brought your musketeers."

"And you should have kept away from Marilyn."

"Stop it," Marilyn said. "I'm with Joe."

They got into the Dodge, the three of them sitting up front, like a row of angry children.

"Joey, tell me about the riddle."

"Later, boss. After we take Marilyn home."

"Now," Isaac said. "I can't stand the suspense."

"Well, stepping on a man's face and throwing him into a blanket, that's a Frannie Meyers special. It was his trademark in Nam. He'd get into a fight with some dealer from the Chinese district, hire a gang of local brats to kick the dealer's brains out, and then stuff him inside an American flag."

"But Mulberry Street isn't Vietnam. Someone would have seen Frannie Meyers breaking into one of Jerry's clubs."

"Not if the door was left open."

"Who would have done such a thing? Raoul?"

"No. Young Robert."

"Betrayed his own dad?"

"Why not? He wasn't exactly in love with the old man."

"And Frannie's coca babies did the job?"

"Yeah, they have a funny habit of wrecking people and places."

"Joey, they're twelve-year-old kids."

"Some of them are fourteen, boss. And I recognized their signature. I've been doing deals in the Bronx."

"What's a coca baby?" Marilyn asked.

"Ah, that's a lovely question of law," Isaac said. "A skunk like Frannie Meyers will hire thirteen-year-old sheriffs to guard his drugs and go to war, because they're untouchable. They can't be tried for murder. They can't be sentenced. They can't sit in jail."

"Yeah," Barbarossa said. "They come with their mothers to juvenile court, sing a sad song, and they're out on the street."

"They're kids," Isaac said. "Kids like to sing."

"Boss, you saw their work."

"Any mutt can step on an old man's face."

"Not with that viciousness. It's their signature. A Bronx trample. Believe it. And Frannie made the flag."

"Suppose it was a different gang, trying to copy Fran."

"I thought of that," Barbarossa said. "But no one can kick like those babies. It was Fran."

Isaac poked his head out the window and waved to his musketeers, who had assembled inside a big brown bus. The bus began to follow Barbarossa.

"Boss, can't we do without your death squad?"

"They're good boys," Isaac said.

"I'd rather trust the coca babies."

Barbarossa drove up to Indian Road with the brown bus behind him. He parked in front of Leo Sidel's apartment house. Marilyn kissed Barbarossa and got out of the car.

"You're going to murder children, aren't you?"

Isaac shook his head. "She's always jumping to conclusions, that daughter of mine."

She touched Barbarossa's ear. "When will I see you, Joe?"

"Soon," Barbarossa said, reluctant to make appointments with Marilyn around her dad. He wasn't going to talk about Tunnel Exit Street.

"Joe, can't you tell? It's Manfred all over again. I know my father. He'll get you killed."

"I'm not Coen," Barbarossa said, and Marilyn ran into the apartment house, her hair blowing against the wind off Spuyten Duyvil Creek.

18

It was called Crazy Corners, where Valentine Avenue bumped into Kingsbridge Road, a little east of Poe Park. But Frannie Meyers' fortress was only a building with a very deep court. He bought the building in 1979 and tossed out every tenant until he became the sultan of Valentine Avenue. He would watch Poe Cottage from his slanted roof. The author of "Annabel Lee" had spent two years in that little bungalow, where his wife Virginia had died. Poe lived like a poor mouse. He had to sell his furniture to bury the wife. He'd married Virginia when she was thirteen. Frannie loved that part of Poe's life. Edgar Poe was his favorite drug addict.

Frannie donated thousands of dollars to the upkeep of Poe Cottage. He was a "citizen" of Valentine Avenue. He wouldn't package drugs at Crazy Corners. He had other outlets—abandoned factories, inconspicuous storefronts, hidden apartments—where he maintained his crack houses and oficinas. Crazy Corners was a dormitory and a playpen for his child wonders, who lived with Fran. Some were orphans who'd disappeared from the Bronx shelter, but most of them weren't. They were kids with a sense of industry in their hearts, who earned hundreds of dollars a day and supported their mothers, sisters, uncles, absentee fathers, and aunts. They were also truants, but no officers from the Board of Education ever bothered about them. Frannie managed to have their names removed from each of their schools' attendance sheets. They were floating brats with their own Board of Ed: Crazy Corners.

It was a six-story brick and stone castle that had been put up on Valentine Avenue during the great building boom of the twenties. Terra-cotta "jewels" decorated the upper tiers of the building. There were goblins and heads of wild geese growing out of the walls. There was a fountain in the great sunken court that had stopped spitting water. The court itself was treacherous. There were holes in its concrete trails. An unwary boy could plunge into a pile of debris. Rats paraded near the fountain. Frannie's boys would chase them with hunting knives and blackjacks. Rat bashing was part of their curriculum.

There had been a hundred and ten apartments, but Frannie tore through the inner walls and now he had a maze of rooms for the boys and half a floor to himself. He wouldn't allow prostitutes on the premises. The boys would meet their chicas at bottle clubs for coca babies like themselves. They'd carry shopping bags stuffed with money from their coca sales, leave the shopping bags behind some counter, and start to dance. But no matter who they were with, they always went to bed alone on Valentine Avenue in the Bronx.

Isaac stood on a roof across from Crazy Corners with Barbarossa and a pair of binoculars. His musketeers were sitting below in that brown bus on the blind side of Frannie's castle. They could have charged Crazy Corners in a minute and a half. They had sledgehammers and tear gas and explosive caps. They had armor-plated shields and shatterproof visors on their helmets. And Isaac had a band of sharpshooters behind the bus. If he had to, he would "levitate" them to the roofs.

He could have invented a little fairy tale around Frannie Meyers and got himself a warrant, but he didn't have the time or the patience. He could have falsified affidavits, manufactured evidence, but he wanted Frannie now.

He'd wander into Frannie's court in a fiberglass vest, provoke the little bastard and his babies, let them take a couple of shots before his musketeers broke into Crazy Corners and captured Fran.

Looking through the portholes of his binoculars, he discovered some of the kids playing basketball in a narrow gym on the second floor. They weren't wearing uniforms like his Delancey Giants. The kids played in their underpants. They weren't cautious. They drove for the basket with all the concentration of young entrepreneurs.

"Ah, shit," Isaac said and screamed into his field radio. "Moses to Captain Blood, Moses to Captain Blood, sink the galleon, send it home."

He tossed the radio into his pocket.

"I'm glad, boss. We can get to Fran without the musketeers. Should we go to our masks?"

"I'm not in the mood," Isaac said. "The kids will laugh at us."

He went down into the street with Joe, put on the commissioner's badge he hardly ever wore, and walked into Crazy Corners. The concrete paths seemed to crumble under his shoes. It was like struggling against slightly hardened quicksand. One of his ankles got lost. He had to hug his own leg to find that ankle again. He hated the idea of mythological journeys. But he could have been entering the wormy regions of his own past. He might have hardened himself against the coca babies if he hadn't seen them in short pants.

"Frannie Meyers," he shouted, "we have to talk."

Windows opened everywhere. Strange hammers began to hurtle down at him and Barbarossa. The hammers were bottles of ketchup distorted by their own velocity and the wind. Isaac and Barbarossa had to duck against the barrage of bottles, which landed with a kiss and a shower of ketchup and glass.

Frannie appeared inside a window frame, with a kerchief around his head and a chorus of boys behind him.

"The Black Stocking Twins . . . Sidel, you look a little naked without your mask."

Isaac displayed his badge. "Fran, I didn't come as a policeman, I promise. Alejo Tomás deputized me. I'm the chancellor's man."

"You and your badge are full of shit, Mr. Deputy Sidel. Tomás hates your guts."

Alejo Tomás was chancellor of all the public schools. Isaac had been battling with him for years over the selling of political favors, the negligence and the corruption, and the wholesale abandonment of schoolchildren. He'd attacked Alejo's cousin, Carlos Maria Montalbán, superintendent of District One B on the Lower East Side. Montalbán had been stealing school supplies and Isaac had involved him in one of his own crusades and got Maria killed. Then he realized how devoted Maria had been to the little girls and boys of One B, how he'd fought against the chaos of the system. And Isaac began doing penance in the public schools. He'd lecture to Maria's girls, attend sewing classes, and he began to make his own peace with Alejo Tomás.

"Alejo doesn't have to love me," Isaac said, pointing to the badge. "I'm still his deputy. And so is Barbarossa. We have to talk about the schoolchildren you're hiding in this castle. Fran, I'm coming upstairs."

"Maricón," Frannie said. "I'll scratch your eyes out."

"Scratch," Isaac said and he ran across the crumbling paths with Barbarossa, while the bottles started to fly.

"It's raining ketchup," Barbarossa said. "I can't believe it."

"What do you expect?" Isaac growled. "This is Crazy Corners. Anything goes."

They galloped across the broken concrete, passed the fountain, and entered the fucking castle. There were no guards at the door. Frannie wouldn't keep any Glocks in the house. He'd never leave himself vulnerable to a police raid. LeComte was his rabbi and his coach. LeComte had helped him memorize all the briar patches in the penal code. The castle was clean. And if there ever was a sudden assault from a rival gang, Frannie would go to the stash of weapons on the roof adjoining his. He owned the entire block, which served as an elaborate tunnel for Frannie and the boys, who could hop from roof to roof. Frannie didn't advertise his status as a real-estate mogul. He was the master of Crazy Corners, and that was enough.

"Boss, you can't reason with Fran. I wear that glove on account of him. He's the guy who crippled my hand."

"I'll remember that," Isaac said. "Come on."

They climbed flights of stairs that were strewn with candy wrappers and articles of children's clothing.

"Joey, are there other dormitories like this in the Bronx?"

"Yeah, boss."

"I must be asleep. I'd better get my ass away from the four-teenth floor."

"Ah, all the commissioners are like you. They think the whole world is Manhattan."

"I travel," Isaac said. "I move around."

"When was the last time you visited Poe Cottage?"

But Isaac wouldn't answer. He climbed and climbed. Boys stood on the landings, watching him as if he were an extraterres-trial who'd arrived on their own planet of the Bronx. But they winked at Joe. They were already involved in Frannie's war with Barbarossa.

"Hey Joey, how you been?"

"Surviving," Barbarossa said.

Isaac wasn't so sure about their national boundaries. Some were Newyoricans, like the late Maria Montalbán. Others were dark- and light-skinned babies from Panama and the Dominican

Republic. A few were refugees from Harlem. He saw black kids with blue eyes, blondies with nigger lips, Chinese with Peruvian cheeks.

He got to the top of the stairs. Frannie was sitting on some kind of throne in a very long room. It was the only chair around. Isaac didn't enjoy the room. It was like visiting Mussolini . . . or Charlemagne. This Charlemagne wore a kerchief, and he had fourteen "peers," boys who stood behind the throne. They wore gold chains around their necks. They had silver bracelets and complicated rings. They carried a Bronx shillelagh, a broom handle with a very sharp nail sticking out of one end. Isaac had never encountered such devoted, heartless boys. His legs dipped a trifle. I'm winded, he muttered to himself. It's only the climb. But he could imagine the boys marking him with their Bronx shillelaghs.

"Hiya, Joe," Frannie said, like some Charlemagne in his chair. "How's the Commish?"

"We're fine, Frannie, fine."

"He wants to arrest my boys with some fucking writ from the Board of Education. They dropped out of school. There were no books. There wasn't even an apple in the lunchroom. I educate them, Mr. Bullshit Deputy Sidel. I teach them how to save."

"And to step on an old man in Little Italy."

"What is this?" Frannie asked. "I thought he was being friendly. First he says he didn't come as a cop. And then he calls me a homicidal?"

"Hearts and flowers, Fran. Why did you kill Don Roberto?"

"Joey, will you please remind the imbecile that I can have him thrown down six flights of stairs. This is my house." Frannie squinted with one eye. "Who's Don Roberto?"

"A puppet master," Isaac said. "Fran, don't play with me."

"I been playing all my life. I played with Joe, and he wears a white glove. And if I play with you, Mr. Deputy, you won't need a glove."

"But I have a gun, Fran. And I can glock you before any of your children put a nail in my head."

"Don't say children. They're my associates . . . young adults. And you can glock me, Isaac. See if I care. You're on a suicide mission. Aint that right, Joey? Because only a suicidal would walk into my house."

"I'm fond of suicides," Isaac said.

Barbarossa started to shake. Suicide talk reminded him of his sister.

"Is it the malaria, Joe?" Frannie asked with a sudden sweetness in his eyes. "Is it catching up with you, kid? I get the shivers every other week . . . and the shits. My associates have to feed me soup."

"I'll cry for you," Isaac said. "I will. But who hired you to whack that old man and steal his dolls?"

"Joey, I'm getting cross with the maricón. He comes here without a hello. He doesn't bring me presents. He plays the truant officer, puts on a phony badge."

"It isn't phony," Isaac said. "It has gold points."

"I've seen better badges in the five-and-ten."

"Kiss my ass," Isaac said. "I'll close all your crack houses, I'll put your little partners in a State farm. I'll shut all the water pipes on Valentine Avenue. I can do it."

Barbarossa nudged Isaac's arm. "Boss, slow down."

"I'm not slowing down. He loses his castle if he can't give me what I want."

The boys behind Fran wet their fingers and stroked the nails on their Bronx shillelaghs. Barbarossa turned around. Other boys had entered the throne room with their shillelaghs. They surrounded Isaac and Barbarossa.

"Boss," Barbarossa whispered, "I'll waste Fran, but I'm not shooting at a kindergarten."

"What kindergarten? You said they were fourteen."

Barbarossa watched the glint of nails as the kids edged closer and closer. He was sad. He didn't want Rosalind to be alone in this world. He shouldn't have brought the Commish to Crazy Corners. Isaac couldn't understand the dynamics of a dormitory. A door opened behind the throne. A woman emerged with an enormous "hat" of orange hair. It was Margaret Tolstoy. Isaac lost his desire for battle. Margaret was right in the middle of Don Roberto's death. It was one more FBI caper.

She fondled Frannie, looking at Isaac with her almond eyes. "He has to behave," Frannie said. "He's in my house."

She approached Isaac, kissed him on the mouth. He couldn't even say "Anastasia." She kissed Barbarossa too, but he could only taste the salt on her lip. She grasped both men by their arms.

"I'm not leaving," Isaac said. "I'm interrogating Fran."

"Isaac," she nibbled into his ear. "I can keep you alive for five minutes, no more . . . Joey, explain the situation to your boss."

"Margaret," Isaac said, "who were you entertaining in that back room? LeComte or Sal Rubino?"

Anastasia shoved Isaac gently to the stairs, walked him down six flights, with Barbarossa behind them, while the coca babies sneered from the landings.

They got to the courtyard, crossed that concrete ocean, and arrived at the cracked cement of Valentine Avenue.

"It's LeComte's party, isn't it? I love you, Margaret, but I'll hunt you down if I have to."

"Promises, promises," she said.

"Where are you going?" Isaac asked, like a jealous husband. "Darling, I have to work."

She stepped into a limo that was parked across the street and disappeared from Crazy Corners.

Isaac fell into Barbarossa's arms.

"Boss," Barbarossa said, "boss."

Isaac opened his eyes. "It's nothing. I have fainting fits. I black out. The whole world spins. I feel better now."

But Isaac was as morose as he could remember. He had an echo in his ear. *Margaret is a murderess, Margaret is a murderess.* And for the only time in his career as a cop he was frightened of the case he had to solve.

19

The whole town had turned into Crazy Corners.

He couldn't find LeComte, he couldn't find Sal. He was living in a castle where every door was closed. LeComte wasn't at his office on St. Andrews Plaza. He wasn't at his usual cribs. Isaac rang the Justice Department in D.C. But LeComte's secretary kept saying he was out on the green somewhere, putting with a group of generals from the CIA. And Sal Rubino wasn't in his Manhattan roost. Isaac couldn't even get to Papa Cassidy, the Mafia's own billionaire and the broker of whatever deal was going down for the dolls. Papa was on some professional junket that never seemed to end. "He's shooting lions in the Sahara," Papa's assistant said. But there were no lions in the Sahara, none that Isaac knew of.

In his idleness he began to plot the destruction of Crazy Corners. Helicopters. He'd attack from the sky. With dumdum bullets and a little Manhattan napalm that could set any castle on fire. He could cajole the Bronx D.A. into lending Isaac some of his subpoena powers. But he'd move without the D.A. He'd clamp Frannie Meyers into leg irons and round up the coca babies, send them to a farm where they'd have to pick vegetables or starve. He'd make them into pioneers. Then he'd look for his Rasta lawyer, Marlon Fitzhugh, to protect him from Frannie's own lawyers and the FBI. They'd scream commissioner's conspiracy, false arrest, and Isaac could advise them to scratch themselves. They could lock him out of One PP. He was a jailbird. He'd already sat in the clink.

His phone rang. It was Mario Klein, the mayor's personal secretary. He ran the City of New York on most days, when Lady Rebecca was on a shopping binge or sleeping with one of her fire chiefs. She'd lost her appetite for the rough-and-tumble encounters with her constituents. She'd stopped calling people "cocksucker." She'd abandoned her abrasive style. Rebecca Karp had no style. She was becoming catatonic. She'd withdrawn inside the whitewashed walls of Gracie Mansion and wouldn't come out. She saw no one besides her secretary.

"Isaac," Mario said, "Rebecca wants to see you."

"Come on, I'm the last person she'd ever want to see. Becky thinks I'm trying to steal her job. Mario, it isn't true."

Isaac liked the little secretary. He was devoted to Becky Karp. He would select the wallpaper at the mansion, prepare the menus with Becky's cook, make her bank deposits, pencil in the time slots for her fire chiefs.

"Isaac," the secretary said, "Rebecca is in too much of a funk to worry about the truth. She's in a black hole, and she asked for you. The woman hasn't talked in a week."

"I'll collect my driver."

"That won't be necessary. I have a car waiting for you at the bottom of Police Plaza."

And so Isaac was driven up to Carl Schurz park in the mayor's battleship, a blue Chrysler with black leather cushions. He had a tray attached to his seat, with a sandwich and a cup of soup, compliments of the Rebecca Karp Reelection Committee. Now he grasped this summons to Gracie Mansion. It was another of

Becky's tricks. Trying to gather Isaac's support in the conspiracy to reelect Rebecca Karp.

He ate the sandwich and drank the soup and was delivered to the mansion's steps. He'd made love to Rebecca in five different bedrooms during the period of their romance, when he'd been *her* Commish and would have his secret sessions with Rebecca twice a month. It was like comfortable incest, brother and sister taking exercise together. But the exercise had stopped. He wouldn't visit the mayor after Margaret reappeared.

Mario Klein welcomed him at the door. The secretary had a cold. He sneezed into a handkerchief. He was wrapped up in a flannel robe. He lived at the mansion with Rebecca, who couldn't bear to be alone. He was in his forties, with a slight bald spot. He had muscular arms and a white mustache. He worked out with Rebecca in the little gym he'd assembled in the attic. He'd become Rebecca's powerbroker, but he could no longer sell her to the City.

"Mario," Issac said, "who's the chairman of Rebecca's reelection committee?"

"I am."

"And whose idea was it for this Cinderella ride?"

"Mine, Isaac. Rebecca is in no condition to have ideas."

"And you're hoping I won't sink her administration."

"That's not asking much. You're her police chief."

"Not to worry," Isaac said. "I wouldn't knock Rebecca out of the box. I don't intend to run."

"We know that."

"Then why'd you bring me here?"

"I told you on the telephone. Rebecca wants to see you."

He led Isaac outside to the porch, where Rebecca sat in a rocking chair, watching a school of swallows dive over the growling waters of Hell Gate. Her eyes had fastened on a particular wing of birds that moved like the little dark points of one perfect creature. She had a blanket around her shoulders. She'd been a beauty queen, Miss Rockaway of 1947, but she looked eighty years old. The texture had gone out of her face. She was beyond the turmoil of any election.

Isaac crouched beside her rocking chair. "Becky, what's wrong?"

Her eyes went off the birds, but they couldn't seem to absorb Isaac, to take him in. He was like a benign stranger who'd come to her porch.

"It's me, Isaac, the Pink Commish."

"The cuckold," she said.

"Becky, that isn't nice. I separated from the Countess Kathleen. Haven't had a wife in years."

"I'm not talking about Kathleen . . . I'm having a breakdown, Isaac. You ran from me. You fell in love with the biggest whore the FBI ever had."

"I won't discuss Anastasia," he said.

"You'll discuss." She started to cry. Her tears were enormous. "I can't walk. My legs are too weak."

"Come on, you have your own gym in the attic. You work out with Mario every morning. You're in better shape than I am."

"Mario, tell the klutz."

"The mayor can't move," Mario said.

"What do her doctors say?"

"Temporary paralysis."

"Temporary paralysis?" Isaac muttered. "Who the hell hasn't had temporary paralysis? Means nothing."

"Isaac, I don't have a single Democrat on my side. The whole machine is against me. And I can't afford to quit. I'll lose Gracie Mansion. It's my house, Isaac. I couldn't live anywhere else."

"Come on, it's a fucking museum four days a week. Do you want tourists in your living room all the time? . . . I'll find you a flat. I'm the PC."

"She's not looking for a flat," Mario said. "Listen to the lady."

"Then what can I do?" Isaac asked, shrugging his shoulders and watching a fireboat race around the bend of Ward's Island.

"You can sit where she sits."

"Mario, I'm dense today. I don't have your lightning mind. I brood a lot. I look at my navel."

"Isaac . . ."

"I give Becky the kiss of death and run for mayor, is that it? Well, I'm not Murder, Incorporated. I don't do hits."

"She won't campaign, Isaac. And she can't win. I've canvased all the precincts. If she ran against Nikita Khrushchev, she'd only get twenty-nine percent of the vote."

"Khrushchev is dead."

"That's what I told you. She can't win."

"Even if Becky bows out, I still might not get the nomination."

"It's a cinch."

"And the Republicans?"

"They'll lie down and endorse the Democratic nominee. They wouldn't dare go up against Sidel, the law-and-order man."

"But the Republicans have Malik."

"A Turk doesn't have a chance in this town . . . they'll come begging and ask you to appoint a few Republican commissioners. And we'll say yes."

"Ah, you'll be my campaign manager."

"Only if you want me, Isaac."

"But I don't have a dime. I can't run without cash."

"No problem. We'll get whatever we need from Rebecca's Reelection Committee . . . with her approval, of course."

"A touch of fiscal magic, huh Mario?"

"It's perfectly legal."

"And all you'll ask is that I save a room for Rebecca at the mansion."

"That's about it. Rebecca would rather have her Isaac than

some pol who's been stabbing her in the back . . . the town loves
you. You'll have to get used to that."

"But will it love me when I can't deliver?"

Rebecca started to cackle in her rocking chair. "I told you he's
a klutz . . . Isaac, this is New York. Nobody can deliver."

"Then why should I run?"

"He's sulking," Becky said. "Because you'll be a player, that's
why."

"I am a player."

"No, you're my police chief. The cardinal's a player, not
you . . . Mario, will ya prove my point? I could have a hemor-
rhage sitting in this chair."

Mario went back inside the mansion and returned with a
telephone. "Isaac, anyone in particular you haven't been able to
reach?"

"Papa Cassidy," Isaac said. "He's shooting lions in the Sahara."

Rebecca started cackling again. "That's Papa's standard line
with retards."

Mario dialed Papa Cassidy, whispered a few words, then hung
up. "Papa's out of town. He'll get back to us."

"After he finishes with the lions," Isaac said, grinning at Mario
and Rebecca Karp. He leaned against the porch rails. The porch
had begun to rot. Isaac didn't hunger for this mansion. Rebecca
could have her fire chiefs and her chair. Isaac would live without
Hell Gate.

He was planning to exit when the phone started ringing.
Rebecca plucked it out of its cradle, and Isaac discovered a
telephone in his hand.

"Sidel here," he said.

"I thought this was the mayor's mansion."

"It is, Papa. But Becky asked me to take the call. I hear you're
in the doll business these days."

"You're mixed up, Sidel. You must be crazy."

"Tell me, Papa, is the Sahara very far from Palermo? Lions

and dolls, that's a beautiful combination . . . how's the child bride? How's Delia St. John?"

"Delia's not a child."

"Does she still dance?"

"Only in my bed," Papa told him and hung up on the Pink Commish.

The mayor had fallen asleep. Isaac and Mario stood at the far end of the porch.

"Is Joey wearing his white glove?"

"Mario, you could ask him yourself."

"I don't get along with Barbarossa."

"Is that why you had your own man drive me up to Gracie?"

"Just ask him about Montezuma."

"What's all the mystery?"

"Drugs, Isaac, drugs. Barbarossa deals. And so does Papa . . . those dolls of yours are a drug scam."

"Mario, keep quiet. I'm the cop. You're a secretary." But Isaac saw dark spots between his eyes. "Montezuma," he muttered.

"Ask Joe. The Maf is bringing horse into the country. That's what the dolls are there for."

"They're museum pieces," Isaac said.

"That's the best alibi there is. Collectors' items. You can move them from gallery to gallery under the noses of every narc. The material arrives, you work a little switch, and presto!"

"But there aren't enough dolls to go around. I met with Rubino. I saw his doll, the brigandess. He keeps her in a safe. And Jerry DiAngelis has five Christian knights in his closet."

"Isaac, they all have hollow insides. I'll bet you my salary."

The dark spots disappeared. Isaac saw a cockroach climb the wall of Gracie Mansion. He wasn't surprised. Rebecca had roach problems at her manor in the park.

"Mario, how did you learn about the dolls?"

"Isaac, I go places. I'm Rebecca's eyes and ears."

The Pink Commish climbed down off the porch. Mario called to him. "Isaac, don't forget us. I'm counting on you to be Rebecca's candidate. If you won't help us, I'll find somebody who will."

"Yeah," Isaac said, "like Montezuma maybe."

20

*M*ontezuma.

It was a call to some battleground, but Isaac couldn't say where. Joe had been the marine, not him. Isaac was the superfly caught in Mafia shit. He paged Barbarossa, and Barbarossa got back to him. He was at Schiller's club.

"Meet me under the Williamsburg Bridge."

"Boss—"

"That's where I conducted all my business when I was a kid. I had my own little sugar market. Leo was my partner, with his short pants."

"But you were glocked under the bridge. It brought you bad luck."

"I don't need luck, Joey. I have you."

Isaac got there first, to the little patch of Sheriff Street that hadn't been lost to housing projects or the ruins of time. It was a dark open-air cave that had once had its own mechanics' row of shops, in a New York where labor had some value, where artisans flourished, where men could hammer angels into any kind of door. The artisans had tiny hats on their heads and thrived on burnt potatoes and rust. They didn't wear plastic guns, like Sidel. They didn't carry Glocks.

He heard the crack of Barbarossa's feet against the cinders on the ground. They stood face to face in the dark, Barbarossa's eyes like blue worms.

"Montezuma," Isaac said.

"Boss, couldn't we have coffee and cake at one of your cafeterias?"

"I like it here."

"You were with Mario Klein, weren't you, boss? I figured he'd get to you sooner or later. But I didn't want to bad-mouth the mayor's man . . . he was my biggest customer."

"You sold drugs to Rebecca's private secretary?"

"I practically lived at Gracie Mansion. He could have fed half a tribe with his habit. He was broke all the time. Then he comes to me with a proposition. He asks me to off this family of dealers, independents who had their own mom-and-pop store. 'Nasty people,' says Mario. 'They're ruining the works.' And he tells me to go and talk to Montezuma, a badass out of Palermo who looked like an Aztec, an Indian. He'd ratted out all his partners in the Sicilian Maf. The FBI had turned him around. He was dealing on his own and doing undercover stuff. I met with the rat. He offers me a hundred thousand to hit the mom and pop. I say, 'Montezuma, what have they done to you?' He won't answer. I find out from my sources that this is a crazy request. Not only is he partners with the mom and pop, partners under the table, but they're *his* mom and pop."

"He asked you to slap his own mother and father? That's inhuman. I'd have killed this Montezuma."

"That's exactly what I did. First we had a fight . . . and then Drug Enforcement comes down on my ass. Montezuma was their baby."

"What happened to the mom and pop?"

"They got slapped."

"Joey, were they puppeteers, this mom and pop? . . . why didn't you warn me about the doll situation, that it was all about drugs?"

"I couldn't," Barbarossa said. "You had Peppinninu on the brain. You were in love with Giuseppina and the paladins. Boss, I didn't want to break your heart."

"That's grand. I have a fucking driver who's into metaphysics, who worries about my heart and soul. You could have gotten both of us killed. You waltzed me around like a blind man."

"I was careful, boss."

"So careful we ran into Crazy Corners and wouldn't have survived if Margaret hadn't been in the back room."

"LeComte wouldn't let you croak. He loves you too much."

"Like you love Marilyn, huh?"

"I'm going to marry that girl. I'm not moving from this bridge until you accept me as your son-in-law."

Isaac was silent. He looked like some clay man, standing in the dark. Then his mouth seemed to crack open. "I'll accept you, accept you in hell."

"That's a pity, boss. We'll have to rot together under the bridge."

"You're my driver. You'll go where I tell you to go."

He lunged at Barbarossa, who swerved around Isaac and sent him flying into the cinders.

"I'm always landing on my ass . . . once you're glocked, you never really recover."

"Boss, I was glocked too."

"Ah, there's no comparison. I was in a coma," Isaac said.

Barbarossa stooped to lift him off the bed of cinders.

"Don't help me," Isaac said and rose to his feet. The dank air comforted him. He remembered the nation of young thieves that would barter under the bridge, hawking whatever wares they had. He'd been much more powerful as a boy with boxes of sugar in his coat than any police commissioner with thirty thousand troops.

"Don Roberto wasn't trampled to death because of his puppet theater. He had other talents, didn't he, Joey?"

"Yeah, he smuggled dope. He must have taken on Montezuma's traffic."

Isaac followed Barbarossa out from under that patch of Sheriff Street. He limped.

"Where are we going?"

"To Chinaman's Chance."

"I'm not in the mood for disco," Isaac said.

"Boss, it's a doper's paradise, the biggest in town."

"Joey, if you had a falling out with Mario, then who's supplying him with drugs?"

"Take a guess."

Isaac started to groan. "Frannie Meyers." And they climbed into Isaac's Dodge.

21

It was a bottle club on the fringe of Spanish Harlem, housed in some cellar a few blocks east of the Harlem Meer, that dead body of water at the upper limit of Central Park. The police would shut Chinaman's Chance, but it kept opening again and again. It had no owner of record, and the property should have been condemned, but no City marshals had come to seize its assets. And Isaac realized who its "owners" were: Mario Klein and the City of New York. The Chinaman's must have been Mario's den.

The Pink Commish was on fire. He went down into the cave with Barbarossa, inside a building that seemed to have no doors. The bouncer wanted to frisk him, but Barbarossa got in the way. "It's all right, Tiny. He's good people."

And Isaac fell into a storm of bodies dancing in the dark. He'd gone from one cave into another. He could recognize Fran's own paladins, his baby warriors who danced with little chiquitas, street girls who looked sixteen going on eleven. He was on fire. Music pounded from the walls, songs that were outside Isaac's vocabulary. He was an old-fashioned constable who believed in lullabies. He'd hardly ever danced, not even at his daughter's weddings or when Isaac himself had married the Countess Kathleen. He was like a bear with a bunch of left feet. His only rhythm would come in the midst of battle.

He bumped into Delia St. John on the Chinaman's floor. She was dancing alone. She wore a fabric that reminded him of the chain mail on a knight. But she had no garments under that "mail," and Isaac wouldn't peek at her breasts or her pubic hair. Malik had been one of her boyfriends. She'd slept with magistrates and lieutenant governors. She was a pornographer's model, playing the perennial child, until Papa Cassidy married her and took her off the market.

"Hello, Delia," Isaac said, taking her into his arms and doing his own kind of bearish walk.

"Hey, I like this slow stuff, Uncle Isaac."

He'd taught himself how to shuffle with the Salome of Chinaman's Chance.

"I thought Papa keeps you locked in the bedroom."

"He does," Delia said, "but I found the key . . . and Papa went away."

"Yeah, he's shooting lions in the Sahara . . . and Sicily."

"Papa hates lions, Uncle Isaac."

He could have kidnapped Salome and disturbed Papa's little vacation, but he wouldn't separate Delia from her dance. He'd get to Papa on his own.

He abandoned Salome and shoved deeper into the bottle club. It was a full house. Narcs and bandidos and coca brats and the prince of secretaries, Mario Klein, dancing with a blonde or a brunette, because Isaac couldn't distinguish colors in this cave. He stole Mario from his dancing partner, seized him by his shirt collar, and trapped him behind a water pipe.

"Montezuma, huh? Are you hocking Rebecca's furniture? Are you planning holdups? How's your fucking habit?"

"Isaac, you shouldn't listen to a thief . . . I do a couple of lines a day. It's nothing. And take your hands off . . . you work for me, Isaac."

"I work for the mayor."

"I am the mayor when Becky is in her rocking chair. Remember that."

"Then fire me, Mario. I'd love it. But the next time you start arranging murders from the mansion, I'll knock you off at the legs. Mario, who's your master? Sal? LeComte? Or the melamed?"

"All three," Mario said. "But you have it wrong. Until Rebecca leaves her porch, I'm the number-one player in town."

"Yeah, I'll remember," Isaac said, twisting Mario's ears. But six men were suddenly behind him, and none of them was dancing. They wore leather coats, like Isaac's musketeers. They were part of his brood, policemen assigned to Rebecca Karp. The mayor had her own detail of six bodyguards and six other escorts. A dozen men who were at Rebecca's call around the clock. They would accompany her on official rides when Rebecca greeted foreign kings, queens, and presidents. They formed her motorcade. They were the tallest, cleanest, most clever cops, handpicked by Isaac's own commissioners and Isaac himself. The chief of the detail was Lieutenant Albert "Wig" Wiggens, the most decorated cop in the City after Barbarossa. Wig had been shot in the head. He'd fallen out a window, chasing bandits. He'd belonged to Special Services and OCCB, the Organized Crime–Control Bureau. He was a black man with a bit of Indian blood, like Barbarossa. His enemies swore that he was part of the Purple Gang, Harlem's own assassination bureau, with branches in Detroit and Memphis and New Orleans. But the Purples had become a mythical gang, almost divine. No one could capture them, and no one had sighted them on Morningside Drive or Mount Morris Park.

Isaac was drawn to Wig. He'd lent him to Rebecca Karp. Wig

had a soft, melancholy voice. He wedged himself between Mario and the Pink Commish.

"Wig, we have a real problem."

"How's that, Commissioner Isaac?"

"I'll have to strangle Mario if he doesn't drag his ass out of here."

"But it's his place."

"Wig, this is a fucking bottle club. It doesn't have a liquor license. In fact, it doesn't have a license at all. It shouldn't exist."

"But it does exist. That's the fun part."

"I could close it down."

"It would open somewhere else. The Chinaman's already had fifteen, sixteen addresses."

"It's a doper's paradise," Isaac said.

"You've been listening to Joey too long. Commissioner, an awful lot of cops come here to dance . . . cops and the mayor's people."

"I could shut down the whole fucking detail. I could reassign you, Wig. You and all your men."

"But meanwhile I'm sworn to protect the mayor and her people . . . let him go, Commissioner, please."

"Wig," Isaac said, "you won't win."

Isaac released Mario Klein and wandered away from Wig. His eyes were smoking. He was on fire. But he couldn't have a shootout with his own policemen in Chinaman's Chance. It would have been a silly ending to his own career. He cornered Frannie Meyers behind a table. Frannie was snorting with a couple of teenagers, little girls with frizzled hair and a zombie's white complexion. The girls scattered when they saw Isaac's eyes.

"You're in the wrong playground, Fran. You should have stuck to Valentine Avenue. You'll talk to me about Don Roberto . . . and the dolls."

"Not here," Fran said, his pirate's kerchief sitting like a dunce cap on his head.

"You'll talk."

"Everybody's watching us," Fran said. "My own kids will call me a rat. I'll meet you in an hour . . . in front of Poe Cottage. Not with Barbarossa. I won't talk around Joe."

"Better not disappoint me, Fran."

And Isaac ducked back into the crowd of dancers, feeling like a maiden aunt. He didn't do drugs, didn't have connections to the Chinaman's teen culture. He met Barbarossa at the mouth of the cave.

"Poe Park," he said.

"What?"

"I have a date with Frannie Meyers."

"Boss, it's a war zone after midnight."

"You'll drive me to Fordham and you'll wait in the car."

"And if it's a trap?"

"I'll sing to my patron saint. Edgar Allan Poe."

The gate to Poe Cottage had been unlocked. Isaac crossed the lawn and stood on the porch, near the cottage's slanted roof. Poe had lived here with his tubercular teenage bride and his mother-in-law, Mrs. Maria Clemm, who was also his aunt. Mother Clemm had to find vegetables and fruit in the country-side of the Bronx to keep the family from starving. Isaac had a quarrel with Poe. He disliked Auguste Dupin, Poe's fictional detective and impoverished chevalier, who could solve a crime with his own "diseased intelligence" and a love of enigmas, conundrums, and hieroglyphics. Isaac would mock Dupin in his classes at the John Jay College of Criminal Justice. "He's all right when the murderer's an orangutan. I'm not Dupin, but even I could uncover the M.O. of an ape. It's not the labs, not the technique, or the linen shirt of a chevalier. It's your informants, the reliability of your rats."

But standing on the gray floorboards of Poe Cottage, without a single light, the Pink Commish began to appreciate the chevalier Dupin. The dolls of Sicily had their own hieroglyphics. And conundrum was only another name for a shitstorm.

Poe Park was caught in its own blue midnight. Isaac could see gangs of junkies outside the gate, hawking stolen video cameras and household wares to motorists on the Grand Concourse. He should have arrested them. He was a cop. But he was waiting for Fran.

He thought of his own bartering under the bridge. If Isaac had been some time traveler, could he have gone back to '44 and arrested little Leo and himself, confiscated all the sugar bags and books of ration stamps? It would have been a merry roust, the middle-aged detective confronting his own boyhood self.

While Isaac pondered, Fran appeared, like a time traveler in a kerchief. Isaac had to read his face in the dark.

"Why all the intrigue, Fran? We could have had a chocolate milkshake at Crazy Corners. Didn't I spot a malted machine next to your throne?"

"The kids use it for drinking blood."

"Afraid of your own warriors, Fran?"

"Sure I'm afraid. I can't meet up with their expectations. I don't have their purity, Isaac. One day they'll build a bonfire on the sixth floor and I'll be in it."

"That bad, huh Fran? Come on. Tell me, did they step on Don Roberto, did they trample him?"

"Yeah."

"And young Robert let you in the door."

"Yeah. It was like clockwork . . . a Bronx commando raid. We weren't on Mulberry Street more than five minutes."

"How much did you pay young Robert to set up his dad?"

"Not a nickel. He hated the old man."

"And who was your employer, Fran? The FBI?"

"I'm not a fucking pigeon . . . I told you. The kids have scruples. They'd punish me quick if I ever hooked up with the FBIs.

I do LeComte little favors, that's all. We're both fighting Jerry D. Jerry wants the Bronx. He can't have it . . . but it was Sal. He's my employer."

"Jesus Christ, Sal belongs to the Bureau. He's LeComte's boyfriend."

"He is and he isn't," Frannie said. "He has his own capers."

"And you think that was one of them? . . . was Margaret Tolstoy part of the package?"

Fran started to twitch. "Forget Margaret Tolstoy. She's my intended."

Isaac clutched the Glock inside his pants. He was getting murderous under the cottage's low porch roof. He could have wasted Fran. Barbarossa wouldn't have whistled. And the baby commandos could have had their bonfire on the castle's sixth floor. "Intended?"

"We're gonna get married soon as LeComte finds another nurse for Sal. I gave her a ring."

"She's always getting rings," Isaac muttered. "She was engaged to Sal's cousins in New Orleans. Martin and Emile. The two cousins gave her rings . . . and tried to kill Margaret."

"She's still my intended. I don't care. She could have a hundred fiancés, a million. Margaret's marrying me."

"Was she at the slaughter, Fran? Did she come with you to Mulberry Street?"

"Nah. The kids wouldn't allow no woman on a raid."

"But she knew about it."

"She's Sal's nurse, aint she? Sure she knew. I don't keep secrets from my intended . . . only my partners."

"Like Mario Klein."

"That son of a bitch, he's partners with everybody. I don't trust him. Mario's been threatening me."

"I thought you're his dealer."

"I am. But it makes no difference to Mario. He sends his sweethearts around with a collection box."

"Sweethearts?"

"Wig and all his people."

"Dollars and dolls," Isaac said. "What did you do with the dolls you found in Don Roberto's cellar?"

"Gave them to Sal. He warehouses the dolls, uses them as coffins."

"To carry dope."

"Or diamonds. Or passports and bonds. It's a Sicilian trick. The first smugglers came from Palermo. That's what Montezuma said."

"Was he a friend of yours?"

"Montezuma was a genius. He revolutionized drug trafficking. The old-line bandits used religious articles. But the carabinieri caught on. They 'arrested' every fucking statue and statue maker. And Montezuma hit on the idea of dolls. He invented a pedigree, some fucking robber with a shriveled prick who carved dolls while he was hiding from the police."

"Peppinninu."

"That's him. Montezuma created his own market for the dolls. He opened art galleries, got in touch with museums. He fakes a new fucking art form. And meantime he's moving drugs from Sicily to Hamburg to Düsseldorf to Marseilles and Manhattan."

"And getting himself killed."

"It was an accident. He shouldn't have done business with Barbarossa."

"Or ask people to murder his own mom and dad."

"I wasn't privy to that information," Fran said.

"The FBIs were running Montezuma, weren't they, Fran?"

"Yeah. But he was also running rings around them until he got burnt."

"And where did Don Roberto fit? Was he Montezuma's people?"

"Yeah. He had his own workshop. He'd find old dolls in some heap, dress them in the right clothes, give them the Montezuma touch. The traffic was exploding. And Montezuma couldn't keep up with his own market."

"Then Montezuma dies, and Don Roberto fills the vacuum."

"Yeah. For a little while. But he took sides in the war between Jerry and Sal."

"He's Jerry's cousin, for Christ's sake. He's a DiAngelis."

"Cousins don't count. He should have stayed neutral, like Montezuma did."

"So your little warriors trample Roberto, you give the dolls to Sal, and now Sal has an inventory. But where does he keep his stock of dolls? With the FBI?"

"Dunno," Fran said.

"And where is young Robert?"

"Dunno."

"Try a little harder, Fran. Because that kid is the whole fucking key. How did Sal get to him?"

"I didn't ask."

"Then give me a description of what happened from the time you arrived on Mulberry Street, blow by blow."

"It wasn't much. Robert lets us into the club. We go down the stairs and surprise the old man. We finish him . . ."

"*And* the puppet theater."

"That was my instructions. 'Leave a message for Jerry,' Sal said. He asked me to total the theater and I did."

"And Robert helped you?"

"Nah. He watched. He didn't smile or laugh or cry. He watched."

"Did he walk out of the club with you?"

"He stayed behind. Downstairs. In the mess."

"Did you catch the look in his eyes?"

"Isaac, there was no look in his eyes. Nothing."

"Where is he, Fran?"

"Isaac, I gotta get out of here. Sal is dancing with Mario, and Mario owns the police."

"I'm the police, Frannie."

"Yeah. You're a foot soldier in center field. And Mario has all the bats and balls. Mario and his henchman, Wig."

"Wig's the foot soldier. I can flop him, Fran, send him to Mars."

"Isaac, will you walk with me? I'm scared."

Isaac took Fran's arm and led him out of the park. It was like strolling with an invalid. Frannie was lost without his throne.

"I'll handle Wig, I promise."

Fran paused in the middle of Kingsbridge Road. "Stay here, or the kids will spot you . . . Isaac," he said, "that boy, Robert, he's in Palermo. I brought him there myself. I was his chaperone."

And Fran continued across the road, disappearing into the sunken concrete of Crazy Corners.

Part Five

22

Isaac returned to One PP and scattered the entire detail of Rebecca's cops, shoved them into exile, like so many lost sons. He found another police lieutenant to put in Wig's place. Lawrence Quinn, a rough, handsome Irisher who could charm Rebecca Karp and dance around Mario Klein. He was the grandson of a homicide detective, with the lantern-jawed eloquence of a boy who'd discovered language in the streets. He'd been part of the detail that stood with Cardinal Jim during the St. Patrick's Day Parade.

"You'll pick your own detail, Larry, men and women who won't dishonor us or disappoint the mayor. And you'll report directly to me, not any of the chiefs."

"Will do," Larry said with all his playful handsomeness. But he was back at Headquarters within a week, his lantern jaw quivering with rage. "Commissioner, you should have told me there would be *two* details."

"What two details?"

"Wig was at Gracie Mansion when I arrived with my lads. He was drinking lemon soda on the porch."

"That's impossible. I flopped him last Monday. I gave Wig

away to the harbor patrol. I put him in charge of all the lobster pots."

"Commissioner, sir, he held a gun in my face. Said we had no business at the mansion."

"Larry, I'll settle this. Wait here."

And Isaac strode across the hall to his own First Deputy, Sweets.

"I flopped Wig. Who let him back inside Gracie Mansion?"

"Me."

"Is it fucking favoritism, because Wig is black?"

Sweets leaned over Isaac with a bloodless anger in his eyes, an anger he'd learned to control. He didn't have Barbarossa's white glove; his huge hands were trembling. He could have squashed the Pink Commish, shoved him into the floor.

"Sorry," Isaac said. "I didn't mean to . . ."

"Protocol," Sweets said. "The mayor can approve her own detail. It's an unwritten law of the Department."

"Did Rebecca complain about Larry Quinn?"

"No, boss. It wasn't Rebecca. It was Mario Klein."

"And a little secretary has more say than I do?"

"Boss, he'll put Rebecca on the phone, and she'll shout whatever Mario tells her to shout."

"It's prejudicial," Isaac said.

"Sure. Me and Wig have our own thing. We're the Harlem Twins."

"You're not from Harlem, Sweets."

"Makes no difference. Harlem is still home country."

Isaac had to drag his tail out of Sweets' office. He went in to see his trials commissioner, Martin Malik, the hangman of Police Plaza. Malik was a Moslem whose dad had come out of Istanbul. The Republicans were grooming him to run against Rebecca as a "minority man" who frightened criminals and cops. Isaac had rescued one of his own detectives, Caroll Brent, from the hangman.

"Martin, I'm worried about Lieutenant Wiggens. He's started a dope club inside Gracie. I'd like to kick him out of the mansion."

"That's easy. Suspend the mother."

"I can't. Mario is protecting him."

"Then go to Poplar Street with your dossier. Give it to Internal Affairs."

"And do what? Investigate Mario and the mayor, start a civil war? But you can do it, Martin."

"I'm not a prosecutor, Isaac. I'm your in-house judge."

"But a word from you, a hint, and Wig would lose his Gracie Mansion address. Martin, he's a menace."

"Then lock him up, but leave me out of it."

Isaac returned to his office. He had to eat his own spit in front of Lieutenant Quinn. "Larry, there's a complication. I'm sort of powerless at the moment. Rebecca's having a breakdown . . . that's confidential. And a new detail might get her anxious. Would you like to guard the cardinal for a couple of days?"

Isaac began to seethe once Larry was gone. He had one of his deputies worm the weekly calendar out of Mrs. Dove, the mansion's chief of staff. A gang of Dutch high-school teachers from Utrecht would tour Gracie's public rooms tomorrow afternoon at three o'clock . . .

Isaac was on line with the Dutch teachers at a quarter to three, Barbarossa beside him, wearing dark glasses. Isaac had his fedora pulled down over his eyes. They got through the gate. The Dutch teachers had adopted them, thinking they were part of New York's homeless population.

There were no other cops in the house. Isaac had summoned Rebecca's entire detail to the police firing range at Rodman's Neck in the Bronx for some phony target practice. Now Isaac was king, with his fedora and the Glock in his pants. But he didn't have the slightest sense of propriety. *I hate it here*, he growled to himself. *I'll never live at Gracie Mansion. Never.*

Aurora Dove, the chief of staff and chatelaine, welcomed all the teachers from Utrecht. She was Becky's girlhood pal, born Annette Davidovich. They'd gone to kindergarten together in the Rockaways. Rebecca was the beauty queen. Aurora was the actress, six feet tall, with reddish hair at the roots. She'd toured America as Lady Macbeth, married a doctor who'd died on her, and was now mistress of the mansion. She'd lost Rebecca's roughened accent. Aurora Dove spoke like a musical dictionary.

"Consider us Dutch," she told the teachers from Utrecht. "The very site you're standing on once belonged to the Dutch West India Company, who sold the land to a prosperous farmer, Sybout Claessen, in sixteen hundred and forty-six. He called his tiny spit of land 'Hoorn's Hook,' in honor of Hoorn, his hometown. He quarreled with the local Indians. The Indians burned the little gardens he'd planted and wouldn't let him build his own mansion. But he had a double dose of bad luck. Hoorn's Hook happened to be a pirates' den. The pirates would bombard Sybout's huts with hot pitch. They drove him off the property. It lay barren, without a farmer's hand, for over a hundred and twenty years . . ."

Isaac was disturbed by this dark tale. It sounded a little phony. "Mrs. Dove," he said, under the refuge of his fedora. "Sybout Claessen wasn't the first farmer on this site. What about the Indians? Didn't they plant corn and squash?"

"I suppose," said Mrs. Dove, already suspicious of Isaac's hat.

Barbarossa had to nudge him. "Boss, you'll let the cat out of the cradle. She'll recognize us."

"You're part Indian, aint you?" Isaac muttered. "Defend your own fucking people."

"The Pierced Noses never got to New York."

"That's circumstance," Isaac said and continued his attack. "Mrs. Dove, I hear old Sybout was a pirate himself."

"Who are you?" asked Mrs. Dove.

"Tommy Netherland," Isaac said. "A boy from Sybout Claessen's hometown."

Mrs. Dove ignored him. She brought the group into the Samuel Dunne bedroom, where the former mayor had lived with yellow tulips on the wall. Sam had been laughed out of office, but his private bedroom had passed into the public domain. He'd had his own rocking chair, like Rebecca Karp. The room was devoid of mirrors. Sam was always suspicious of his own face. Isaac was forlorn in the Samuel Dunne bedroom. He'd once served under Sam.

"Boss," Barbarossa whispered, "what are we doing in Sam's bedroom? I'm tired of this shit."

"Shhh," Isaac said. "We'll have our reward."

They followed Mrs. Dove to the basement, which housed a miniature museum. The current exhibition, "Bouwerie Lane," charted the Dutch influence on modern New York, from the introduction of almshouses, to public hospitals and synagogues, to Peter Stuyvesant's pear tree. Isaac and Joe hid behind a huge cardboard replica of the first almshouse in North America as Mrs. Dove marched upstairs with her troop of teachers. She turned out the lights, and Isaac had to fumble in the dark with a box of kitchen matches he'd brought to the mansion. He kept striking matches against the sole of his shoe.

He searched and searched, groping for hidden doors, but it was Barbarossa who stumbled upon a long metal chest in a tiny alcove behind the museum. Isaac snapped open the lock on the chest with a huge pair of pliers he'd kept under his coat.

Three Giuseppinas were lying in a metal grave, like sisters to Sal Rubino's doll. Three brigandesses in their armor and colored skirts. Isaac undressed one of the dolls, plucked off her helmet, her plume of hair, her armored coat, sleeves, leggings, and shoes. She was a bald sister with dark eyelashes and a red mouth. Isaac picked her up and smashed her against the wall. One arm fell off and revealed a hollow cave that went from her shoulder to her wrist.

"Coffins," Isaac said. "Come on. We're taking the other two as hostages."

"Isaac, we can't walk out of Gracie with a pair of dolls. Mrs. Dove will catch us. Mario can send us to jail."

"And expose whatever network he has? Not a chance."

Each of them carried a doll up the stairs, the clanking armor creating a terrific din.

Mrs. Dove leaned against Rebecca's staircase, smoking a cigarette. She didn't blink at Isaac or Joe or the noisy dolls.

"Hello, Dove," Isaac said, behind his hat.

Mrs. Dove took a Police Special off the bottom stair and aimed it at Isaac's heart. Isaac wouldn't cover his own heart with a doll. He smiled. "Do you have a permit, Dove?"

"You're trespassing," she said.

Isaac used his own diseased intelligence, like Auguste Dupin. Dove was no simple chatelaine. She was part of Mario's gang.

"Shoot me, Dove. I don't have all day . . . I'm the Pink Commish. How can I trespass in a building I'm paid to protect?"

And the two constables walked out the mansion door with their dolls, Barbarossa dreaming of Dove's black and bitter eyes.

23

There was bewilderment at One PP. The Pink Commish had introduced his own strange museum. He kept a pair of warrior women in his office, huge dolls in body armor, right next to the begonia. He would hold conversations with the dolls, address them both as Giuseppina. But none of his men could tease the dolls' history out of Isaac. He'd turn mute, stare at the walls . . . until Isaac's own black giant came in to examine these giant dolls.

"Isaac," Sweets said, "help us out. Are they souvenirs from one of your battlefronts?"

Isaac roused himself from his own reverie. "Has Mario been screaming? Did he tell you that we raped Rebecca? Did you know that her fucking housekeeper carries a gun?"

"The dolls, Isaac, what about the dolls?"

"Lemme finish. Mario is a user, Sweets. He smuggles dope, and the mansion is his hideaway."

"Then we'll bust the son of a bitch. Is that what you want? We could bring the whole City down on our backs. Return the dolls."

"No."

"You captured them from Gracie, didn't you? That's why Mother Courage pulled her gun."

"Which Mother Courage?"

"The housekeeper, Mrs. Dove."

"The dolls are carriers, Sweets, drug boats. To bring heroin into the United States."

"Did you find any heroin in the house?"

"No. Not yet."

"But the Black Stocking Twins did one of their famous searches and seizures."

"Sweets, we weren't even wearing our masks."

"What happens now?"

"We wait."

"For God and the Devil?"

"Both," Isaac said. "It's a question of who comes first."

"Watch yourself. God might get crazy and steal your Glock."

Sweets walked out and left Isaac alone with his pair of Giuseppinas. But the Pink Commish didn't have to wait very long. God *and* the Devil showed up in the person of Frederic LeComte, wearing his habitual blue on blue. His mouth seemed missing. His nostrils sucked air without any real sense of a nose. His profile was like some artificial creation. LeComte was the nearest thing to an invisible man. He could have faded into any background with his blue coloring. It bothered Isaac, who was his protégé. LeComte had put his ass on the line and named Isaac Justice's first Alexander Hamilton Fellow, a philosopher-sheriff who would go from town to town, giving speeches on the vagaries of crime. But Isaac had disappointed Justice and embarrassed the hell out of LeComte. He'd fallen in love with LeComte's own undercover agent, Margaret Tolstoy; he'd shot Sal Rubino during his time as a Hamilton Fellow; he'd befriended Jerry D., LeComte's number-one nemesis.

"You've been ducking me," growled the Pink Commish.

"I haven't."

"You've been ducking me, I said. You closed the door. I can't get to Papa Cassidy or Sal, and you've been letting Margaret scribble Valentine cards to Frannie Meyers. I don't like it."

"She can't stick to one fiancé. The girl has to keep her options open. You might move into an early grave."

"LeComte, you want your microphones and mine picking up that little patter? The prince of Justice threatening his own Hamilton Fellow?"

"It's not a threat. You've been messing around with some dangerous people."

"Like whom? Montezuma's ghost?"

"You're a pisser, Isaac. You really are. That man was the overlord of Palermo."

"Until you turned him around. And he got careless. This is America, LeComte. Federal informants don't usually hire someone to cancel their own mom and dad."

"Barbarossa isn't 'someone,' Isaac. He's the best hitter in town."

"Sure. That's why he's my chauffeur. He hits all the time."

"And helps you steal objects from the mayor's museum. You'll have to give them back."

"Fuck you, Fred."

"You're muddying the waters, meddling in a critical investigation. We have the whole Sicilian drug mart on the run. Should I tell you the street value of the heroin and cocaine that's involved?"

"Street value doesn't mean shit. It's an invention of the FBI."

"But you could never guess the volume of traffic that's coming through."

"Where? In the bodies of Sicilian dolls? Who's your partner? Peppinninu? You sent Frannie and his children downtown to stomp on Roberto DiAngelis."

"Did not. That was Sal's idea."

"And who owns Sal? The Bureau."

"Don't get naive on me, Isaac. Sal is in business for himself. Don Roberto was double-crossing him. He tried to have Sal killed. He was the biggest heroin smuggler in the United States."

"LeComte, I met the man. He roosted in the cellars. He was a puppeteer."

"It was an act. Jerry D. was trying to impress you. Heroin and coke, that's what the war inside the Rubinos was all about. Who would control the distribution, Jerry or Sal."

"The melamed couldn't have been involved. He despises drugs."

"Dream a little more, Isaac. He was the mastermind."

"The melamed had Jerry's soldiers killed for handling drugs."

"Not for handling, Isaac. For ripping off the melamed's couriers and mules."

"I would have known. I'm not blind. I have my intelligence teams. How long has this been going on?"

"Years and years, Isaac. Years and years."

"And you never told me?"

"How could I trust you? You crawled into bed with Jerry and the melamed."

"That's why you made me your Hamilton Fellow. To get me as far as you could from the field."

"It was only one of the reasons. I admired you, Isaac. I wanted you in my camp. You have your poetry. You were much more than a cop. You cared, Isaac, cared about all the little kids."

"Yeah, I was your private shill. With his own baseball team. The Delancey Giants . . . I'm going to Palermo, LeComte. And don't you try to stop me."

"Jesus, you'll ruin everything. What's in Palermo, Isaac?"

"Young Robert. I'd like to hear from him why he set up his own dad. He might be able to give me a lesson in loyalty."

"Don Roberto wasn't his father. The boy was an orphan. He was apprenticed to Roberto when he was eight or nine."

"As a puppeteer?"

"No, no. He was the next Peppinninu. He could carve like a motherfucker, copy the patina of old, rotting wood."

"And the dolls in my office are his? They have Robert's mark?"

"Naturally."

"Ah, the orphan artist. Learned to hate his master, huh? Confused him with some dream dad."

"It's simpler than that. Roberto was cheating him, taking all the profits."

"And Sal got to the orphan, huh?"

"How? From his wheelchair? It was your long-lost love, Margaret Tolstoy."

"I forgot," Isaac said, his heart boiling up the blackest kind of blood. "She's Sal's arms and legs. Margaret was the conduit. Did she seduce young Robert?"

"Didn't have to. The boy was game."

"Then why did he bolt?"

"Wasn't cowardice, Isaac. We advised him to scram for a while, to crawl back into the nest. We flew him to Palermo. Margaret and Fran were his babysitters."

"Margaret and Fran," Isaac said. "Margaret and Fran."

"Isaac, I can't let you go to Palermo. I'm sorry."

"Will you steal my passport?"

"I'll do worse."

"Good. Because I intend to meet with the kid."

"I can deliver him to your office."

"I don't want him delivered."

"You'll never survive Palermo," LeComte said. "Palermo chews up police chiefs."

"If I don't come back, LeComte, I'll will you the dolls."

"You'll will them to me anyway."

"Not a chance. The dolls stay in this office until I'm pronounced dead."

It took a phone call. Isaac was allowed to enter the melamed's retreat on Cleveland Place, where he lived with Jerry and his daughter, Eileen, who was Jerry's wife. But Jerry had been absent from the household. He was either at the Baron di Napoli or with Raoul and Alicia in Bath Beach. The melamed had to share his daughter's sorrows. She'd badgered Jerry, asked him to steal Raoul from his comare so that she could raise him as her own child. She'd suffered through Jerry's war with Sal and she required some visible benefit—the boy Raoul. She wouldn't scheme with Jerry's captains, wouldn't hand out bribes. She sat at home, preparing meals for people who had disappeared on her. Isaac could read all the pathology in her face, like some fucking doctor of the soul. She was a widow with a live husband. And Isaac couldn't console her.

But he did eat her Jewish pasta, sitting in Jerry's chair.

The seat next to Isaac's had once belonged to Teddy Boy, alias Nose, Jerry's little older brother, who'd become a rat for the FBI and was killed in Central Park during a ball game between Isaac's Delancey Giants and Cardinal Jim's Manhattan Knights. Eileen had been fond of that murderous halfwit. She mourned Nose with the empty chair, blamed Isaac for Nose's death. He was careful around Eileen, like some penitent. It was a cockeyed world where the Pink Commish had to apologize for his very own life.

"Delicious," he said, his mouth stuffed with noodles.

"I'm happy for you," Eileen said, with a cigarette dangling from one side of her face. Her hair had gone white during that war inside the Family, when her husband was in constant danger and she didn't hear from him for a month.

"Isaac, have you seen the little prince?"

"Yes." He couldn't lie to Eileen.

"My own father shields him from me."

"Eileen," the melamed said. "Eileen."

"You hypocrite. My husband has Raoul, and what do I have? I'm his wife. The little prince belongs to me."

"But his mother is entitled—"

"Entitled to what? She's a whore."

"But she's the one who gave birth to Raoul, she had the labor pains."

"Like a common cow. Jerry can have his comare. I want the boy."

"Isaac," the melamed said, the veins bunching on his forehead in a blue design. "Will you reason with my daughter?"

"He has nothing to do with this discussion. He killed the baby."

"The baby was on the rampage," the melamed told her.

"Honor him," Eileen said. "He was my brother-in-law."

"He sold us to the FBI."

"What could he sell? His pants? His shoes? Jerry never sat in jail because of him . . . Isaac, your soldiers didn't have to shoot Ted. They could have captured the baby."

"Eileen," the melamed cried. "He wasn't capturable."

"I want Raoul. Isaac, you kidnapped him once. Kidnap him again."

"Wish I could," Isaac said. "But it would cause a catastrophe."

She glared at Isaac and the melamed. "You had your pasta. Get out of my kitchen."

Isaac tramped into the melamed's room and sat beside the melamed on a narrow bed. The melamed had no one to warm his bones. He'd never taken a mistress.

"She didn't even offer us dessert, that daughter of mine."

"Ah, Iz. She's upset. Jerry's with Alicia all the time."

"She drove him crazy. *Raoul, Raoul, Raoul.*"

"She can't have a child, so she dreams."

"I'm hungry," the melamed said. "I don't think straight without ice cream."

"We could go to the corner."

"What corner? I'm bedridden. I haven't recovered from my stroke."

"Stop it, Iz. You run to Ratner's twice a week."

"I'd be lost without my own cafeteria. I'd starve to death. But I'm glad you could come. Eileen's more human with another man in the house, even if she hates us both for not bringing her Raoul . . . Isaac, what's wrong? I couldn't enjoy the noodles. You kept giving me funny looks at the table."

"I'm old-fashioned," Isaac said. "I always thought you wouldn't lie to me beyond a certain point."

"That's true. But sometimes the point can change."

"Especially when it involves drugs."

"You know my policy. I'll hurt anyone, even a captain, who touches that crap."

"Some lullaby, Iz. Don Roberto smuggled for you. You're the biggest dealer in town."

"LeComte's been singing in your ear."

"No. He supplied one detail. That your fight with Sal Rubino wasn't a popularity contest. It was about the Family's own Sicilian connection."

"Isaac, I'll faint if you start giving me a sermon on Peppinninu. Can I help it if you decided to fall in love with dolls that duel?"

"Ah, they weren't made for dueling, Iz. They're fragile under their battle clothes. They have hollow insides like any coffin that carries dope."

"The dolls were never my idea. But we couldn't let Sal ruin us. He was getting rich off Jerry's own vassal, Roberto the puppet maker. We had to take Roberto from him."

"That's how the war started?"

"We collected Roberto. Sal decided to kill our men."

"And Montezuma?"

"He was caught in the middle. But we had the dolls, Isaac. We had the dolls."

"Sal could have hired his own carpenters."

"He did. But they couldn't produce quality stuff. And that jeopardized the whole venture. You have to have the illusion of an illusion, or it wouldn't work. Museums were involved. And galleries with sensible clients. One mediocre doll would have soured the deal. That's what I learnt as a melamed. You want to cheat, stick to the authentic as much as you can. Roberto was nothing until the boy came along."

"Young Robert."

"He had the magic hands. That puppet maker plucked him out of a street in Palermo. He had no name, no identity in America, nothing. He was Roberto's nameless wonder. The boy worked day and night, and that wasn't enough. The dolls were perishable, Isaac. They could only be used once. But they wouldn't break in transit, they wouldn't come apart at the seams. They had no seams, and they couldn't spill your goods. Robert glued a doll in his own special way. He filled in every crack. He sanded down the imperfections. And then he had to create the bumps and scars of a Peppinninu. The boy was worth millions. It boggles the mind. Took him twenty hours to seal the goods inside a doll. It was snug as the tomb of a god. You couldn't get in without a chisel and a pair of heavy hammers. You had to manufacture your own split line. And if the split was too deep, the bags would break and you'd have yourself a heroin storm."

"Iz, I'm ashamed. A melamed talking like a drug lord."

"Sonny, I did what I had to do. We jumped into the market to stay alive. And don't let LeComte fool you. He has his own little government."

"And Montezuma was part of that government, right?"

"Isaac, you have a problem. You're a police chief. Your eyes and your ass are locked in Manhattan. You have to start thinking global. Nothing moved without Montezuma. He found the nameless wonder for Roberto. He stroked the mafiosi in America and Palermo. He was LeComte's partner and registered spy . . .

until he bumped into a crazy wall. Barbarossa. And now there's complete chaos. Shipments are lost. Customers complain. Dolls that should have gone to some museum end up at a puppet show. Their arms and legs start bleeding powdered blood. And the young maestro is missing."

"He's gone to Palermo," Isaac said.

"We know that. But we can't rush in like strangers. It's perilous without Montezuma. I've been negotiating to get the boy back. But I can never tell who I'm negotiating with. The wind? The trees? A don who died last month?"

"I'm going to Palermo," Isaac said.

"Isaac, it's not a city for strangers. It's hard enough for us. Jerry has cousins in Palermo, and he's still a stranger."

"I'm going to Palermo."

"Always the crusader, ready to rescue a lost boy."

"No, Iz. You have it wrong. I'm hoping the boy will rescue me."

24

He wouldn't let Barbarossa accompany him on his crusade. "It's perilous," he said, copying the melamed's diction. "Both of us out of the country. Anything could happen."

"Boss, you'll need our masks in Palermo."

"It's one Twin to a continent, Joey. That's how it has to be while Mario is in the mansion and Wig is running loose."

"You have a battalion of detectives."

"I have you."

"You could close Mario's shop."

"Rebecca would open it again. She's under his influence . . . Joey, did you ever sell drugs to the melamed's people?"

"I'm not that dumb."

"But you were out there, Joey, buying and selling. You had your customers, Mario himself. And your contacts. Didn't you have a hint that the melamed was doing heavy business?"

"He's a rabbi, boss."

"Not a rabbi, a schoolteacher without a school."

"Isaac, if he was dealing, I would have known."

"He tricked us, surrounded himself with his own fucking piety."

"He's not the invisible man."

"But he's the melamed. He hasn't left a trace."

"There's always a trace, and I'll find it."

"Watch the street, Joey. And my brother Leo . . . and Marilyn. But no romance."

"Boss, how can I promise?"

"No romance."

Isaac had a sudden pull of dread. He was leaving Barbarossa in a mine field, but he didn't want Joey to die on him, to become another Manfred Coen. Ah, he missed that dead angel.

Joey brought him to JKF. They were the Black Stocking Twins. They had certain rights and privileges. They hugged outside the Alitalia lounge. "Boss, did you forget your mask?"

"Nah. I have it in my pocket."

"It's your only weapon. They'll shit in their pants when they see you wearing the mask. They'll think you're the Devil."

"I am the Devil," Isaac said, and Barbarossa left him there.

Isaac had to borrow off his pension to finance the trip. He had no money in the bank. He gave all his excess capital to the Delancey Giants. He didn't have the Catholic Church behind his team. The cardinal could beg or borrow to finance the Manhattan Knights. Isaac had to steal from his own pockets. He'd booked a room at the Palazzo Palme. It cost a billion lire a night, something like that. Isaac couldn't seem to count in Italian money. He wasn't searching for bargains. He could have discovered some pensione near the railroad station, but he had a sentimental attachment to the Palme. Richard Wagner had stayed there with his family, had completed *Parsifal* in the middle of a plague. Isaac had done his homework.

Palermo was a poor miserable town until the Saracens captured it in 831 from the Byzantine kings, who couldn't have bothered with a dusty island outpost. It flourished under Arab rule, became a second Cairo, with palaces and libraries and mosques, with scholars and magicians who settled there and lived without violence. The Normans took it from the Arabs in 1072, kept some of the magicians, and Palermo continued to thrive. It flowered in the twelfth century, had its own small renaissance, while the rest of Europe was pissing in its pants. But the renaissance didn't last. Palermo fell into its own dark age. There was insurrection after insurrection. There were bloody wars. The Bourbons seized Palermo, then the British. But it prospered in the nineteenth century, was known as "Paris of the Palm Trees." The Palme was a British inn when Wagner lived there and wrote about Parsifal, that melancholy knight, and his quest for the Holy Grail. Isaac was on his own uncertain quest in Paris of the Palm Trees.

There were two uncertain characters waiting for him in the lounge. Frannie Meyers and his fickle fiancée, Margaret Tolstoy. Her hair was polished silver this afternoon. Isaac would have to make an inventory of all her wigs. Her almond eyes bored right into his gut, where the worm had been. He was hopeless around Anastasia, a puppet strangling on his own strings.

Isaac managed a growl. "Go on home to LeComte."

"Can't," Frannie said. "We're your official babysitters."

"I don't need Judases and Jezebels."

"He's nice, isn't he, Fran?" Anastasia said.

"He can't help it. He's the big cop. He has to complain."

"Are you getting married in Palermo?" Isaac asked, his brown eyes on Anastasia.

"No, darling," Anastasia said. "We're all sharing the same suite at the Palme."

"Hell we are. I'm not living around lovebirds."

"Commissioner, watch your mouth," Frannie said.

"Isaac, you'll never find Robert without us. And you'll never leave Palermo alive."

"I'll take my chances."

"There are no chances in Sicily," Anastasia said. "There are dogs and children and lots of dead people . . . I visited Palermo in 'forty-three, with my Uncle Ferdinand."

Frannie started to brood. "Uncle Ferdinand?"

"Didn't you know, Fran?" Isaac said. "Margaret was married when she was eleven. Her uncle was emperor of Odessa and the Black Sea. He was a fucking war criminal with his own puppet state, Russian Roumania."

"I was in Palermo during the Allied bombings . . . with a bunch of Gestapo generals."

"She was everywhere," Isaac said. "Paris, Palermo, Lower Manhattan. The little wandering bride."

She slapped Isaac's face. The slap seemed to vitalize him. It was almost as savage as a kiss.

"The prefect of Palermo had his tongue cut out for annoying the mistress of a certain general. Rats slept in my shoes. All the heroes of the Luftwaffe had to pretend that the piss they were drinking was champagne."

"I hate champagne," Isaac said. "And I'm not a hero."

He crept onto the plane with Anastasia and Fran. Isaac had the window seat, above the starboard wing. Anastasia sat between her two warriors. Fran was very troubled. "Margaret, I'll start to worry that you're holding his hand and I won't be able to sleep."

"Shhh," Margaret said. "Close your eyes."

Fran obeyed her and fell asleep.

Margaret curled against Isaac, while he thought about that prefect who'd lost his tongue to the Nazi war machine.

There was a short delay in Rome. Fran had bloodshot eyes. He kept changing hundred-dollar bills for packets of lire. Isaac had spent eight hours in the air stealing kisses from Margaret Tolstoy.

He could imagine his old age, looking for Margaret among all her boyfriends and basket cases.

"I don't want Frannie in our bed," he told her.

"He's my fiancé."

"I'll kill him, I'll bury him at the Palme."

"He's fond of you, darling, or you wouldn't be here. Frederic gave him the golden route, Palermo to Poe Park. You shouldn't begrudge Fran."

"And Sal's so generous that he lends Fran his nurse?"

"Sal has no choice. He's a little doll-crazy, like you. And he smells dollars. He can't afford to lose Palermo."

"I'll smash the whole operation, I swear."

"It's Palermo, darling. Remember that. You'll have to study the art of whispering."

They arrived at Punta Ráisi, where the airport cops wore handguns above their pelvises like obscene toys. A coach with ancient wooden chairs that reminded Isaac of a donkey cart drove them along the sea. Anastasia pointed to a tiny clot of land with a tower in the middle.

"The Isle of Women," she said. "It's empty, dear. It was once the pasture for girls who got pregnant by Norman knights. The locals were superstitious. They would have ripped apart the wombs of these girls and squashed their unborn babies against the rocks. But the knights were civilized. They rowed their sweethearts to the little island and left them to live or die. The girls had to eat grass. They built a tower with their own bloody hands. They went into labor, howling like wolves. The children were born with green spit on their bodies. The locals were terrified. They begged the knights to do something about these devil babies, and the Normans did. They rowed out to the Isola delle Fémmine, but they didn't have the will to destroy their old sweethearts and a brood of children with a green crust. They rowed this strange family to a much more isolated island, but it didn't matter much. They all died of some disease, like loneliness or heartbreak."

Isaac couldn't get those mothers and their green children out of his mind.

They rode into Palermo on the Via Libertà, passing palm trees and a garden that made Isaac dream of Miami. Libertà was very wide. Palermo had that curious smell of talcum powder and gasoline. It wasn't unpleasant to Isaac. Mothers and daughters in the streets had the same swollen faces. Isaac wondered if they were secret survivors of that deserted island. He couldn't keep his eyes off the skeletal men of Palermo, who peered into his little bus with broken, brutal looks.

It's the sun, Isaac sang to himself. It reduces everything. Robs you of your brains.

He arrived on the Via Roma and the Grand Hotel delle Palme. It was a sunburnt palace, darkened with time. Young men rushed out of the hotel in military tunics and tore the luggage from Isaac's fists. Miami, Isaac muttered. Miami with a touch of the Sicilian sea. The front desk was near the door. It was very discreet. Isaac signed a little card for Anastasia, Fran, and himself, collected all their passports, handed them to the clerk, and was taken to his suite. It was a field of windows decorated with dark furniture.

Margaret wouldn't let him shower or shave, or worry where he would sleep and who he would sleep with. "Fine," he said, "bring me the doll maker. I have to talk to young Robert."

"Darling," she said. "We're being watched. I picked this suite on purpose. It's a glass cage. We have to go sightseeing."

He couldn't even comb his hair. He went down into the lobby with Anastasia and Fran, crossed a maze of sitting rooms, with an enormous flow of people. The lights were very dim. Isaac had found his proper cave, a dark, forlorn city of dreams inside the

Grand Hotel. He recognized Papa Cassidy in one of the rooms where Richard Wagner must have contemplated Parsifal. Papa sat alone, reading some darkly inked edition of the *Financial Times.*

Isaac bolted from his babysitters and sat down next to Papa, nearly in his lap. "How are the lions?"

"What?" Papa muttered. Then he recognized Isaac and started to moan. "You're out of your element, Sidel. This isn't baseball in Central Park."

"No. It's lion country. And the Sahara is just outside the door."

Papa appealed to Margaret Tolstoy. "Put him in some kennel, please, before he hurts himself."

Isaac pulled the newspaper out of Papa's hands and sat nose to nose with the potentate. "I memorized all your fucking routes. Are you buying dolls, Papa? Are you dabbling in the heroin market?"

"Sidel, you've gone over the edge. You don't even have City Hall behind you. And Palermo is none of your business. I don't have to check my itinerary with a rotten little police commissioner."

"But you ought to check Delia's itinerary. I loved dancing with her at the Chinaman's."

"Shut your mouth, Sidel."

Margaret and Frannie Meyers seized Isaac by his armpits and dragged him away from Papa Cassidy. "Darling, we're only guests here, and Papa is part of the furniture. The Sicilians like his money. He does an awful lot of laundering for the little kings of Palermo."

"Take me to the kings."

"Shhh," Margaret said. "The Palme is their personal souk, not ours."

"Yeah," Isaac said, "it's a clearinghouse for mutts like Papa Cassidy."

"Whisper, darling, it's essential. The walls have ears. And I'm not talking about microphones. The grandmas at this hotel are loyal to their kings."

"Kings," Isaac said, "every mother is a king."

The Maf of Palermo was a very special breed. Mountain rats in stone caves, they weren't like the barons of Castellammare del Golfo, who'd maintained their medieval roots and familial ties with the dons of Manhattan, the Bronx, and Bath Beach, lending out their underlings or selling them off. But the dons of Palermo had little sense of family. They'd kept to their own caves, these princes and kings of chaos. They bribed and killed and had little focaccerias where they devoured pieces of flat bread baked in olive oil. And when the carabinieri came after them, the kings dove into the depths of their caves. No one, not even the kings themselves, could determine the beginnings or endings of their domains. Two kings could rule the same street. They had their own nurseries, where young children could be educated as "ghosts" who would disappear from ordinary school life and start to steal and deliver special favors to a king. The graduates of these ghost schools might die at ten or eleven or become future kings.

It was Palermo, where an unpopular judge might find ground glass in his soup. Journalists who delved into the mysteries of the kings might not survive their supper. Omertà, the vow of silence that every Mafia buff talked about, was misunderstood. Silence wasn't a vow in Palermo. It was a way of life. Skeletal men and enormous women. The perfume of talcum powder mingled with gasoline. Ah, Isaac was getting to like Palermo. But Anastasia wouldn't let him off his leash.

She drew him out of the hotel and got him onto a bus with Fran. Isaac couldn't find a single person who paid the fare. It must have been a city of Robin Hoods, where bandits robbed everybody and subsidized the rich and the poor.

"Anastasia," Isaac groaned, "we're too conspicuous."

"Darling, we're supposed to be conspicuous. The safest ride in Sicily is on a bus. Anyone who's curious can tell that I don't have a shotgun under my skirt."

"And what about me?"

"You're the sleepy-eyed magician, Isaac of Delancey Street." The three of them changed buses and passed under the Porta Nuova, with its own Chinese chapel on top. The road started getting narrow. Anastasia shoved Isaac down the stairs of the bus. They went into a coffee bar and had a briosch con gelato, ice cream inside a bun. It seemed like a crazy idea, munching ice cream and a regular roll. But he had four brioschi con gelato with different flavors. He would have had five if Anastasia hadn't dragged him out of the coffee bar.

They landed on the Via Cappuccino, turned several corners, and entered a catacomb. It was a fucking house of the dead, filled with mummified corpses and skeletons, arranged according to rows. There was a line of bishops, wearing pointy hats, soldiers with smiling jaws, a panel of children in dolls' costumes, doctors in rotting clothes, all held up by wires and strings. Isaac was startled by the different expressions a skull could have. The skeleton soldiers and bishops seemed more alive now, with all the deep pain of the living. The women had their own separate wall in this society, like some segregated synagogue of the soul.

The Pink Commish started to cry.

"What's the matter?" Margaret whispered in his ear.

"I'm crazy about all these skeletons."

"Darling, that's why I brought you here."

"Now I know where Peppinninu got his inspiration. From these dolls of Palermo. He must have been an embalmer or a monk who dressed up skeletons on a lot of walls."

Fran looked very pale. "I'm sick," he said. "I need fresh air."

"In a minute," said Isaac of Delancey Street, who wanted to grab his own inspiration from these dolls. He saw skulls with tufts of hair, skeletons wearing neckerchiefs, like banditi. He saw looks of such sorrow, he could have demanded his own niche in the wall.

A professor arrived with a mob of students. He spoke English with a German accent. His clothes were a bit too tailored in this catacomb. He had a magenta-colored jacket.

"It's ingenious, eh? To visit your loved ones after they've departed. And it's not as morbid as you think. Do I sound sacrilegious if I say the soul is still there? Or at least the reminder of a soul. The body dies, but you still have your loved one. You can visit a mother, a father, a child who died in infancy. You can talk to the dead, even as the fluids drain."

Fran rushed out of the catacomb. And Isaac had to follow. But he would have liked to have a dialogue with this professor of the dead.

25

Anastasia brought him to a palace where the Normans had lived. He found the throne room of Roger II, first king of Sicily, whose palace had risen out of the ruins of an old Moslem fort. There were mosaics in Roger's room: antelopes and Sicilian tigers in a big heavenly garden. But he wanted young Robert, not the dream park of a twelfth-century king.

"No more sights."

"We're hunting," Anastasia said.

"Yeah. Tigers on a wall."

He returned to the hotel. Anastasia claimed one of the bedrooms for herself. She closed her door and Isaac sat with his other babysitter, who couldn't stop shivering.

"I'm dead."

"Ah, you miss Poe Cottage, Fran, that's all."

"I'm dead, I told you . . . she's not my fiancée. I live in a fucking circus. I stretched myself too far. I should have given the Bronx back to Jerry D."

"And lose Poe Park?"

"Commish," Fran said, "I already lost it." And he vanished into his own bedroom.

Isaac knocked on Anastasia's door. She called out to him. "I'm asleep."

He entered the bedroom. She stood beside the bed, wearing a holster.

"Fran isn't my babysitter. You are. You're dumping him in Palermo. Fran is the reason for this trip."

"He went into the wrong cellar. He didn't have any license to kill Don Roberto. He took money from Sal. He freelanced with his children's army."

"But young Robert was his accomplice."

"Robert's a psychopath, like most artists and magicians. He was paid to deliver dolls, not to sacrifice his own teacher."

"I'm in the dark," Isaac said.

"Darling, that's what makes you adorable."

"Where'd you get that Glock? You weren't wearing a holster on the plane. I would have felt it near your heart. Was some Sicilian CIA man on our bus? Did he pass you the gun while I was watching the palm trees?"

"Darling, I can always get a gun. I'm LeComte's handmaiden."

"I'll bet you are," Isaac said. "I'm not leaving Fran in Palermo. I'm not abandoning him."

"He has no future in America. The children are on to his favors for the FBI. They'll trample him the first chance they get. And Jerry D. knows he killed Don Roberto."

"Who told Jerry?"

"I did. Fran has to stay here. And don't bother sneaking out of the hotel to look for Robert. You'll never find him. Every street is its own country. That's why we had to behave like tourists. So the little kings and their ghost children would get used to us. I'll take you to Robert."

"When?"

"Tomorrow," Anastasia said.

And he walked out of her room. She'd manipulated Isaac, called him darling and treated him like a pet bear. She'd have

gone to bed with Isaac, hugging that holster. No, she wouldn't
have gone to bed with him at all.

Isaac had to coax Frannie out of his bedroom. Fran sat over his
morning grapefruit, with lumps of sugar in his mouth. Coffee
had spilled on his pajamas. His hand was trembling, the way
Barbarossa's used to tremble. Isaac was guilty about Joe. He'd
left him in the badlands of Manhattan and the Bronx. Isaac
couldn't even trust his own department. The mayor's detail had
more clout than Police Plaza.

"Come on, Fran. Get dressed. Margaret's taking us to
Robert."

"I can't go," Frannie said. "I have to finish my grapefruit."

"I want to see you both face to face. Then I'll understand some
of the bullshit . . . how much did Sal pay you to pop Don
Roberto?"

"I didn't do it for Sal. I don't like wheelchairs. I did it for
Robert. He couldn't escape without giving Roberto a send-off. I
loved every minute."

Isaac tore off Fran's pajamas and dressed him in his pirate's
clothes, with the kerchief around his head. Jesus, Isaac thought.
Fran looks just like a bishop in that catacomb of the Capuchin
monks, a guy without his vital fluids.

"She'll kill me."

"Who'll kill you, Fran?"

"My fiancée."

"I thought you weren't really engaged to Margaret."

"I am . . . and I'm not. It depends on who's asking and what
benefit it brings . . . Commish, we're not safe. People have a
habit of dying around Margaret Tolstoy."

"We'll be careful," Isaac said. "I'll hold your hand."

The three of them walked out of the Palme, and Isaac still
couldn't tell the baby from the babysitters. They landed on the

Via Riccardo Wagner, behind the hotel, with its green shutters. There were potted plants along the street. Isaac could have entered that same heavenly garden on the walls of King Roger's throne room. But the garden didn't last. Garbage pails appeared. A mangy starving dog crossed Isaac's path. Frannie shuddered, and Anastasia pulled him onto a side street that was so narrow, there was hardly room for Isaac or Fran between the walls. Clots of laundry hung from balconies over their heads.

The street widened again, and cars with crazy drivers seemed to come out of nowhere. Isaac had to dodge them like a matador. He had no grasp of Sicily. The street curled into alleys and other streets, tiny vicolos with their rat dogs and men who watched Anastasia with dull brutish eyes. Were they ordinary stragglers or the vassals of those little kings, undressing Margaret in their locked imagination?

Margaret led her own lost children into a small cemetery that grew right out of a courtyard. There were angels and cupids on the tombstones, and photographs of the dead, like medallions. Isaac had an odd feeling of peace, as if he'd arrived at some soothing necropolis where the living and the dead manufactured their own space and time, and no one was allowed to intrude.

They sailed beyond the cemetery and fell upon a bombed-out zone near the port of Palermo. Houses lay in ruin. There were hills of rubble strewn with the crushed wheels of bicycles and baby carriages.

"The Allied bombings?" Isaac asked. "That was over forty years ago. The little kings ought to practice some industry."

"They do," Anastasia said, and Isaac began to see nests of people within the ruins. "Darling," she said. "This is Palermo. It doesn't pay to rebuild."

"Where's young Robert?"

"Open your eyes."

They'd come to a piazza with a little park. It was cluttered with a curious junglelike growth, banyan trees with roots snaking along the ground, strangling other trees. Each banyan was its own forest, with a little empire of trunks and roots growing out of every limb, like twisted chains, or the maddening hair of some Medusa. A man in a black leather coat stood inside the crazy complex of a banyan tree. He didn't have the raggedy look of an apprentice puppeteer. It was Robert, without his master, like a young Sicilian god. He didn't have spiky hair in Palermo.

"How are you, Mr. Isaac? I'm touched. Really, I am. The biggest police commissioner in America comes all the way to Sicily to visit the doll-maker's boy."

"You're not Roberto's boy. You never were."

"I'm all the boy he ever had. I ate his shit. He swindled me."

"That's the life of any apprentice."

"Yeah, it breaks my heart . . . hey, Frannie, aren't you gonna give your partner a little fucking handshake?"

Fran kept behind Isaac. "We're not partners."

"You're slipping, Fran. Lying to the commissioner like that." Robert stepped out from the confines of the banyan tree. His coat wasn't black. It was dark blue. "Hello, Margaret. Haven't hugged you in a while."

The Pink Commish was beginning to like this boy less and less. But he still couldn't fathom young Robert. All that bravura was very thin.

"Why did you pretend to be Roberto's child?"

"He wanted it that way. It made him feel that a miserable fuck like him could have a family. I played along. What else could I do, Mr. Isaac?"

"Have him killed."

"I had to make my bundle . . . so I cannibalized Roberto. I became him."

"Then why did you run to Palermo?"

"You'll have to ask my padrone."

"Jerry DiAngelis?"

"Christ, you are a little dumb for a detective. You're being jerked around."

"Who's your padrone? LeComte?"

"That pencilhead? I didn't cut my fingers, crawl on my belly day and night, to build Peppinninus for the FBI."

"Who's your padrone?"

"Haven't you figured it out? Follow me, Mr. Isaac."

Robert left the forest of banyan trees, with Isaac and Fran and Margaret behind him. He waltzed them through winding streets. Isaac began to hear a loud clatter on the roofs of certain cars. Robert started to laugh. It was a hailstorm. But Isaac had never seen such hugh hailstones, beautiful balls of ice that could bend a man's back.

"The wrath of God, huh Mr. Isaac?"

And Robert danced in the hail, twisting his own body to the bite of the stones until he fell. Isaac lurched to pick him up.

"No," Robert said, with a line of blood across his mouth. The hailstones stopped falling. But a fierce rain flooded the streets. The town had no drainage system. Cars stalled. The lights went out all over Palermo. It was darkness at noon.

Robert rose to his haunches. He let the rain lick at him. Isaac stood in an enormous sea. Palermo, he said to himself. He was Margaret's magician, the rain god.

The storm turned into a drizzle. Isaac trudged across the sea to a jewelry store on the Piazza San Domenico, with darkened windows. He followed Robert into the gioielleria. It was another cave, filled with voices. The lights came on again, and Isaac found himself with a gallery of grandmas, wives, and little girls on a tiled floor. A man stood behind a long counter with a jeweler's glass in his eye. He had very dark hair and the chiseled features of an Aztec Indian. Isaac didn't even have to guess. It was Montezuma, risen out of whatever grave the FBI and the Drug Enforcement geniuses had prepared for him.

Margaret and Fran had come into the store with Isaac. Frannie's face was white. He kept shivering at this Christ with the magnifying glass in his eye. Isaac was an imbecile. Montezuma and Sal were both jewelers. They had a dealership in diamonds, dolls, and junk.

Montezuma screamed at the grandmas, tossed them out of the gioielleria with the whole brood of wives and little girls, closed the shop, and welcomed Isaac into the back room with Margaret and Robert and Fran, who couldn't stop shivering.

"Frannie," Isaac said, "he's not a fucking ghost. LeComte resurrected him. He's done it before, with Sal."

"Bravo," Montezuma said, removing the glass from his eye. "But it wasn't the same thing. Sal had a case of lead poisoning. He nearly died. The FBI surgeons had to carve a new body for him. Half of Sal is missing. Takes him a month to have an erection. Ask Margaret. She's his nurse. But I didn't take one hit. I was wearing a fancy vest with a bag of animal blood. Barbarossa shoots me. The bag explodes and I have my own red river."

"It was a setup. You asked Joey to kill your mom and dad."

"My mom and dad? They were amateurs, comedians with a candy store full of drugs, compliments of the FBI. We counted on Barbarossa. He's a hothead and a moron, like that other boy you had. Manfred Coen."

Coen, Isaac thought. It always comes back to Coen. "Montezuma, the first assassination might be fun. But you won't survive the second."

"Commendatore, it's disrespectful to threaten me in my own town. I could have had your throat cut at the airport. Ask Margaret. I did Frederic a favor."

"Fuck your favors."

"I can see why Margaret fell in love with you in the middle of the war. You're a reckless prick. I like that."

"And you're an FBI rat."

"Can't be helped, commendatore. Can't be helped. LeComte

caught me with my pants down. Had to do some tricks for him and all those other narcs. But that never hurt my business. I made LeComte very rich, so he could buy his field equipment and arrange a lot of busts."

"But the little kings must have known you were partners with LeComte."

"It's on account of the kings that I had to play dead."

"They can't be that blind. You have a jewelry store. Any grandma can give you away."

"You missed the point. I am dead. I went through the ritual of dying. The FBI powdered my face. I napped a couple of afternoons in an open coffin. The little kings couldn't risk flying in to my funeral. They never travel. But they sent their associates, all the jackals they could spare. They stood over my coffin with their stinking breath. I rode to the cemetery in a silver truck. I climbed out of the coffin, had a game of solitaire, while the coffin was lowered into the ground with a rubber doll inside. And what can the kings do? There were witnesses to my burial. You can't dishonor a dead man. The kings have to ignore me, pretend I don't exist, or they will disgrace themselves. But every ounce of heroin in Palermo has to come through my door. That's ideal, eh? I'm rich. The kings are rich. LeComte is rich. And Robert might be rich if he had some brains."

"Roberto was stealing from you, right?"

"I had to put him in charge while I was dead. He controlled the traffic. He began to plunder and mark up the price of every doll. I couldn't come to Manhattan. Roberto knew that. I was preparing my own surprise. And then young Robert does that foolish thing with Sal. I would have frightened Roberto back to tranquillity. Not kill him. Robert isn't always reliable with the dolls. The maestro had to oversee his work."

"Padrone," Robert said, "I shouldn't have—"

"Shut up. I need an indemnity, someone to serve as a ransom. I've decided on Fran."

"You'll put him in charge of a ghost school, he'll train orphans and brats."

"And what did he do in the Bronx? That crib he had, Crazy Corners, was a ghost school. I gave him the idea. Fran was our little king."

"Well, I'm taking him home to the Bronx."

"It will have to be in a hearse."

"Montezuma, I'd love to start a ghost school. I'll be your little lamb."

"Margaret," Montezuma said, "will you enlighten this poor fuck."

"Darling, Fran stays with Montezuma."

"But he hasn't packed," Isaac said. "His clothes are still at the Palme."

"There's no reason to pack. He can live at the Palme."

"He'll get lonely," Isaac said.

"Lonely for what? America?"

"Poe Park and his baby commandos."

"Darling, they'll kill him if he ever goes near Valentine Avenue."

"Let's leave it to Fran," Montezuma said. "Where would you like to live?"

"The Palme Hotel in Palermo," Fran said, like the principal of a ghost school. And Isaac was in the mood to destroy the jewelry store and its jeweler. He could feel the boiling bags of blood in his own heart. "Montezuma, you didn't work for Jerry DiAngelis or Sal. They were conveniences, mules with lots of money. The morphine base arrives by boat from Turkey, it's refined into heroin in some fucking Mafia ranch in the mountains, it's compressed and packed into narrow bags, and the bags are squeezed into the hollowed ribs of the dolls. Now each doll is a masterpiece, and it goes through customs like some lamb of God. You open art galleries in Düsseldorf, Manhattan, Cologne. You bribe curators. You have your own banker, Papa Cassidy. But how did LeComte uncover your scam?"

"I got careless. Killed a man. It was a stupid fight. Over drug money. The Feds were like a gang of grave diggers, going deeper and deeper into my past, so I went to church, a church called Frederic LeComte, and I got my salvation. But I had to give . . ."

"You let him into your big secret and sold a few of your friends. And when the kings were about to kill you, you staged your own death. Whose idea was it to borrow Barbarossa?"

"He was perfect for the part."

"But who recommended him?"

Montezuma smiled. "Mario Klein. But it's your fault. The most decorated cop in New York dealing drugs to the mayor's secretary. It's a scandal."

"Padrone," Robert said, "tell him the cop's code name."

"Why not? It has a nice ring. 'Montezuma's Man.' "

Robert and Montezuma laughed.

Montezuma's Man. Isaac had been a dolt about young Robert, the ghost child who'd had a smuggler's education. His own pilgrimage to Palermo was poorly planned. He couldn't rescue Robert. There was nothing to rescue him from.

Isaac himself was a ghost child among ghost children.

"Commendatore, you have a devoted sweetheart. She brings a pistol into my establishment, hides it under her heart. And if I moved against you, she would splatter my brains on the wall. But I don't mean you any harm. I've given you an audience. Now you'd better go . . . but not with the dottoressa. I have things to discuss with her. You can find the Palme on your own."

He didn't return to the hotel. He wandered across Palermo with a picture in his head: Frannie Meyers shivering in Montezuma's back room. Isaac deserved whatever punishment he got. Mario

Klein had been correct. The Pink Commish wasn't a player in Palermo *or* the city of New York. And Isaac had a terrific attack of jealousy. It was Montezuma who must have told Margaret about the Isola delle Fémmine and its lost tribe of women and children. Montezuma was the real magician, the maker of myths. And Isaac was one more ridiculous knight.

He stumbled upon an outdoor market where people carried vegetables under their arms in paper horns. The vegetables were like long green noses. He nearly tripped over a rooster in the street. He saw a pingpong parlor close to the Piazza Verdi. But he didn't have the heart to watch pingpong in Palermo. He would have thought of Coen. He had a cappuccino at the Gran Café Nobel. He walked outside into the dusk. There were no street lamps, and the town turned to midnight as darkness fell.

He bumped along in the blackness. He saw cubes of light in a couple of windows. He could discern the face of a Japanese tourist in front of him. The tourist had a little money bag tied to his wrist. A boy on a motorbike darted out of some street corner and swiped at the money bag, but the Japanese tourist wouldn't let go. His body twisted as the motorbike dragged him along. Then the bike stalled, and Isaac felt a fury rise up from his throat. He knocked the boy off his bike. The tourist stumbled with him, bound to the boy. They both danced in the dark. Isaac caught the glint of a knife. He socked the boy over the saddle of his bike.

"Puttana di mèrde," the boy said. He'd cut the strings of the money bag and freed himself from the tourist. But he'd lost his purse. He hobbled away without the bike. The tourist was also gone. Isaac stood alone in that early midnight and couldn't contain his anger. He started to smash the bike. He broke the handlebars, twisted the headlight off its mount, tore at the fenders until a gang of older boys emerged and watched the spectacle of a madman destroying a motorbike.

The boys hissed at him. Ah, Isaac muttered to himself, ghost children coming out of the closet. There were ten of them, twenty, clutching thick wads of paper knotted with wire.

"Orso bianco," they called him. Isaac the polar bear.

They whacked him with the paper clubs, punishing Isaac . . . until Margaret appeared with her Glock.

"Dottoressa," the boys shouted at her.

Margaret shot the motorbike. The boys scattered into different streets.

Isaac wouldn't even thank her. "It was Montezuma who told you that story about the women's island. He's another fucking fiancé."

"Isaac, we'll have an army here in a minute. Don't talk. Your tongue is bleeding."

"Montezuma's Man," he said. "You knew all about Joe. Le-Comte fixed it so that Montezuma could have his own little death and Joey would be on a string for life. What kind of fucking people are you?"

"Darling," she said, "people just like you," and she carried Isaac away from the carnage of a wounded motorbike.

Part Six

26

Barbarossa would meet Marilyn Daggers on Indian Road, where he could also watch Isaac's little brother Leo. He was some kind of sheriff and minstrel who couldn't sing. He would have gone to Tunnel Exit Street with Marilyn and rolled around with her on Roz's bed, but he'd promised Isaac to look after Leo. And Joey, who'd been a wild man without an address, would dream of settling in with Mrs. Daggers.

"Jesus," Marilyn said from Leo's divan. "I almost forgot. I keep confusing husbands. I was never legally married to Mark. I was his squaw . . . I don't have to run to Reno for a quickie divorce. We can get married. Any time. Any place."

"Tell it to your dad."

Marilyn began to flail at him, while Barbarossa held her in his arms. "Damn you. He can't negotiate my life."

"I'll marry you, Mrs. Daggers. But not behind the boss's back."

"I already told you. I'm not Mrs. Daggers. And we can have a shotgun wedding," Marilyn said. "I'll hold the shotgun on dear daddy Isaac."

Barbarossa almost laughed. He saw a black man from the

window, downstairs on Indian Road, with the Hudson's waters behind him. It was Wig, chief of the mayor's detail, spying on Marilyn and Joe.

"I'll be right back," Barbarossa said. He put on a light lumber jacket and went downstairs with a twitch in his jaw that was like the prelude to a kill. Wig shouldn't have haunted him. Not on Indian Road.

Barbarossa crossed the street and approached Wig, who stood near a fence with that spectacular look of the Purple Gang: brown leather and a gold medallion hanging from his neck. No one could ever find the Purples. They were cool aristocrats of mayhem, renting themselves out on some mythical basis.

"You shouldn't have come here, Wig. Persecuting me and my woman."

"Aw," Wig said, fondling the medallion. "I wouldn't mess with Marilyn the Wild."

"She's Mrs. Daggers. Show her some fucking respect."

"Wouldn't hurt a hair on her head."

"But you came to Indian Road. That's criminal."

"Couldn't find you, kid. I looked everywhere. Sherwood Forest. Chinatown. I visited your pingpong table. All I got was a load of crap."

"I go where I want," Barbarossa said. "I'm Isaac's driver."

"But the great man is out of town. He's with them Sicilian mothers, and I had to see you."

"Wig, if I catch you on Indian Road again, or anyplace near Mrs. Daggers and her Uncle Leo, I'll kill you, Wig."

"That's okay. But Mario wants to meet with you."

"He can pick up a phone."

"He's not too fond of telephones. He sent me."

"Yeah," Barbarossa said. "His packager."

They stood by the fence, the two most decorated cops in New York, with scars on their faces, little wounds. They'd both lived with the tiger, toyed with its teeth. They fell off roofs, they'd both been glocked. They were reckless warriors who robbed drug dealers and were captains of their own ambiguous country.

"I can drive you, Joey."

"I have my own bus," Barbarossa said.

"Then you drive me. We're expected at the mansion in twenty minutes."

Barbarossa went back upstairs. He hugged Marilyn and Leo. "Lock the door," he said.

"What's the matter, Joe?"

"Ah, it's some stupid business. But don't you answer to anybody. No one gets in here but me."

"That's glorious," Marilyn said. "We're under house arrest."

"Listen to him," Leo said, feeling the urgency in Barbarossa's scarred mouth.

"If something happens, you sit here, you call Sweets. He'll come with his cadre."

"You're scaring us," Marilyn said.

"Baby," Barbarossa said. "It's the best I can do."

He rode down to Gracie Mansion with Wig beside him in Isaac's black Dodge. Wig wouldn't shoot him in the car. Joe would have to kill Wig one day and suffer the consequences.

He drove through the gate at Rebecca's mansion. He saw the other members of her detail in long leather coats, like Isaac's marksmen and musketeers. They sat on the front porch, whittling pieces of wood. The porch was littered with their shavings. One or two of them had shotguns at their feet. The mayor was in her rocking chair. Mrs. Dove, Rebecca's chief of staff, was feeding her lentil soup with a large spoon. The giantess seemed to frown at Joe from the roots of her red hair. But it was Wig who scolded those other policemen.

"Hey, you're marking up the mayor's floor."

The policemen crouched on the porch in their leather coats and picked up the shavings while Wig went into the mansion with Barbarossa. Mario was in his tiny office near the pantry.

He had a photograph of Fiorello LaGuardia, the first mayor to occupy the mansion. The Little Flower was a frenetic man who would often serve as a magistrate or fire chief or commander of the harbor patrol. Isaac always talked about the Little Flower, who was his hero as a child. He'd made war on slot machines, he read the funny papers on the radio to the children of New York. Isaac discovered Dick Tracy through the voice of Fiorello LaGuardia. Barbarossa was a bit resentful that he didn't have his own Little Flower. Isaac was the lucky one. All Barbarossa had was Chief Joseph, a noncombatant warrior who died in his own tent.

Mario Klein was wearing a velvet jacket, a silk tie, and a pair of slippers that seemed to complement his white mustache. He looked like a naval explorer who'd been driven off the sea, a doomed admiral exiled to a closet. Joe had been his dealer. He understood Mario's Napoleonic moods.

"Joey," Mario said, "you'll have to make up your mind. Either you sink with Isaac or survive with us . . . Wig, explain him the facts of life."

"Joe, Isaac is one fucking lonely cop."

"He's a voice in the wilderness," Mario said.

Wig rolled his eyes. "Mario, will you let me finish?"

"You don't have to finish," Barbarossa said. "Mario wants his dolls back."

"That's correct."

"And you'd like me to steal them from Isaac's office."

"You're the only one with enough leverage. His sergeants are scared of you. You could walk in and walk out."

"Wiggy," Barbarossa said. "I'm disappointed. I mean, I'll have to off you or vice versa. We always knew that. But why would I betray my own chief for some little Napoleon who thinks he's Rebecca Karp?"

"I don't think I'm Rebecca," Mario said. "And you're standing on a cliff. You've been dealing, you've killed people. The FBI can end your career, and Isaac can't help. He likes to cry about schoolchildren. He can't save you, Joe."

"And you can."

"Yes. I can make you captain of Sherwood Forest, get you a disability pension. You have a sister to support."

"Mario, please don't mention my sister."

"I won't," Mario said. "I won't. But it's a point of honor. I can't have Gracie violated like that. It's supposed to be impregnable. It's the mayor's house. I was holding the dolls for a client. Isaac destroys one, and steals the other two. I'm under a cloud, Joey. I can't have that."

"But you have the resources, Mario. Tell young Robert to replace the Peppinninus. He's the doll builder."

"It's complicated, Joey. He can't just build a doll on command. He's a little cracked in the head, or he wouldn't have murdered his own meal ticket . . . the dolls that Isaac has are crucial to me."

"Tough," Barbarossa said.

"Aw," Wig said, "be kind to the man. He's trying to spare you some grief."

"Like what, Wiggy?"

"You've been leading a double life, kid. It could catch up with you."

"And what about your double life?"

"Me, kid? I've been reborn. I'm becoming a priest."

"Yeah. The spiritual advisor to the Purple Gang."

"Quit the backbiting," Mario said. "We don't have the time. Look around you, Joe. Rebecca is in permanent retreat. Every little putz on the City Council has to kiss my ass. I'm the kingmaker. I can fuck anyone out of his career. And Sidel is no exception. I sit with all the federal attorneys. You and Isaac had your little romance as the Black Stocking Twins. Isaac's baby brother is a shoplifter, a common thief, and his daughter, Mrs. Daggers, is a bigamist. That girl has peculiar ideas about marriage."

"She's not a girl," Barbarossa said.

"Joey, wake up. Join our team."

"I have my team," Barbarossa said and walked out of Gracie Mansion. There were no more whittling policemen on the porch. Rebecca's detail was gone. She sat in her rocking chair, all alone, watching some inner turbulent sea. But she looked up at Joe. Her hair hadn't been combed. Her mouth was wet.

"Barbarossa, is that you?"

"Yes, Madam Mayor."

"You're in trouble."

"Trouble?" said Barbarossa, like Becky's own child.

"You've been tricked. Run on back to Indian Road."

27

He drove to the northern edge of Manhattan with his sirens drowning the City's noise. He should never have trusted Wig. He was a rotten negotiator. While he'd talked about the dolls, Rebecca's detail snuck out of Gracie Mansion, and Joe was left with his prick in his pocket. Now he'd have to waste the whole detail *and* Mario Klein.

There were tears in his eyes, and he wasn't a crier like his boss. He was something of a stoic, like that lost Indian chief who went into battle backwards, with his ass facing his enemies. Joe parked the car. He couldn't see any signs of malice near Leo's apartment house. He looked up at the windows. He found nothing but vacant glass. He didn't use the elevator. He climbed the stairs, took the six flights in great galloping strides. He was clutching his Glock, and he couldn't even remember having unholstered it. In his own mind, he was already in the middle of a firefight.

Leo's front door was open.

He could see the skirts of long leather coats. Barbarossa rushed in. "Freeze," he said, the gun in his white glove. And he fell upon the Pink Commish, surrounded by his musketeers, grim men who could have been the doubles of Rebecca's detail.

"Boss, I figured it was a trap. I . . ."

"Where were you, Joey?"

"With Wig and Mario. It was Rebecca who warned me from her rocking chair."

"From her rocking chair," Isaac said. "That's grand. I come to Leo's, I find seven of Wig's soldiers picking their teeth in front of my daughter. This time I'll fuck them out of their pensions with or without Malik. Seven soldiers."

"They're cops, boss, they're your soldiers too."

"They're animals," Isaac said. He was also wearing a leather jacket. Palermo must have changed him. He had the Devil's own darkness under his eyes.

"Where's Marilyn . . . and Leo?"

"I sent them out for a little R and R. Leo likes to shop at Alexander's. I'll cripple him if he lifts anything. Marilyn didn't want to move. 'I have to wait for Joe,' she said. 'I have to wait for Joe.'"

"I told her to call Sweets if—"

"I'm not blaming you, Joey. I blame myself. I ought to resign. There I am, worrying about young Robert. LeComte endorses my trip to Palermo. He lends me Margaret. He's my rabbi all of a sudden. He was moving merchandise, Joey. He wanted me out of the way. And Margaret is his little angel. That's what hurts. She's stringing me along, pretending to be my guide. It was a stall."

"Boss, did you get to use your mask?"

"No, I didn't have the occasion. But I should have, Joey."

He walked into Leo's bedroom with Barbarossa and shut the door so Isaac's musketeers couldn't listen. It was like the bedroom of a little boy. Leo had maps on the wall of Marco Polo's route to China. He had a photograph of Isaac and himself as children in a cave that Barbarossa instantly recognized. It was that touch of Sheriff Street under the Williamsburg Bridge. Leo's desk and bed were gorgeous pieces of maplewood. The desk was much too little for a man. But Isaac hardly noticed. The furniture must have been as familiar as the corns on his feet.

"Boss, is that Leo's school desk?"

"Yeah, he inherited it from me. But I didn't bring you in here to talk about desks. I have regards," Isaac said, "from a cadaver."

His boss was the Devil, that much Barbarossa knew. Only the Devil could have come out of Sicily with those darkened eyes.

"Which cadaver, boss? I know a bunch of them."

"Montezuma, the cavalier of cavaliers."

"Boss, he was buried in a box . . . out in Queens. I went to the funeral."

"And Montezuma was laughing his ass off inside the hearse. It was an FBI caper, Joe. LeComte was behind it."

"Boss, I don't mean to brag. But when I kill a man, he stays killed."

"He was wearing plastic putty. The FBI dressed him to take the kill. He had a bag of blood under his coat. All you ever saw was the bag break."

"I saw him dead."

"Joey, he runs a jewelry shop in Palermo. I met with him. I have witnesses. It was a brilliant stroke. The little kings of Palermo can't touch him, because they're supersitious bastards, and meanwhile LeComte has you hooked for life."

"I'm going to Palermo," Barbarossa said. "I sock a man, and he starts selling jewelry. I have to sock him again."

"Are you blotto? It's a blessing. You're off LeComte's list. You're free."

"Free, huh? Free to live under a pingpong table, free to drive you around, but am I free to marry Mrs. Daggers?"

"Leave my daughter out of it," Isaac said. "She's a fucking victim of marriages."

"I want your blessing, Isaac."

"Joey, we have work to do. LeComte is the master of disinformation. He goes into business with Montezuma. He's partners with Sal and Jerry D., and they're blind to the whole schtick. He uses their soldiers, he uses me . . . and you. He sets up the biggest drug cartel in creation and runs it like a little king. He controls all the traffic. He makes millions, and when he's ready to pounce, he'll pounce. Montezuma is registered to him. Le-Comte is clean. He can't get hurt. But he's behind the times. He doesn't understand chaos. He doesn't appreciate nonlinear twists."

"Boss, what's a nonlinear twist?"

"Turbulence," Isaac said. "Everything in nature leads to turbulence. It's at the heart of every form. Singularity. That's what baseball is about. Singularities inside a field of order. Nine men. Nine positions. A pitched ball."

"Boss," Barbarossa said, "I can't talk baseball right now. Please. I have a headache. I was with Rebecca on her porch. I had to go eyeball to eyeball with Wig. I was worried about Marilyn. And you tell me Montezuma walked away from his own burial. Do we go to our masks? What's the plan?"

"Turbulence," Isaac said. "We destabilize LeComte and his cartel."

"Yeah," Barbarossa said. "With a shitstorm of singularities."

And they walked out of Leo's bedroom together, the Black Stocking Twins. Barbarossa's hand tingled under the white glove. He owed LeComte a lesson in turbulence. It annoyed him that Montezuma was alive.

28

The Pink Commish had to practice his own art of Zen. He meditated in front of the dolls in his office, the two Giuseppinas. He begged them to forgive his vanity, his self-righteousness, his overreaching nature. He was the prince of nothing. He wasn't worthy of being their very own knight. He locked himself in with the dolls for two days. He wouldn't accept any nourishment. He sipped a glass of water. He had no hunger pains. He sought a koan that would deliver him from the world of police chiefs. But he couldn't discover any surge of enlightenment. He was Isaac, son of Joel, brother of Leo, father of Marilyn, estranged husband of Kathleen, ambiguous sweetheart of Anastasia, lapsed comrade of Jerry D. and Isadore Wasser the melamed, former beneficiary of Frederic LeComte, boss and spiritual twin of Joe Barbarossa, enemy of Montezuma, mourner of Manfred Coen . . .

He woke from a turbulent dream, kissed both dolls, left his office, had Moros y Cristianos at his Newyorican café, and began calling in whatever cards he had as Commish. He went into the chambers of judges who still admired him, he met with Alejo Tomás, the schools chancellor, he met with Cardinal Jim, he courted the district attorneys of Manhattan, Brooklyn, and the Bronx, told them about the cartel, he sat with Democratic *and* Republican Party chiefs, talked like a mayor, barked like a mayor. It was mostly bluff. He schemed with Becky's other commissioners, promised whatever he could. He drove a wedge between them and Mario Klein.

"There's a rumor running around that the lad will be indicted," Isaac said in his best policeman's brogue. "He's been warehousing drugs in Rebecca's basement. Wouldn't count much on Mario if I were you. But I can't say more. I'll prejudice our case."

He didn't have a case. He had cries and whispers, nothing at all.

He chatted up certain art patrons, friends of the Police Athletic League who frequented Manhattan galleries. "Dolls," he said. "Masterpieces of the Sicilian puppet theater. Knights and warrior ladies in skirts. You couldn't miss them. They'd haunt your memory. They're three feet tall . . . ah, the Lucifer Gallery on Madison and Fifty-seventh. Near St. Patrick's Cathedral. Neighbors of Cardinal Jim."

He arrived at the Lucifer with a fire marshal who owed him favors. And Barbarossa. Isaac was carrying documents with fabricated violations. He'd woven a little tale around the Lucifer. He could have simplified his life with a search warrant. But he loved to maneuver in the dark. Isaac the enchanter, with stories to tell.

And he had to smile, because his own diseased logic had paid off. The girl minding the gallery was Monica Bradstreet, whom he'd met at the Green Hut with her dollish face, the specialist on puppet theater who pretended to work at the Museum of Natural History. She was one of LeComte's creations, borrowed from the FBI.

"Hello, Dr. Bradstreet," he said.

The gallery had precious little art. It looked like a Mafia laundering operation, an outfit that was meant to lose money. A couple of carved heads and a pudgy Don Quixote holding a pathetic lance.

"I'm not Dr. Bradstreet."

"Yeah, and I suppose we never met."

She had a glorious mouth, and if Isaac hadn't been in love with Margaret Tolstoy, he might have had more of a crush on Monica Bradstreet.

"What are you doing here?"

"Having a look." He pointed to the fire marshal. "Jonah, I smell a leak. Don't you?"

"Definitely," the fire marshal said. "The walls feel wet."

Dr. Bradstreet picked up her telephone and started to dial.

"Monica dear, if it's LeComte you're calling, or the President of the United States, I have the same sad story. This is my town."

She stopped dialing. "Where's your warrant?"

"Wouldn't want me to bother some judge or the district attorney, would you, dear? I'd have to arrest you, and it would be an embarrassment to the FBI. One of their agents charged with murder."

"You're out of your mind, Commissioner Sidel."

"Ah, you remember my name . . . excuse me, have to follow that leak," Isaac said, breaking into the gallery's storeroom. He didn't find any dolls, but there were plumed hats and decorative pieces of body armor. It was like a clothing shop for Peppinninus, a lost land beyond the ruinous doors of reality.

Isaac took everything.

Dr. Bradstreet taunted him. "You won't be so eager tomorrow."

"Tomorrow, dear? Better give up your lease. Because I will be back with a warrant. Tell LeComte to strike Lucifer off his phantom books before I grab the whole fucking inventory."

She turned to Barbarossa. "How is Montezuma's Man?"

"Doing fine," Isaac answered, and the three men strolled out of the gallery, their arms laden with metal furnishings.

"Boss, who's Montezuma's Man?" Barbarossa asked, under all the miniature gloves he had to carry.

"It's not important."

"Who's Montezuma's Man?"

"Ah, that's your nickname in FBI circles . . . means nothing."

"Montezuma's Man," Barbarossa said. He waited until the fire marshal emptied his load of armor into the trunk of Isaac's car and started back to his own station. "I'm the patsy, boss, aint I?"

"No. They scheme. They use people. They build their scenarios. They tied you to me, that's all. They remembered my attachment to Manfred Coen, and . . ."

"I'm not Coen," Barbarossa said.

"Joey, you can't let LeComte get your goat. We'll fuck them, I promise. Body and soul."

Isaac returned to Police Plaza, locked the armor in his own closet. He communed with both Giuseppinas and went to see his First Dep, bringing him a doll's iron glove. But Sweets wasn't in a welcoming mood.

"You were in Palermo, huh?"

"I left you a memo, Sweets."

"You were out of communication for almost a week. That's reckless and irresponsible and illegal. You're the Commish. Your ass belongs to the City of New York. I'm only the First Dep. I can have a private life. But you're the number-one public servant, after Rebecca Karp. And you follow your personal vendettas."

"That's some personal vendetta. A drug cartel run out of Gracie Mansion."

"LeComte's casting a wide net. He'll bring in all the big and little fish."

"Has he bought you, Sweets? Has he bought the Department?"

"Don't say that."

"He's not the PC. He can't fish or fuck over our heads. I'm breaking up Rebecca's detail, and don't bother lecturing me about protocol and unwritten laws. Wig's men were up on Indian Road, harassing my daughter. They laughed in Leo's face, said how they were going to toss him out the window if he didn't lick their shoes."

"You should have told me that," Sweets said.

"I'm telling you now. You can have the Department, but give me a week."

"While you pile contraband in your office?"

"That's not contraband. They're my sisters. The two Giuseppinas."

He left Sweets. He had an appointment with his Rasta lawyer, Marlon Fitzhugh. Isaac could tell from the look on his sergeants' faces that Marlon had arrived. They couldn't get used to dreadlocks on the commissioner's floor.

Marlon was stooping over the dolls when Isaac opened his own door. "Magic mamas," Marlon said. "Are they African?"

"Could be," Isaac said. "Black brigandesses . . . I need advice. I have to take on LeComte, cut off his bases in Manhattan. He has Justice behind him. He has the edge. I have to invent affidavits, stretch a couple of warrants, make a few false arrests, steal private property, close a discotheque, wrestle with FBI agents, storm Gracie Mansion, kidnap Rebecca maybe. How much time do I have?"

"Until you're arrested or killed?"

"Both."

"Isaac, I'm not an oracle. I'm a Rasta who went to law school. I get the runs around white people."

"I'm white people," Isaac said.

"You're the lion of Judah. A white boy with a black man's heart."

"How much time does this lion have?"

"That depends on whether he's a candidate. A white boy can get away with a lot of crooked shit if he decides to declare."

"I can storm Gracie Mansion if I agree to run for mayor?"

"That's correct."

"I can kick ass?"

"The mayor's always the Man, even if he wears a skirt, like Rebecca. Mr. Lion, are you gonna run?"

"I'll think about it, Marlon."

"That's not good enough. You're out in voodoo land. They'll triangulate you, brother. Catch you in a cross fire. Are you gonna run?"

"No . . . yes," Isaac said.

Marlon clutched Isaac and kissed the future candidate. "Our king."

"Christ, I'm a cop."

But Marlon combed his dreadlocks with one long metal tooth and disappeared on Isaac, the loneliest lion of Judah.

29

He had thirty musketeers.

They rode behind Isaac in a green bus with wire dug into the windows. He went up to Frannie's old fortress, with Barbarossa and Chancellor Tomás, who was a graduate of the Golden Gloves. Tomás could have been a professional boxer. He had the wind and the hand power and that sense of lightning in his legs, but he chose politics, and not palookaville. He'd married the Bronx Democratic machine. He presided over a system of graft. Isaac had feuded with Alejo, fought with him about the concerns of schoolchildren. They'd had a shoving war two years ago at the governor's Manhattan Ball. But Isaac had to give up this vendetta if he wanted to get near the schools. He'd established a grudging alliance with Alejo. And Alejo could deliver the Bronx machine to Candidate Sidel, who was behaving like a reluctant bride. He'd announce, he said, but not until next week. He had to clear his plate at Police Plaza. Still, Alejo had agreed to accompany Isaac to the ghost school at Crazy Corners, where Fran's brats had outlawed themselves from the Board of Ed.

"Isaac, it's impossible. A whole tribe of children quitting public school at nine and ten."

"Alejo, most of them quit long before that."

"I have my own policemen," Alejo said. "I would have heard about it."

"Not from your castle on Livingston Street. This is Valentine Avenue."

"Hombre," Alejo said. "I grew up around Poe Park. I played stickball on Valentine Avenue."

"That was another lifetime, Alejo."

Isaac, Tomás, and Barbarossa entered that sinister, sunken courtyard of Crazy Corners, with thirty musketeers standing out on the street. No ketchup bottles fell from the windows. Nothing exploded on the concrete. There weren't any war cries. Just a spooky silence as Isaac crossed that concrete ocean and entered the building with Joe and the chancellor. He never drew his gun. He discovered a few boys sleeping under the staircase, clutching the torn edges of a communal blanket. He climbed up the stairs, meeting dull-eyed boys, who did a slow dance around Isaac and the chancellor.

"Told you, Alejo. It's a ghosts' college."

They continued to climb.

Alejo's shoulders started to sag. He stopped a boy, spoke a few words of Spanish.

"Pappy," the boy answered. "We all alone."

Isaac couldn't disguise his own pity. They were mean boys who would have kicked Frannie to death for his association with the FBI. But they were forlorn without Fran, little instruments without a family. Who had poisoned them against their president? It must have been LeComte . . . or his angel, Margaret Tolstoy. LeComte was always disrupting families he helped to build. Fran had become a liability to LeComte, and he sat in exile at the Palme Hotel.

The chancellor whispered into his portable telephone. And Isaac wondered if Alejo was buying school furniture at half price, or politicking with the Bronx machine. He got to Frannie's throne room on the sixth floor. It reminded Isaac of a ravaged opium den. Children lay near the walls, sucking some kind of candy. Their eyes couldn't focus. They'd withdrawn into their private moon.

"Fantasmas," the chancellor said. "Isaac, I don't have the finances to deal with ghosts."

"Alejo, we can't leave them here."

The chancellor stooped over several children and scribbled on a pad until a man in a red cape arrived. It was Cardinal Jim with a small colony of monsignors.

" 'Lo, Isaac," the cardinal said, with a runty cigarette in his mouth. Isaac wouldn't answer.

"I had to call Jim," the chancellor said.

The cardinal pleaded with the Pink Commish. "I'm not a leper. This is my parish."

The monsignors began administering to the moon children. They reached into the military bags they were carrying and removed bits of nourishment.

"You could have warned us, son," the cardinal said to Isaac.

"Jim, they were ordinary bandits until a week ago."

"Bandits without a bloody soul."

"They might not have agreed with you . . . they lost their president."

"I'd love to meet that man," the cardinal said. "I'd sock him in the nose, do much worse."

"He provided a home, Jim. They were wandering the streets."

"Then it's a shame on all of us. I'll have to go into the till and get us an emergency fund. I'll send the lads to one of our retreats. And then we'll worry about their schooling . . . by the by, do you think there's a second baseman among them? Your own lads are in trouble."

Isaac stared at the cardinal with an angry grin. "Haven't had time to consider the Delancey Giants."

"They're battling my lads next month."

"Forgive me, Jim, but I'm getting fucked by the FBI."

"Bite that tongue of yours. You're around children."

"They'll teach you a thing or two, Jim, when they recover from their moon sickness."

"You're the one that's moon sick. Running for mayor."

"I'm the people's candidate," Isaac said.

"Well, you're not mine. You don't belong at Gracie. You're a policeman. The mayor has to bend. You don't have a political bone in your body."

"You shouldn't discourage him, Jim," the chancellor said. "He's our choice."

"Then the Bronx is daft," the cardinal said, chewing his cigarette. "Joey, will you escort your chief out of the building? I'll swallow him the minute he's mayor."

Isaac had to laugh. "You're my rabbi, Jim. I'm counting on you to deliver the religious vote."

"I'll deliver you to hell . . . get out of here, Isaac, or we'll never cure the hearts of these children."

Isaac whistled on the ride down to Rebecca's mansion. Battling the cardinal always seemed to rouse him, put him in the mood for another fight. He had thirty musketeers behind him. He intended to crash the gate.

The guard was gloomy inside his shallow box. "Commissioner, sir, I have orders from the Green Room not to let anyone in."

The Green Room, the Green Room, Isaac muttered to himself. Mario had established his own headquarters inside the mansion's walls.

"Officer, you happen to work for me."

"I work for the City, sir. The mayor says no visitors."

"The mayor . . . or Mario?"

"Sir, it's pretty much the same thing."

"Surrender your badge," Isaac said.

"I can't, sir. I'm sworn to protect the mayor and all her people."

"Joey, arrest the son of a bitch. He's breaking the law."

Barbarossa had to whisper in Isaac's ear. "Boss, he's right. Besides, he controls the gate."

A woman walked down from the mansion with half of Rebecca's detail. She was wearing high heels and a light-skinned holster. It was Monica Bradstreet, who must have gone to the FBI's ghost college at Quantico.

She shouted at Isaac. "You're a pest, Commissioner Sidel."

Wig was with her, and the seven cops who'd deviled Leo and Marilyn on Indian Road.

"These men are no longer peace officers, Dr. Bradstreet."

"Commissioner, I've deputized them. They're temporary marshals. And I told you, I'm not Dr. Bradstreet. I'm Special Agent Smith of the Atlanta field office, on assignment."

"To fucking Frederic LeComte."

"I'm not allowed to discuss that, Commissioner. And you are trespassing. I've been empowered to seize property at moments of crisis. You're standing on federal grounds. And you're congregating in an unlawful manner, violating the civil rights of the mayor and persons in her employ."

"Joey," Isaac said. "I can't keep up with all that crap."

"Boss," Barbarossa said.

Isaac pressed against the gate. "Go on, shoot me, Dr. Bradstreet. Frederic will love you for it."

"Boss," Barbarossa said.

"Joey, I have thirty sharpshooters. She has shit."

"Boss," Barbarossa whispered. "It will never go down. Massacring an FBI agent and your own cops."

"They're not my cops. I suspended them. And LeComte can't improvise his own laws."

"Boss, he can."

"Come on. We'll put on our masks. We'll surprise Dr. Bradstreet."

"Boss."

Isaac stood frozen. He was like a disenfranchised puppet, a wooden knight without the gift of intelligence, or a human heart.

A tall man suddenly appeared. It was Alejo Tomás.

"Wig," he said, in a gentle voice. "Will you get Mario, please?"

Wig dialed Mario from the telephone in the guard's box. He uttered two or three words. And Mario arrived in slippers and a bathrobe, nursing another cold.

"Mario," the chancellor said, ignoring Special Agent Smith. "You'll have to let Isaac in."

"I don't get it," Mario said. "I'm preparing papers, Chancellor Tomás. Rebecca is asking him to resign. He'll lose everything if he opens his mouth. The mayor's prepared to fire him."

"Mario, you'll have to destroy those papers."

"Why?"

"He's our king."

"Sidel a king? He carries a gun in his pants like a hoodlum."

"But that hoodlum will be the next mayor of New York. He's our king."

Mario Klein sneezed into a red handkerchief, rolled the handkerchief into a ball, stepped around Wig and the special agent, shivered once, and opened the gate for Isaac Sidel.

30

He didn't stay very long. He scattered Wig and all his men, called Police Plaza and invited Lieutenant Larry Quinn to form his own detail once again. He couldn't really punish Mario. But he could surround him with detectives who were loyal to the Pink Commish. The special agent picked up her handbag, tightened her holster, and left those grounds she'd anointed for the FBI. Isaac admired the pull of her calves. He couldn't seem to get angry at Monica Bradstreet Smith. He was grateful to Chancellor Tomás, but he had to ponder Tomás' roll in this palace putsch. Was Alejo Tomás Frederic's new man in the Bronx, an FBI sleeper? Half the world was FBI. But Isaac didn't care. He was a wooden knight with his own fucking heart, and it ripped at the sad picture of Rebecca Karp. She'd grown worse since his last visit. She'd become a chronic rocking-chair case.

"Becky, Becky," he said. "We'll repaint the master bedroom. This is your home for life."

There was a fleeting warmth in her eye, then it passed. "Cocksucker," she said in her cracked voice, which was like a pale song with a lot of static. "You could still lose the election."

"Yeah, and the moon could run to Mars . . . Rebecca, take care. It's Mario who's the cocksucker, not me."

He marched into Mario's office. "You'll close shop, understand? No dolls, no heroin, no cocaine."

"Isaac, I have my own habit."

"Then sniff airplane glue. I don't want the mansion involved in LeComte's drug capers. Mario, we're starting a new marriage. Me and you. I won't bother searching the basement. But get rid of all your stock. Don't disappoint me, Mario."

Isaac walked out of the mansion with Alejo Tomás. He was still suspicious of the chancellor. Mario was a dwarf. Tomás was the kingmaker.

"Don't want to sound surly, Alejo, but I'm the police commissioner, and I can't get through the gate until you come along. Did you follow me from Poe Park? Did a sparrow land in your ear?"

"It's no mystery, Isaac. The sparrow was Cardinal Jim."

"Should have figured. He has the best spies in town."

"You're wrong. Jim worries about you. But he can't meddle. He realized you were locking horns with that little shit."

"Alejo, honest to God, are you FBI?"

"I'm schools chancellor, Isaac, and boss of the Bronx. I don't need LeComte's special agents."

Alejo ran out of Carl Schurz Park like some Golden Glover, and Isaac stood there, watching the rise and fall of a chancellor's shadow. He'd never get far in the universe of Manhattan, no matter who called him king.

⚔

He lived in that speckled world of a candidate who was about to declare. Reporters parked outside his office. A television crew from Munich wanted to spend seven days and nights with him. "And sleep in my bed? Nothing doing." Women would hug him in the street. "Our king." But Isaac couldn't concentrate on his most immediate tasks. He dreamt of Palermo. He couldn't forget the hailstorm, the lights that went out all over the place, the brioschi con gelato, the skeleton bishops in their long hats. Palermo had captured him, become his mythical kingdom. And then he'd rage against LeComte and Margaret Tolstoy. He went on a midnight tour with his musketeers and shut down Chinaman's Chance. He could have arrested Delia St. John for exhibiting herself in a club without a license, but he wouldn't get at Papa Cassidy through his child bride, and Delia wasn't even a proper child. He closed all the clubs she'd ever danced in. It wasn't out of spite. They were drug cribs. He began to realize that Delia St. John must have been a spotter for Le-Comte, the girl who traced the routes of LeComte's drug cara-van. Wherever Delia danced, that's where the drugs could be found.

He hadn't bagged a single ounce of heroin. He had to act on blind faith—and his diseased logic—that he was slowing Le-Comte, hurting his caravan routes. He couldn't fuck LeComte in Düsseldorf or Cologne. But the caravans had to end in Man-hattan, and Isaac would break him here. The town was getting very tight on anything to cook, shoot, or blow. Isaac had an active barometer on all this: the methadone clinics were filling up with poor souls who couldn't find any junk on the street.

He sat in his office and waited . . . waited for what? He was Charlie Chan, the infallible detective who could read the dark-ness, discover ribbons of light. Those ribbons arrived in the shape of that former dead man, Montezuma. He wore dark glasses. He was incognito. The collar of his coat was up around his ears, like a commonplace assassin.

"Cavaliere, how is the jewelry business?"

"Bene," Montezuma said. "But I have other grief. Young Rob-ert. He's been plotting with the little kings."

"But you're his padrone," Isaac said. "He owes you every-thing."

"He has different ideas. I couldn't even run to the bank. Had to escape with the shirt on my back."

"And jewelry in your pockets."

"Niènte. I'm a pauper, Don Isacco."

"Cavaliere," Isaac said, "no titles. I'm not part of your clan. And why should the little kings suddenly turn against you?"

"La dròga," Montezuma said. "The flow has stopped. I can't provide the kings with their ration of dollars."

"Then go to LeComte," Isaac said. "He's the fucking mastermind."

"Frederic has abandoned me."

"Then what can I do, cavaliere? I'm a police chief who's ready to resign. I don't have Frederic's resources."

"But you could hide me, signore."

"Where? I have a railroad flat on Rivington Street. I . . ." And then Isaac remembered. He did have an odd piece of real estate, a house he might inherit. He dialed Gracie Mansion and got Lieutenant Quinn. "Larry, the mayor is going to have a guest . . . how long? Dunno. He's a jeweler by profession. He can repair all the mansion's clocks . . . his name? Montezuma. And Larry, he's not to leave the house . . . recognize him? You can't miss. He looks like an Aztec."

Isaac put down the phone. "There, it's done. You'll live at Gracie Mansion."

The cavaliere tried to kiss Isaac's hand. "Padrone," he said.

"I'm not finished with you. This isn't Palermo, and I'm not Santa Claus. You want asylum, I'll give you asylum. But you'll pay with your blood, cavaliere. You'll talk Margaret Tolstoy."

"Signore, what can I possibly tell you about LeComte's favorite girl?"

"Did you sleep with her, cavaliere?"

"She was a twelve-year-old bride . . . in Odessa."

"I didn't ask you about Odessa."

"But it's important. She visited Palermo with her husband,

Antonescu, the Butcher of Bucharest . . . and a bunch of Nazi generals. That's where I met her. Before you ever did."

"If it's another one of your phony resurrections, I'll . . ."

"I was a boy," Montezuma said. "Eleven years old, waiting on tables at the Palme Hotel."

"It always comes down to the Palme," Isaac muttered.

"It was a honeymoon hotel for the Nazis . . . Wagner, Nietzsche, the German High Command. And she was having lunch with the generals. She was Magda then. Magda Antonescu. She noticed me. I spilled soup on a general's lap. I was punished. Magda screamed at the generals for slapping a gypsy boy."

"You're not a gypsy," Isaac said.

"We're Sicilians. We have gypsy blood. We've had so many conquerors, we've all been fucked in the ass. Phoenicians, Greeks, Carthaginians, Romans, Byzantine kings, Muslims, Norman knights, Catalan counts, Bourbons, the British, Mussolini, Hitler, General Eisenhower . . ."

"Cavaliere, save the laundry list. It's nineteen forty-three. You're a busboy at the Palme. What happened?"

"We were children. We didn't have time for romantic interludes. Bombs were falling. The generals could have been eating shrapnel with their soup."

"What happened, cavaliere?"

"We kissed twice . . . in a closet."

"She was already a bride," Isaac spat. He was numb with jealousy. Nothing was sacred. Not even his own wartime idyll. He didn't count Antonescu. Antonescu was an adult. But Montezuma had been there first. "And afterwards?"

"Signore, we met by chance. I didn't have a clue that she was part of Frederic's entourage. We recognized each other . . ."

"And resumed your fucking romance."

"There wasn't the same passion. She was FBI material. I treated her like that."

"And I could kill you, cavaliere."

"But you won't."

"Yeah, that's my nature. I'm tight as a tit. But I can't let you walk out of here alone. You have enemies all over the world. I'll have to lend you Barbarossa. Remember him? Good luck, cavaliere."

He sat in the car with Joe. He couldn't have told Sidel that he'd lived with Margaret for a month while young Robert was preparing a new shipment of dolls. He'd taken all his meals with her, at the Palme, where they'd flirted in a closet thousands of years ago. The Palme had its own magic force. The hotel of musicians, philosophers, kings, and Magda Antonescu. The cavaliere had to reconsider. Had Margaret blinded him to young Robert's maneuvers? Was *their* lovemaking only a stab in the back? But he couldn't ruminate very long. This driver of Sidel's was a dangerous man.

"I apologize."

Barbarossa said nothing.

"I was under orders, Joe."

"Don't you ever call me Joe. I'm Mr. Barbarossa, you scumhead. The boss is a baby. He believes your lies. But I know what you are. An FBI suck. You don't move from Gracie, *Montezuma*. That's where you have your wet dreams. You can plot with Mario all you want. But if you walk out of the mansion, you won't survive that walk."

"It was LeComte's game, *Mr. Barbarossa.* I had to disappear. LeComte picked you as the agent. He never consulted me. He didn't eat your bullet, I did."

"I'd like to strangle you with that bag of blood you were wearing over your armored vest. Did you laugh a lot, Montezuma? Did you say, 'Joey's a fool,' to Lecomte's other people?"

"There were no other people," Montezuma said. "Just Margaret Tolstoy."

"Did she laugh too?"

"Not at all. But she did think it was clever."

"Well, 'clever' won't get you out of the mansion, Montezuma. Nothing will."

He deposited the cavaliere.

His face was quivering on the drive up to Indian Road. Montezuma's Man.

He couldn't hide his own particular wound from Mrs. Daggers. They kissed on Leo's divan, fumbling with each other's clothes.

"What's wrong, Joe?"

"Had to deal with a ghost," he said. "It's nothing."

"You're the ghost," she said. "Like Blue Eyes. My father always wins."

"I'm not Coen," he said, and his pager started to sing. It was Roz's nursing home. He dialed Macabee's. Roz had slashed her wrists with the shards of a broken mirror she'd hid in her room. His love for Mrs. Daggers and his work for the Pink Commish had blunted his devotion to Roz. He'd neglected his suicidal sister. Macabee's had got her to the Allen Pavillion. That was Barbarossa's one piece of luck. The hospital was five minutes from Indian Road.

Marilyn wouldn't let him run there all alone. Rosalind lay in a room overlooking Spuyten Duyvil Creek. Both her wrists were bound with gauze. She wasn't pale. Joe had never seen her with such a rosy complexion. She smiled at Mrs. Daggers. Her lips were as red as those dolls of Isaac's, the two Giuseppinas. But Roz wasn't a brigandess.

"Is this your sweetheart, Joe, the girl you want to marry?"

"Mrs. Dag-dag-daggers," Barbarossa bumbled.

"I'm Marilyn Sidel," Marilyn had to say. She wasn't hysterical, like Joe. The two women seemed to calm him. They laughed like sisters under their own private sun.

"I wasn't depressed or anything," Roz said. "It happened. I didn't hear voices. It happened."

Joe was blubbering.

"He's a crier," Marilyn said, "like my dad."

"No," Roz said. "It's something new."

"Men," Marilyn said. "They can't control themselves."

"But Joe's a doll," Roz said. "I raised him. Did you know that?"

"He doesn't like to talk about his personal history."

"We have an Indian chief in our past. Joey's named after him."

"Ah," Barbarossa said. "You shouldn't boast. Mrs. Daggers will think we're royalty or something."

"We are royalty," Roz said. She looked up and saw a man. He must have been born under Saturn's rings, he had such a blackened brow. It was Sidel. The nursing home had called his dispatcher, looking for Joe. And Isaac had to bum a ride up to the Allen Pavillion. He hadn't expected to meet Marilyn with the suicidal sister. He was carrying flowers and chocolates he'd swiped from concessioneers next to Police Plaza. He didn't really know what to bring. But he could smell a marriage. Both these women were in love with Joe. And Isaac would have to accept his own twin as a son-in-law.

Barbarossa.

31

He'd never accumulated so much power by doing nothing at all. He inhabited this fat country of the future king. His silence bothered the political chiefs. They couldn't bear the uncertainty. He had a visit from the Republican Party boss, Tyson Hammer.

"We could run Malik. But we'd rather keep him under wraps. He'll be our own dark horse for the governor's seat."

"What are you saying, Ty?"

"We'll consider a fusion ticket."

"Not a chance. I never voted Republican in my life."

"All right. We'll go through the motions. But I want assurances that you won't hurt us."

"How can I hurt you?"

"By waging war on the Republican Party."

"That's not my style."

"Your own Party will pressure you, Isaac. They'll want scapegoats. White Anglo-Saxons. Rockefeller. The big banks."

"You have my word, Ty."

"Then we'll support you . . . via the back door. No Republican candidate will have a bad word to say about Isaac Sidel."

"Come on, Ty. I'm the Pink Commish. They'll call me Stalin's baby brother."

"Not if they want to hold onto their heads."

"I don't mind a fight."

"Isaac, whoever our man is, I'm warning my captains to vote for you."

"That's indecent," Isaac said, smiling at Tyson Hammer. But he brooded after Hammer left. Isaac was a little too electable. He'd have to go against straw men, run without a race.

He couldn't keep clear of the petitioners outside his door. But he didn't have the heart to deal with a fucking army. He'd flown out of Palermo with Margaret Tolstoy and hadn't seen her since. They'd held hands in the sky, drank Alitalia wine, kissed, and then Margaret had crawled back into her usual black hole of being Sal Rubino's nurse.

Isaac stood near the door and peeked at all the petitioners. Christ, there was a brat among them, the little prince, Raoul, with his enormous eyes. Isaac had to encourage this baby Galileo. "Come in, come in." Raoul darted into Isaac's office. He couldn't take his eyes off the two Giuseppinas.

"How's your dad?"

"He's in trouble," Raoul said, like the consigliere of his father's clan. "Jerry wants to see you."

"And he sends you to sit in my outer office? . . . where's the melamed?"

"He couldn't make it. Grandpa Izzy's in mourning."

"He's not your grandpa. And what's he mourning about?"

"The money he's losing because of you."

Isaac muttered good-bye to his warrior ladies and followed the little prince. Papa Cassidy was in the vestibule, with Isaac's other petitioners. Isaac whispered in his ear. "Home from the Sahara, eh, you son of a bitch?"

"We have to talk."

"Tell Delia I'm sorry about Chinaman's Chance."

"Isaac," Papa said, and the Pink Commish whirled past him with Raoul. He didn't have to collect his wits. He followed the little prince. They trudged under the arcade of the Municipal Building, sidled around City Hall, which seemed like a huge enchanted cottage without Rebecca Karp, and entered Rowena's Restaurant. Rowena was a fallen beauty queen, like Rebecca. She'd been Miss Long Island many years ago. Her restaurant had become a hangout for female detectives and assistant district attorneys. It was always jumping with women. But Rowena rarely surfaced. She would count receipts in a back room. And Isaac began to wonder if Raoul had gotten lost. Rowena's wasn't a Mafia haunt. He nodded to the female detectives, who'd never encountered Isaac at Rowena's in the company of a little boy.

"Hello, Commissioner." Rowena herself had come out of isolation to greet the Pink Commish. She was sixty or so. She'd bonded with Rebecca, catered most official functions at City Hall, and was president of Lesbians for Rebecca Karp.

"You're not dethroning our sweetheart, are you, Commissioner?"

"I have her blessings, Rowena, I swear."

"That's not how Mario tells it. He says she's a prisoner at the mansion."

"She's withdrawn from the world. But she's no prisoner. I'll take you uptown. Ask her yourself."

"I believe you, Commissioner. But I can make trouble. You might not get to Gracie without the lesbian vote."

She brought Isaac to a table across from the bar, where Jerry DiAngelis sat in the kingdom of his white coat. Raoul immediately climbed on his lap, and Rowena disappeared.

"I don't get it," Isaac said. "Rowena's Restaurant?"

"It's flooded with lady detectives," Jerry said. "I'm safe at Rowena's."

"Safe? The war is over with Sal."

"That's part of the predicament. Sal is dead."

"Don't kid me. Sal dies and I don't even hear about it? Who's police commissioner?"

"He drowned in his bathtub. LeComte buried him in some backyard."

"I have my own rats, Jerry."

"But they're compromised. You pay them with the money you get from LeComte . . . Isaac, dead is dead."

"Is Margaret in the story? She was looking after Sal."

"How the fuck should I know?"

"You tried to kill her at Chinaman's Chance."

"Yeah, and you stole my kid . . . it's memories, Isaac, that's all. And we have a real problem. I mean, young Robert's on the rampage. He has a loose wire in his brain. He isn't satisfied with the puppets. He wants the whole mountain."

"What mountain?"

"All our junk."

"I happen to admire the boy. You shouldn't have advertised him as your own little cousin. You lied to me, you put on little puppet shows, pretended that the dolls were part of your fucking history."

"Hey, not so loud," Jerry said. "Raoul is here."

"He ought to learn about his dad . . . you used me, and I don't like it."

"Everybody uses you," Jerry said. "You're Sidel. You cry like a baby. You fall in love with a phantom. *Peppinninu.*"

"You and Sal concocted that tale with a little help from Montezuma and the FBI."

"I'm entitled," Jerry said. "You have a twin. Well, I have a twin, a poisonous twin. Sal. I hated him, but sometimes we had to dance. And we needed you to get LeComte off our back."

"But Sal was LeComte's favorite little man."

"He was . . . and he wasn't. I'm talking millions, Isaac. And here I am, Jerry D., in a partnership with Sal Rubino and the FBI. And I'm getting fucked. Don Roberto's mine, young Robert's mine, and I'm getting fucked. LeComte borrows my ideas, my men, and keeps trying to indict me."

"You shouldn't have gone into business with the FBI."

"Did I have a choice? LeComte has the trade routes. He has the galleries, he has connections with all the museums. We couldn't have gotten the junk through customs without Le-Comte."

"And what did the melamed have to say? He's not stupid."

"We didn't have a choice. LeComte is the only game in town, that's the bottom line. It costs money to have your own mob. Can you figure the handouts I have to make? I'm the boss. I have captains. I have crews. I have to find them work. I have to beat LeComte's indictments. It's no picnic. I have six lawyers on retainer, around the clock. They have to bribe witnesses. That doesn't come cheap."

"Are you sure you want to tell me that?"

"Isaac, my lawyers can wrap you in a blanket. They'd destroy you in open court. You're a police commisioner, a baby."

"Montezuma's alive."

"Of course he's alive. And he's running from Robert. You put him up at the mansion. That's clever, I have to admit."

"You and Izzy are as bad as LeComte."

"Isaac, it's dangerous. Robert's making up his own rules. He killed Sal."

"Robert's here . . . in Manhattan?"

"He's a citizen," Jerry said. "Robert was naturalized. He can come and go."

"And you're scared of one little doll maker?"

"He has those cavalieri behind him, the little kings."

"The kings never travel."

"Yeah, but they can hire an awful lot of substitutes to travel for them . . . Isaac, we're talking Sicily. That's one crazy island. Robert must have a Christ complex. He's doing God this year. I have six lieutenants guarding Alicia alone."

"And you let Raoul come up to my office without an escort?"

"Who's gonna harm him inside Headquarters? . . . and I had soldiers stationed in the street. I'm Jerry D. I don't take chances."

"And what am I supposed to do?"

"Find Robert. You found him once . . . in Palermo. Find him again. Meet with that maniac. Because I can go to the cannons, Isaac. I'll fight the cavalieri, I'll steal Palermo from them, I'll throw Sicily right into the sea."

"Jerry, you couldn't take the Bronx. Forget Sicily."

Isaac shook hands with the little prince and walked out of Rowena's.

32

He was lonely for the dolls, but he didn't return to his roost. He was sick of Republicans and Democrats. He envied Rebecca and her rocking chair. She'd become her own Manhattan melodrama. Would any other metropolis allow a sitting mayor to retire from politics and rock in an enormous upright cradle?

Sidel had his usual eyes in his ass. A gang of monkeys was following him. He didn't like it. Was it the little kings, or their American surrogates? Had young Robert come to claim the two Giuseppinas? Isaac wasn't giving them back. His warrior ladies were the only ones who could relax him. He'd go for his Glock if he had to, he'd shoot to kill.

He avoided his flat on Rivington Street. Robert's henchmen could dim the lights in the hall, catch Isaac, and toss him down the stairwell. What would he dream of during that descent? His few moments with Marilyn when she was a little girl? His barterings under the Williamsburg Bridge? His first encounters with Anastasia? His fall into adulthood had left him with very little. He had nothing but his own mayoralty to look forward to. He had to find a rocking chair and put it next to Rebecca's.

He went to Ratner's because it was an open place. He could

view his adversaries while he drank lime jello and munched on poppy-seed cakes. Only what would a gang of substitute kings look like? He had six poppy-seed cakes. And then he groaned. LeComte had walked into the cafeteria wearing a blue leather coat, like some Neo-Nazi.

"Aren't you going to ask me to sit down, Mr. Mayor?"

"LeComte, I could shoot your fucking eyes out. No jury would convict the PC."

"I'm proud of you," LeComte said. "My protégé."

"Are you listening, LeComte? This is my cafeteria. Anything goes."

"They screamed on the Hill when I named you my first Hamilton Fellow. 'That bum,' they said. 'He's the Pink Commish.' And I answered, 'What a strategist. He excites people. He's good for the system.' And they said, 'A panther's never good. He's wild. You'll have to kill him one day, Frederic . . . build a cage around him that's so big, he'll never be able to tell the difference.' "

"Is that what you are, LeComte, my circus trainer?"

"Not bad," LeComte said, inside the comfort of his Neo-Nazi coat. "Mr. Mayor, you're becoming a poet."

"LeComte, you have it wrong. I'm part of your animal act. You're the poet. You created Peppinninu."

"Not really. It was Montezuma's idea. I stole it from him . . . and the Maf. Isaac, you have to understand the equation. If you want to control drugs, you enter the marketplace. The Drug Enforcement people haven't done shit. What does it mean to kill a few banditos? The empire is always there. It has its own life, outside the banditos. We call it 'skeletal structures.' You can't destroy a skel. You can only build onto it. So I built."

"Your own fucking machine."

"I borrowed, I drank the Mafia's blood. And now I run the Palermo Pony Express."

"Pony Express. That's cute, LeComte. I hope I smashed a couple of the ponies' legs."

"You did. That's the thrill of it. That's what I was counting on."

"A fucking chaos factor."

"Jerry DiAngelis is finished. He doesn't have a dime."

"And Sal Rubino's dead."

"An unfortunate accident. He had a morbid love of dolls. He was a sentimentalist, raised on puppet theater. But he shouldn't have let young Robert into the house. He shouldn't have let young Robert into the house."

"You're repeating yourself, LeComte."

"Am I? Robert suckered him, sweettalked Sal, told him he was bringing a new doll, and Sal couldn't resist. Robert cuts his babysitter to pieces, baptizes Sal in his own tub, and steals back the queen of Sal's collection."

"Giuseppina," Isaac said.

"I told you. He was a sentimentalist. You can't trust a doll maker when it comes to his own dolls, and Robert was never reliable. He had a notion in his head to recall whatever dolls he could."

"What about my collection of Giuseppinas?"

"He's superstitious about police stations."

"Who was the babysitter?"

"What?" LeComte said.

"The bodyguard Robert ripped with his knife."

"One of my Mormons. Lowenblum. A very good boy."

"And where was Margaret?"

LeComte ordered a poppy-seed cake. But he didn't clutch it in his fist, like a boy from the Lower East Side. He dissected the cake with his knife and fork. It was a brutal operation. Isaac couldn't imagine a poppy-seed cake devoured in such surgical bits.

"She's gone native," LeComte said, while the bones in his jaw worked overtime.

"Will you translate that fucking FBI parlance?"

"Margaret has flown the coop. You think Robert could have gotten upstairs if Margaret had been around?"

"Where is she? In Odessa?"

"Palermo. She's underground."

"Can't you shape a deal with the cavalieri and get her back?"

"Isaac, the cavalieri don't shape deals."

"Then snap your fingers, LeComte. You can rob commandos from all your agencies. Have them parachute onto the roof of the Palme Hotel."

"They'd get stripped of their chutes before they ever landed on the roof. It's Palermo, Isaac, the city of corpses. You know that."

"Then how come Papa Cassidy can sit at the Palme like his own little king?"

"He was only a supplicant, Isaac. He brought dollars into Palermo. And you should be nicer to him. He's going to be the treasurer of your campaign."

"I'll kill him first."

"Isaac, you can't win without Papa Cassidy. He draws big money."

"Then I'll go for the little bucks."

"There are no little bucks in Manhattan."

"You're wrong. I'll collect dimes from grandmas. I won't take your drug money. How does it feel, LeComte, to be the number-one traficante? The FBI feeding horse to kids . . ."

LeComte had a sliver of cake on his lip. He touched his mouth with a handkerchief. "The horse was there . . . and now it's gone. I took it off the street."

"You, LeComte? It was me and my musketeers."

"And that was written into my scenario. I centralized the

distribution. And then I chopped off its arm, thanks to my own cavaliere."

"I'm not your cavaliere, LeComte. I'm the worst dream you ever had in your life."

He was meticulous now, because he had to retrieve Anastasia from this new black hole she was in. LeComte might have been lying, but it wouldn't have made much difference. The Pink Commish was returning to Palermo. If Margaret was out on some mission for LeComte in the Sea of Japan, he could still go and visit Frannie Meyers at the Palme, if Frannie was alive. But he wouldn't create a black hole for Sweets, saddle him with an absentee Commish.

He sat with the giant. He wrote a letter of resignation, handed it to Sweets. "I'm gonna run. I could announce this minute, but I'd rather not. I can't afford the publicity right now. Give me five days. If I'm not back, go with the letter. You don't have to cover my ass. I can't promise what Rebecca will do. But it won't matter. If I win, you'll be my Commish."

"It's Margaret Tolstoy again, isn't it, Isaac? Why are you involved? She's just another caper."

"I gotta go."

"And what if I put my letter of resignation on top of yours?"

"Ah, you wouldn't do that. The whole Department would land in a shitstorm."

The giant hugged Isaac. "Be careful, boss . . . Palermo is another planet."

Isaac grabbed the two Giuseppinas, hid them in the back of his car, and went up to Gracie Mansion with Barbarossa.

"I got me a passport," Barbarossa said.

"What the hell for?"

"Palermo."

"Forget about it. I can't protect you, Joey. I'm resigning in a couple of days. And you'll be a renegade cop attached to a renegade ex-Commish."

"That's my funeral. We're the Twins."

"Wait in the car," Isaac said, and walked into the mansion. Mother Courage made him a cup of tea. "Thank you, Dove." Was she angling to remain chief of staff during the Sidel administration? He didn't feel like the City's future king. He was only one more man inside a labyrinth.

The mayor was asleep in her rocking chair. Mario was in some far corner of the house, avoiding him. Isaac climbed upstairs to Montezuma's bedroom. Montezuma was curled up on a window seat, watching the water. He sat in his slippers and faded corduroys, like a warlord at the end of the world.

"Cavaliere, I need your advice."

Montezuma turned to look at Isaac. He'd been crying.

"Sorry," Isaac said. "I didn't mean to . . . it's hard to live in exile."

"On the contrary. I love it, signore. I have a river all my own. I'm treated like royalty. I was remembering my childhood . . ."

"At the Palme Hotel."

"Yeah, at the Palme . . . and before. How can I help you?"

"Margaret's disappeared."

"I'm not surprised," Montezuma said. "She's looking for Odessa."

"Come on, cavaliere. Don't play innocent. She's in Palermo. Why did she run away from LeComte? I thought she was a career girl . . . you spent more time with her than I did. *Tell me.*"

"She was tired of wearing wigs, of not remembering who she was at night, of being the wet nurse of criminals."

"Cavaliere, she could have come to me."

"Perhaps," Montezuma said. "But you're also a criminal, if you'll allow me to say so."

"Cavaliere, you don't have to be polite. I am a criminal. I

agree. But Margaret should have gone to Paris. She speaks French. She lived in Paris with Antonescu."

"Palermo was where she had her honeymoon . . . with me. I'm joking, signore. She couldn't escape LeComte in Paris, even with all her wigs. But in Palermo anything is possible."

"Is she with Robert? Would Robert take her in?"

"Anything is possible."

"Then give me a fucking opinion."

"She's with Robert," Montezuma said. "If Robert is in Palermo."

"And how can I get her back?"

"You can't," Montezuma said. "But you could bring her flowers, signore. Margaret loves white roses, with long stems. And I'd bring a babysitter with the flowers."

"What babysitter would you recommend?"

The cavaliere smiled. "Who else but Montezuma's Man?"

"I thought so," Isaac said. "Montezuma's Man."

Part Seven

33

She lived at a broken palace near the harbor, on a vicolo without a name. It was a blind alley with a little crumbling bridge that connected Margaret's palazzo to a palazzo across the street. The old woman who attended Margaret called her "dottoressa," but Margaret had no degrees. She'd gone to junior high with the gypsy, Sidel, and that's where her education ended . . . until her kindergarten classes with the KGB. She'd had only one address: Little Angel Street in Odessa, where she'd starved with Uncle Ferdinand and eaten the flesh of little boys from the lunatic asylum. The dottoressa was a cannibal and a whore and a nurse for the FBI. She'd lost her patient, Sal Rubino. The maestro, young Robert, had murdered Sal, and Margaret was in mourning. But she couldn't recall the name or number of the street where she'd lived with Sal. It was one more vicolo in a life of vicolos.

—Dottoressa.

The old witch, Giovanna, was calling to her from below. Margaret found her little basket with its long piece of rope and let it out the window. She could tell when Giovanna started to tug. Margaret would count to thirty and draw up the rope, length by length. And she'd have her paradiso of wine and cheese and roasted red peppers in a sea of olive oil. It was all part of the same pretense that she was a prigioniera at the palace, that she belonged to Robert, like some Arabian horse or wife, and not to the eyes of Palermo. The door wasn't locked. She could wander the streets day and night, and she often did. The darkness reminded her of that other darkness, the catacombs under Odessa, where the partisans and pirates had their own mirrored world, with Little Angel Street and Magda Antonescu.

Robert had "captured" her the day she arrived. His workshop was in the palazzo across the bridge. He would stage puppet shows for the cavalieri, those dons with tiny shotguns that seemed to fit the dimensions of their bodies. No woman was invited to the puppet shows, except for Margaret, the maestro's Roumanian-American mistress, horse, and wife. She was "una matta," touched in the head, and the cavalieri could ignore her without offending Robert.

She would steal the little black cigars from their mouths, and the cavalieri refused to notice. They were the only ones who didn't call her "dottoressa." She was the devil lady who'd entangled Robert, caught him in the trap of his own affections, and Margaret had to laugh, because it might have been true. She'd wanted a vacation in Palermo, a long rest, a honeymoon of her own, and Robert had imposed himself upon her bachelor honeymoon.

But he didn't destroy the privacy of her palace. He would wait for Margaret to cross over that crumbling bridge to his little museum of dolls. And if the two of them made love, it was in a comradely way, like brothers or sisters with a homicidal bent. Whatever contact they had was enough.

Mostly, Margaret was by herself on that nameless vicolo, where her past would also impose itself, and she would suck at the dark cigarettes and dream of the days when there was no

Margaret Tolstoy, and she was Magda Antonescu, a little Nazi
queen in a place called Paris . . .

Magda had a rocking horse and a dollhouse that reached the
chandeliers. Her windows faced the cimetière, with its own
dollhouses for the dead, and when she stood out on the balcony,
she often felt that the dollhouses belonged to her. She was twelve
years old. She slept in Uncle Ferdinand's bed, with little chocolate boys under her pillow. The chocolates came wrapped in
silver and were called "nigger babies." She would eat them in
the middle of the night, after Uncle Ferdinand made love to her
and fell asleep in his silk pajamas. He would touch her gently
and ride on her, blowing air out of his cheeks, and then he would
curl up like a nigger baby on his side of the bed.

Magda had no complaints. She was a married lady, but she
wasn't allowed to wear a wedding ring. Uncle Ferdinand advertised her as his niece. He was the finance minister of Russian
Roumania, a new country on the Black Sea. The country was
called Transnistria, but it wouldn't be ready for another month.
Meanwhile they lived on the boulevard Edgar Quinet.

It was January 1942. Magda counted her nigger babies while
Paris starved. The admiral who lived upstairs had turnips for
breakfast, turnips for lunch. He'd lost his entire fleet. He was
considered quite crazy because he wore a yellow star over his
heart. French admirals weren't supposed to wear a yellow star.
The police arrested him, but the little führers at the Service Juif
didn't know what to do with Admiral Antoine Gabriel. A tailor
would arrive to tear off the yellow star, and the police would
send him home.

Once, while she was on her rocking horse, Magda saw the
admiral wandering in the cimetière. He stooped and began to
scrub the stone of a particular dollhouse. Magda ran downstairs

in her winter coat, crossed the boulevard Edgar Quinet, and entered the cimetière, which had its own boulevards, like a separate city inside the walls of Paris. She stopped in front of the admiral, who was still scrubbing the dollhouse.

"Monsieur l'Amiral?"

He turned around. His eyes were red. He was wearing another yellow star.

"Ma petite reine nazie."

"Is your wife resting inside the little house?"

"Yes. Now go away and let me have some peace. It's a cemetery, child. Not a Nazi brothel."

Magda ran out of the cimetière. She returned to her rocking horse and cried.

Uncle Ferdinand brought her to a big hotel on the boulevard Raspail. The Germans were having a soirée at Gestapo Headquarters. Magda wore a red dress with a sash around her shoulder. Uncle had a dark cloak and all the medals of a Reichskommissar, but he was the kommissar of a country that didn't exist. She'd met Ferdinand when she was nine. He'd been her ballet master in Bucharest. He'd pulled her out of an orphanage and she started to live with him when she was ten and a half. He'd woo her with nigger babies. She didn't understand all the fuss and fury of sleeping with a man. Every night, a little before eleven, she grew into a rocking horse.

There were generals at the soirée and Obersturmführer Kleist of the Service Juif and Lieutenant Lodl, who was her favorite policeman. Lodl didn't have a uniform. He looked like a boy who might have stepped out of her dollhouse with an eagle's eyes. He would dance with Magda, do funny faces, and mimic Ferdinand and all the other kommissars.

He let her have a sip of champagne.

"Lodl," she said, "do you know the admiral who lives in our building on the boulevard Edgar Quinet? Why does he wear a yellow star?"

"Because he's a pest. He doesn't have one Jewish aunt. And he wants to embarrass the Service Juif. But I'd rather dance than talk about Admiral Gabriel."

They were in the ballroom on the first floor, which looked out upon the Bon Marché, where Uncle had found the rocking horse, stealing it right out of the store window. She danced with Lodl and Führer Kleist and policemen from the Service Juif. No one questioned her relationship with Ferdinand, who was going to govern Bessarabia and deliver all the wealth of the Ukraine. He'd been one of the first Roumanian Nazis, the Butcher of Bucharest, who beat up all the gypsy Jews.

The generals drank and drank. Lodl fell down once. Führer Kleist collected him and walked with Lodl into another room. She could hear them from outside the door. She'd been around so many Germans, she could dream like a Nazi and talk their talk. She didn't really listen until they mentioned "der jüdische Admiral."

—Lodl, I'm sick of police stations. I'm sick of warnings. I'm sick of having our own tailor destroy the yellow stars. I want him to disappear.

—When, Herr Obersturmführer?

—Tonight. Collect him after curfew. Take him to the cemetery. I've left the gate open for you. Put a cloth around his head and kick his brains out. Let the gardien find him in the morning. We'll round up some hooligans and blame it on them.

—But he was a war hero, Herr Obersturmführer. If he's found with the yellow star on his chest, it will make a martyr out of him.

—Then tear off the star after you kick him to death. Lodl, I leave it to you.

She didn't say a word. Uncle Ferdinand brought her back to the boulevard Edgar Quinet in a Nazi limousine.

"I'm proud of you," he said. "You were the queen of the ball. The Fritzies couldn't take their eyes off you. You had the whole Paris Kommando at your feet."

"They're going to kill the admiral," she said.

"Keep quiet."

"They're going to murder him in the cimetière."

"That's none of our business. If he wears the star, he has to pay a price."

Ferdinand made love to her without taking off his silk pajamas. It wasn't a very long ride. Magda felt more like a camel than a rocking horse. Ferdinand fell asleep. Magda searched for her clothes. The moon was out, and it lit the bedroom like a lantern. Magda wore her nightshirt, her slippers, and her winter coat.

The moon came down to meet her as she crossed the boulevard. The gate was unlocked. She entered the cimetière and watched for Lodl. The dollhouses couldn't seem to comfort her in all that moonlight. She'd been born in a hospital for bastard children. She'd been raised like a bastard in a little crèche. Her keepers watched her dance naked when she was five or six. A Roumanian Nazi like Ferdinand had to steal her from the State. He was much more kind than all her keepers. He wouldn't touch her privates without saying "please." He lent her his name. *Antonescu.* He got her to Paris where she could study with the best ballet masters. He wasn't cruel. He kissed her and bought her a dollhouse that was large enough to live in.

She kept counting her own fingers in the cimetière. "Un, deux, trois . . ." The gate started to creak, and there was Lodl and a Gestapo stooge, dragging the admiral along the frozen grass. She could see his yellow star in that crazy, mellow moon.

"Admiral Scheisse," Lodl said, "you have a little time to repent. Sing us a nice Christian song."

Magda jumped out from behind a tree.

"Lodl, how are you?"

She looked like an ordinary ghost who'd dropped off the moon.

"Herr Leutnant," shouted the stooge, "is this a Französiche elf?"

"No. She's Herr Antonescu's niece."

"Dracula's little daughter. She comes here to drink blood."

"Idiot," Lodl said. "This is a cemetery. There is no blood."
And he stared at Magda with his eagle's eyes. "Mädchen, I
will take you home."

"Not without the admiral," she said.

"Do not complicate my life, little one. You're trespassing. This
graveyard is the property of the Reich."

"Herr Leutnant, I could strangle Dracula's daughter for you,"
said the stooge.

Another figure leapt into the light. It was Uncle Ferdinand in
a bathrobe and his boots.

Lodl bowed to the new lord of the Black Sea. "Herr Antonescu, please take the little one. We have to finish something."

"Not tonight," Ferdinand said. "It's unwise to murder a
French admiral during a full moon."

"Do we have to discuss this in front of the child?"

"You've already discussed it. That's why I'm here. And don't
make me remind you, Lodl, that I'm attached to the SS. You
might end up in Bessarabia, working for me."

Uncle Ferdinand was holding a black pistol in his hand. It was
a toy he'd borrowed from Magda's own dollhouse. But it seemed
real enough in the light. Lodl left with his Gestapo stooge.

Uncle Ferdinand lifted the admiral off the grass and wiped
some blood from his mouth.

"You're a Nazi like the others. Why did you help me?"

"Because of her," Uncle Ferdinand said, pointing to Magda.

"Ah," the admiral said, "ma petite reine nazie."

"Call her what you like," Uncle Ferdinand said. "I couldn't
care less. And if I were you, Admiral, I'd get out of Paris. I'd
wear all my medals day and night. And I'd forget about yellow
stars. They're unbecoming to an admiral."

"I don't agree," the admiral said, and he walked out of the
cimetière with Ferdinand and Magda, who grabbed Uncle's gun
and pretended to fire at a very fat moon.

Margaret heard a funny sound on that crumbling bridge between the palazzos. It was the light peck of a man's feet. The young maestro had never visited her until now. He had crimson marks on his cheeks. Robert was in a homicidal mood. But he was secretive with Margaret.

"You look pale," he said. "You never go outside."

"I'm in mourning," she told him.

He laughed like a wounded monkey. "Mourning, dottoressa?"

"Yes," she said. "I'm Sal's widow."

"You were his nurse. And he was hoarding my dolls, dottoressa. He was dancing with the FBI."

"That's not the reason, Robert. You'd come to kill him, that's all. You'd have killed the melamed and Jerry too . . . anything and everything to do with the dolls."

"They took advantage. I was their little prodigy, someone to pet and stroke. I wanted my Peppinninus back."

"Stop it," she said. "You carved them on command."

"It's still *my* collection, dottoressa."

"Yes, the prodigy speaks. Don't give me that nonsense about the grieving artist. You grew up. You discovered that the dolls were more valuable as museum pieces than heroin boats. It's ironic, isn't it? La eroïna isn't as powerful as the world of art. You began building other boats. But you never told Sal or Jerry D."

"Dottoressa, they had the same idea. Sal and Montezuma and the FBI man were overwhelmed by the success of their own story. But I got there first . . ."

"You don't have all the dolls."

"I can manufacture replacements, dottoressa. And the little kings are on my side. Suddenly they love the art market."

"They love their pocketbooks, Robert. You would have killed Jerry's little boy, wouldn't you?"

"Why not? Anything to scare him. He'll have to withdraw. The Peppinninus are all mine . . . dottoressa, your cavalier is in Palermo. At the Palme."

"Robert, I have so many cavaliers, I can't count."

"It's not a game, dottoressa. The policeman is here . . . with his shadow. I won't give you up."

"Robert, we're neighbors, you and I, nothing more."

"I won't give you up. And I warned that fucker not to come here again."

"That's Isaac," Margaret said. "He's always following me. But I'll send him away."

"I don't think so, dottoressa." He clutched that carving knife of his, the knife he would employ to cut a man's throat or create his Peppinninus. She'd lived with assassins all her life. Robert was the most curious. He was cruel and he wasn't. He was one more character on this island of exquisite corpses.

He didn't threaten Margaret with his knife. He ran the blade across his cheek, drew a narrow line of blood. He had all these tiny scars crisscrossing his face, like his own dolls, who were another kind of exquisite corpse.

He returned to his palace. Margaret put on the hottest lipstick she had. She'd have to play Mamma Mafia, or she couldn't get Isaac and Barbarossa out alive. The little kings had their own network of grandmas at the Palme. She started to walk down the steps. Why was she so dizzy? She hadn't starved herself. But one foot wouldn't follow the other. And then she realized the significance of that old witch who fetched Margaret's food. Giovanna was bleeding Margaret little by little. That paradiso of wine and peppers was a poison kit. But Margaret disciplined herself, counted "un, deux, trois," grasped a wet wall, and descended the palace's winding stairs. *Un, deux, trois, un, deux, trois.* She'd become a paradox of arms and legs that had forgotten how to walk in the womb of her palazzo.

She started to cry. "Little Angel Street." Home is where the heart is. That's the first maxim she'd memorized at Isaac's public school. But the heart didn't have a home. Uncle had his own palace on Little Angel Street. The palace was very cold. She had a new rocking horse called Sasha. She would have orgasms on that horse. Sasha could make her into a music box.

Margaret arrived at the bottom of the stairs. The old witch was waiting for her with the round eyes of a lupara under her shawl, that dreaded shotgun of these little people.

"Witch," Margaret said, "out of my way."

"No, dottoressa."

"Sì," Margaret said.

But this Giovanna struck her on the forehead with the shotgun's lip, and Margaret fell to the palazzo's earthen floor. She didn't float into some lousy dreamland. She felt the puzzle of words. Home is where . . . home is where . . . And some kind of storybook seemed to take over her senses. She had a liquid voyage inside her own head. She'd gone back to Little Angel Street. The ground was covered with crocodiles. The crocodiles were eating her legs. They had disgusting pink snouts. But they couldn't handle Margaret. They were all toothless wonders. Margaret laughed.

"Silenzio," the old witch said, and struck her with the lupara again and again.

34

He wasn't Charlie Chan. He didn't have a fucking prayer of finding Margaret without Frannie Meyers, and Fran wasn't registered at the Palme Hotel. The little kings would descend upon him, that much Isaac knew. He needed some lightning act of imagination, but the lightning wouldn't come. He had a Sicilian fruit salad with Joe. And then he conjured up Margaret's tale about that island of lost women, the Isola delle Fémmine. Montezuma had taught that tale to her. Pregnant women and Norman knights.

And Isaac went down to the port with Joe. He stumbled upon a marina. But none of the locals would take him to the Isola delle Fémmine. It was a haunted island. They didn't want Isaac's money. He offered a fucking fabulous sum. A fortune in traveler's checks. The more he persisted, the more they withdrew. And Isaac was growing into Charlie Chan again. It was l'Onorata Società, the Sicilian Maf, that these mothers were afraid of.

He found a Yankee captain on a little yacht who was bumming around from sea to sea. The captain wouldn't hear of Isaac's checks. "Put your money away. The pleasure is all mine."

And Isaac cruised out of the harbor on a boat called the *Appo-*

mattox, with Joe and a captain who could have been a CIA plant from Palermo Station. He didn't care. He'd sell his stinking body and soul for a ride to the Isola delle Fémmine.

The captain had a beard, and called himself Beard. Isaac didn't like the metaphoric jungle between a name and a face. Beard's beard. But he had to trust the son of a bitch. There wasn't even a skeleton crew on the yacht, not one galley slave. Captain Beard was his own pilot and cook. That should have signaled something, rang a fucking bell, but the Pink Commish was desperate. He kept one eye on Beard and also watched the receding roofs of Palermo. The boat rocked in its own blue cradle, and the whole town sank into the Tyrrhenian Sea. Isaac was the sailor now, his own Sinbad, with the water pulling him toward that little island.

It was a rocky scrub of land, good for goats. Sinbad Sidel was standing near the prow, while Captain Beard searched for some tooth between the rocks, a cove where he could park the *Appomattox* and wait for Sinbad and Barbarossa. He didn't ask them what they were doing on a deserted island. And Sinbad had never properly introduced himself.

"I'm Sidel," he said. "Police commissioner of New York. And this is my deputy. His—"

"Keep it simple," Beard said. "I'm not much for names. I have a rifle in the hold. I could lend it to you."

"Thanks. We'll do without the rifle."

Isaac and Joe climbed down a little ladder and leapt onto the rocks.

"Boss, you should have taken the rifle."

"Come on, Joe. It could have been a booby trap. We'd look ridiculous with a gun exploding in our faces. You're the soldier. You've been to Nam."

"I never soldiered," Barbarossa said. "I played pingpong at the American Embassy, I dealt drugs, but I never soldiered."

"Ah," Isaac said, "you know what I mean."

And they scampered off the rocks and shoved toward the heart of the island, which contained that mythological tower where all the women had wept. Only the tower was much more than a myth. It was strewn with rubble from Norman times. Isaac and Joe were two dusty knights searching for human signs. They discovered a condom on the ground, a wine bottle dug into a hole, toilet paper lying there like the scattered wings of a scarf. Furtive lovers, Isaac imagined, or modern pirates moving their bowels in complete isolation.

But the tower was a little too picturesque.

Isaac could live without a leap of imagination. The Isola delle Fémmine was a drug colony posing as a deserted island. It was a fucking heroin farm, with a lab for the production of "la morte bianca," the little white death.

The Black Stocking Twins went to their masks.

Isaac screamed, "Mamma Morte!"

A man with a machine pistol jumped at Isaac from the tower door, stared at the masks, and ran back inside the tower.

Isaac and Barbarossa ran after him. They'd entered a cave with a very high roof. The machine pistol had disappeared. Little men hopped around in the irregular light. They looked like Turks. Isaac saw bottles and jars and vats in this distillery. Frannie Meyers sat on a stool near the "kitchen," the cooking works. He didn't respond to the masks.

"Frannie," Isaac said. "It's me."

Frannie was crying now. "I can't move," he said. "Montezuma put me here. I can't move. Where's Joey?"

"Jesus," Isaac said, "you hate each other."

Barbarossa touched Fran's shoulder. He was still wearing his mask. "It's all right, Fran."

"Joey, will you take me back to Saigon?"

"Sure," Barbarossa said. He picked up Fran and carried him out of the cave.

The Twins took off their masks.

"I can walk," Frannie said. "I can walk."

Barbarossa let him down.

Fran was wearing a poncho. He had a bitter smile. "Crazies," he said, "run for your life. This is holy ground. It belongs to the cavalieri."

"Don't rush me," Isaac said. "Didn't Montezuma make you the principal of a ghost college?"

"He did," Frannie said. "You're standing on it."

"Where are the pupils?" Isaac asked.

"On vacation. Hombres, how did you get to this island?"

"A captain brought us," Barbarossa said.

"With a beard?"

"Yeah," Isaac said. "Captain Beard . . . he has a little yacht."

"He's the cavalieri's boatman," Fran said. "He hauls their junk. And he didn't even shoot your eyes out. He's a retired secret-service agent from Malta. The cavalieri love to use Brits."

"He's an American," Isaac said. "His yacht's the *Appomattox*. That's where Lee surrendered to General Grant. At Appomattox."

"Don't teach me history," Fran said. "Beard is a Brit." And he led the Black Stocking Twins away from the captain's little cove. The three of them marched across the island. Isaac cursed the stark vegetation. He had stones in his shoe. He couldn't see the walls of Palermo from this miserable spot. It was like the fucking end of creation. A volcanic island without a volcano.

They arrived at another cove, far from the *Appomattox*, where Fran had his own tiny boat. But a pirate stepped out from behind the rocks with a very long rifle. Captain Beard.

"Steady, lads," he said. He'd lost his Civil War accent.

"Malta man," Isaac muttered.

"Tosh," the captain said. "A police commissioner on Fran's little island. That's a bleeding shame . . . you're our warden, Mr. Meyers. You're not entitled to your own private guests."

"True," Fran said.

Isaac heard three quick claps from under Fran's poncho. Beard fell off the rocks and landed belly-down in the sea. But Fran had set his poncho on fire. Barbarossa slapped at the fire with his white glove. The glove turned black.

It wasn't much of a mystery. Fran had the missing machine pistol under his poncho.

Fran stared at the dead captain floating in the water.

"Never liked him," he said.

35

Isaac had a school principal on his side. Frannie Meyers. He and Barbarossa were Fran's ghost children, lost boys in Palermo. The Pink Commish bought white roses for Margaret Tolstoy, but how could he deliver them? Fran struggled to arrange a meet with the young maestro. "Tell him," Isaac said, "tell him I have two of his dolls."

Isaac kept the Giuseppinas in his bedroom at the Palme. Fran moved in with Isaac and Barbarossa. He had to make sporadic dashes into young Robert's neighborhood, near the Via Pappagallo. He couldn't stay long, or he'd lose his life to the little kings and their band of Brits, those Malta men, like Captain Beard. The Brits were all over the fucking place. They'd already killed journalists and mayors and policemen in the back halls of the Palme Hotel.

The Palermitans were frightened to death of these ex–British agents, who could seize a restaurant or a cinema at will, and then vanish into some vicolo. The police were powerless against the Brits, who had the little kings behind them. Fran stopped foraging. And Isaac grew sick of eating endless meals at the Palme, surrounded by ancient widows, the only ones who could afford the full pensione besides Isaac himself. He was fond of a Sicilian fruit salad called "macedonia." Isaac wondered if Alexander the Great, king of Macedon, had brought the first fruit salad to Sicily.

"It's no use," he said, after eating his fifth macedonia with Joe and Fran. "I'll have to get to Robert on my own."

"Boss, it's murder out there."

"I can't wait. Margaret's not coming. And that little prick Robert won't meet with us."

He went upstairs to get the dolls. Joe and Fran stood behind him. "We'll back you up," Fran said. "You'll never get near Robert. The Brits will pick you clean. They'll grab the dolls, your shoes, your life . . ."

"I'll have to risk it."

He walked down from the Via Roma, crossed the Vittorio Emanuele to the Via Pappagallo and that piazza with its forest of banyan trees, where he'd met Robert once before. He was carrying the two Giuseppinas in his arms. He didn't advertise himself. He stood there in that forest. He couldn't tell much about the Brits. Little gangs gathered around Isaac, but no one menaced him. And then he saw Robert within a maze of roots, wearing a crimson shirt.

"I played here when I was a boy," Robert said, without acknowledging Isaac or the Giuseppinas.

"Boy? What boy?" Isaac said. "You were born a puppeteer."

"You're confusing me with my knife," Robert said. But he wouldn't take the dolls. Isaac had to stand there with those two curious children in his arms, three feet high. His head seemed lost among their limbs.

"I've been guarding them for you, maestro. *Your* dolls."

"I don't want them, Mr. Isaac. They were gifts to Mario Klein and the mayor of New York. You'll return them . . . with my compliments."

"They were carriers," Isaac said, "boats for la morte bianca.

You can't deny it. I was at your heroin farm on the Isola delle Fémmine. I found Fran. He was all strung out. Barbarossa had to hold him like a baby."

"But he's alive, Mr. Isaac. And that's an accomplishment. You can have him. I'm not interested in Fran. But the dottoressa stays with me."

"I'm going to marry that girl."

"She's not a girl, Mr. Isaac. She's our local goddess. And the best neighbor I ever had. I wouldn't know what to do without the dottoressa. There's only a small bridge between us. That comforts me. I work on my marionettes and think of her."

"Then you'll have to find another goddess."

"I could have had you slaughtered in your bed at the Palme, but I didn't. I admire *babbas*, policemen with romantic ideas."

"You're mistaken. I'm not a babba. I'm an assassino, just like you."

"The people you kill don't stay dead."

"It's very dashing of you, Robert, to drown a crippled man in a tub of water. I was getting fond of Sal. He was crazy about your dolls. You shouldn't have killed him . . . Robert, you can have all the cavalieri in the world, and all the men from Malta. It won't save you. Because I'm going to wrap your fucking neck around a tree."

The maestro started to cackle in his crimson shirt. He took out his knife and slashed one of the Giuseppinas across her eye. Isaac was horrified.

The cackling stopped, and Robert seemed to dissolve inside his shirt. He was the spiky-haired apprentice again.

Isaac turned around. Jerry DiAngelis was behind him, with the melamed. They had their own escort, five Brits, hurly-burly men with speckled beards. Isaac felt a bleakness in his heart.

"You made up with Jerry, didn't you, Robert?"

"He returned all the dolls," Robert said. "He hates LeComte. I hate LeComte. That's almost like a marriage."

"You're going for museum money now. That's the catch. Isn't it, *Peppinninu?*"

"Mr. Isaac, I'm only a carpenter," Robert said.

"And the latest in a fucking line of bandits and pricks."

"Robert," Jerry said, "don't listen to him. He likes to rave. Give him back the bimbo, Margaret Tolstoy."

"He's a babba policeman," Robert said. "What the hell does he mean to you?"

"I can't afford to have him killed."

"Yeah," Robert said. "You want a mayor in your Family."

"It's not like that," Jerry said. "Raoul is fond of him, and so is the melamed. But it's not like that. We'll all be hounded. The babba is running for office."

"Then I want some compensation."

"You can talk dollars," the melamed said. "We're not stingy people."

"Rabbi," Robert said. "Keep your dollars. I want flesh. The policeman has to give me Barbarossa. He'll be my monkey. And when I tire of him, I'll cut his throat."

"That's fine with me," Jerry said. "You can have Barbarossa."

Isaac had to hug the dolls to his chest, or he would have attacked the three of them, and all five Brits.

"Not in your lifetime," he said. "Barbarossa isn't for sale."

"Come on," Jerry said. "It's like baseball. You're shaking up your team a little . . . we have to give Robert something, for Christ's sake. That's how things are done on this island. Robert will look bad. How can he face the little kings? He has to have a monkey."

"Then I'll wear the leash."

"Who would believe it?" Jerry said. "You'll be mayor in six months, our next king."

"Niènte," Isaac said. "You get nothing. You and the cavalieri are kissing cousins . . . ah, I should have figured. The melamed would never have made a deal with LeComte. You were just tickling him. That breakdown in the heroin traffic didn't cost you a cent. It was a lullaby to put LeComte to sleep. The dolls were only a diversion."

"Not a diversion. Call it a sideshow. We had a lot invested in the dolls. LeComte never knew."

"And while Margaret was gone, you encouraged Robert to go after Sal."

"Jesus," Jerry said, "Robert tried to kill me too!"

"But he didn't get very far, right, Iz?"

"We saw our chance," the melamed said, "and we took it. It's called creative management."

"No, Iz. It's murder à la mode. And when the Black Stocking Twins arrived, you got scared. You thought Margaret and Joe and me might corrupt young Robert. So Jerry brings you along to make a good impression on the cavalieri, like pious puppets."

"Babba," Jerry said. "I save your ass, and you call me a puppet? . . . Dad, let's leave him here. You travel four thousand miles after you had a stroke, and he spits in our face."

"Yeah," Isaac said. "It's just like Rowena's Restaurant . . . a little acting class."

He dropped the Giuseppinas at Robert's feet, stepped outside that little wall of bearded Brits, and removed himself from Robert's playground of banyan trees.

Margaret was at the Palme when Isaac returned, wearing her red wig. She had bruises on her forehead, and her face was sallow.

"I'll kill Robert and his Malta men."

"It's nothing," Margaret said. "I had an argument with a witch . . . stop crying or I'll run away."

"I'm not crying. I had flowers for you. And they're all dead."

"Why did you drag Joey along?"

"He's my twin . . . ah, Montezuma told me to bring him."

"My poor dumb darling, it was Montezuma's way of getting Joey killed."

"Nobody dies," Isaac said. "Not while I'm in Palermo."

But he was shivering in his bones. He didn't want another Blue Eyes. Marilyn would scold him into eternity. And Isaac would be a lone rider with a useless stocking mask.

He had his own honeymoon with Margaret for half an hour. He kissed her bruises, and then they all had to catch a plane. Margaret never returned to her palace. She sat beside the window while Barbarossa slept near Frannie Meyers, and her own dumb darling held her hand. She thought of Little Angel Street and the admiral's turnips and the big dollhouses in the cimetière, and she wondered what the hell it meant to be a child. The big bear wanted to marry her, but how could Dracula's Daughter become a mayor's wife?

"I'll go to LeComte," Isaac said. "I'll buy you back from the Bureau. They'll never deport you, Anastasia. I'm king of the Democrats. That fuck will have to listen."

"Shhh," Margaret said, closing his mouth with a kiss in front of all the stewards and stewardesses. Margaret had a vegetarian meal. She couldn't bear the odor of meat after her days and nights as a cannibal in Odessa.

"You'll live with me . . . right away."

"Shhh," she said. But she did start to dream of herself as the mistress of a mansion, La Signora Sidel. She carried that picture off the plane with her. But it didn't last beyond the passport control. She had to leave Isaac and Barbarossa and Fran and get on a separate line. She was an alien who didn't even have a green card. LeComte wouldn't allow her one. She had a Roumanian passport, invented by the FBI. Her status in America would always be ambiguous.

There was a familiar face behind the control booth. It belonged to LeComte's girl Friday, Special Agent Monica Bradstreet on loan from Atlanta. LeComte was sleeping with her, as he slept with all his girl Fridays. Monica was some kind of ninja who could have knocked Margaret on her ass.

"Frederic's waiting," she said.

And Margaret had to accompany Monica Bradstreet across a labyrinth of aisles and into a U.S. Customs interrogation room. She didn't even have the dignity of being alone with LeComte. Monica stood beside him with a notebook in her hand. LeComte was wearing a powder-blue shirt that Margaret had given him for one of his phony birthdays. LeComte loved to feed on his own image of a mystery man. He was constantly changing addresses and birthdays, but he couldn't crawl out from under the color blue.

"What happened to your face?"

"It's the Sicilian sky," she said. "Bad for the complexion."

"Margaret, you had your fun . . . now it's over."

"You squealed to Isaac, didn't you? You told him where I was, sent him on a sucker's bet. He was your carrier pigeon."

"He's the Pink Commish. He brought you back to civilization."

"I liked Palermo," she said. "I had my own palace."

"You walked out on Sal. He couldn't survive without his nurse . . . Margaret, you got him killed."

She would have struck LeComte, but she couldn't fight the little boy blue and his ninja.

"Frederic," she said, "Sal would be alive if you wanted him alive. You got sick of him. He was one more broken-down jeweler . . ."

But she did miss that man in the wheelchair. He'd become part of Margaret's own skin. "If you hold me too long, Isaac will put on his mask and start ripping up the airport with Barbarossa."

"He can have the golden goose," LeComte said, while his ninja smirked into her notebook. "But you're mine, Margaret. Remember that . . . tell me about the little master."

"Robert? He doesn't whimper in the middle of his orgasms,

like Frederic LeComte . . . are you taking that down, Monica dear?"

"I'm laughing my heart out," LeComte said. "You're a stateless little bitch. The Roumanians won't even recognize you as one of their nationals. You can't afford to be a badass. Now what about Robert? He's been silent all of a sudden."

"He's meditating. He likes to lick blood out of old pieces of wood."

"Robert's much more clever than that. He's gone into partnership with himself . . . what are his trade routes?"

"I didn't ask Robert about his routes. I was his concubine, Arab style. We never spoke. Monica's younger than I am, and she doesn't have varicose veins. Have Robert fall in love with her . . . meanwhile, Frederic, get fucked."

She kissed LeComte on the forehead, walked out, got past the Customs declaration booth, and found her little trio of men.

"Baby," Isaac said, "what took you so long?"

36

There was a panic among the Party bosses. The Pink Commish wasn't even a registered Democrat. Isaac had to scribble his name in front of a little old lady at the Board of Elections. He thought of Sweets. Rebecca wouldn't move from her rocking chair, wouldn't sanctify him as her PC.

For the third time in two years, Sweets was Acting Commish. He moved back into Isaac's office and summoned Barbarossa to the commissioners' floor. Joe didn't get along with the black giant. Sweets would probably take his gold shield away and banish him to Sherwood Forest.

"You'll guard the boss," Sweets said. "I'm assigning you to Sidel. He was already wounded once . . . a hospital case. I don't want it to happen again."

Police inspectors scurried out of Barbarossa's way. He was marked by Sidel. He was the chauffeur and confidant and lawless twin of the Democrats' new dark knight, their vigilante cop, the Pink Commish who was running for mayor.

Isaac couldn't go anywhere without a band of photographers. The constant, crazy traffic exhausted Barbarossa. He had to shield the boss, protect him from male and female admirers, the lovelorn, the wounded, the misfits who tried to grab a piece of Isaac. Suddenly the boss was famous. It had nothing to do with the Democratic machine or the campaign itself. There was no campaign. The dark knight had to be out looking for the holy ghosts of Manhattan and the Bronx, the witches of Queens, Brooklyn, and Staten Island. He searched the sewers and the subways for some strange grail.

And on one of these quests, with people all around him, Isaac whispered in Joe's ear. "We have to whack Montezuma, but I'm not sure how. We could stick him in Rebecca's basement, but he'd start to stink . . . ah, he's only a rat. Let him stay where he is."

Frannie Meyers would have been another guest at Gracie Mansion, but he couldn't seem to get along without Poe Park. Barbarossa had to move him back to Valentine Avenue. He had a whole castle to himself, Crazy Corners, with the broken concrete and his king's chair. The castle was overrun with rats. Barbarossa had to hurl chunks of debris at them.

"Fran, you don't have to stay. I could find you a boarding-house."

"I live here," Fran said. "It's my home."

They'd been enemies half their lives, they'd scarred each other, planned each other's deaths, but their battles had given them a language and a history, and they were almost bedfellows now, intimates of their very own war.

Barbarossa went from Poe Park to Palisade Avenue and his sister Roz, who had her old room at Macabee's. Her wrists had healed. Her hair was whiter at the roots. Joe couldn't forget that absolute blondness she'd once had.

"I have my own beautician," Roz said. "Mrs. Daggers. She came up from Indian Road to do my hair."

Barbarossa saw the penciled lines under his sister's eyes. She looked like an aristocratic Mama-san in the French Quarter of Saigon, the widow of some plantation owner who'd fallen on hard times. No matter how long he lived, he couldn't graduate from Nam: the drug-dealing marine with his own pingpong table.

He was feeling guilty under Roz's gaze. He hadn't gone to Indian Road since he returned from Sicily. He loved Marilyn the Wild, but he was frightened of the wounds she could open in him, that fucking tenderness. He'd have to kill Isaac to keep her.

"She loves you, Joe. Don't come here again until you see her."

But there were complications now. He was shadowing Margaret Tolstoy. She wouldn't settle in with the boss on Rivington Street. She'd disappear for days, and the boss would mope.

"Doesn't leave a message . . . I'm telling you, Joey. She has the hots for another man."

There was only LeComte. The little boy blue had his claws in Margaret. Joe tracked her to one of LeComte's cribs, and while he stood in the hall and waited for her to come out, a woman approached with slightly greenish hair. It was Monica Bradstreet. She smiled at Barbarossa and then her feet were in his face, and he was lying on the floor. *Montezuma's Man.* He hadn't even blocked her kicks with his white glove. He didn't have a white glove. Monica must have pulled it off his hand and he had to stare at his own raw fingers and the mottled skin that was the color of a turkey's neck.

He blinked and clutched the wall. Margaret was standing over him. She'd found his white glove. She had to help him squeeze his raw fingers into the fingers of the glove. He scratched the wall with his gloved hand and rose up until he landed in Margaret's arms.

"You shouldn't have tangled with Monica Bradstreet. She's a ninja."

"Next time I'll know," he said.

"And why are you following me?"

"The boss is cracking up. He won't drink his jello. He can't remember any of his speeches. He'll run against himself and lose . . . the blue boy is blackmailing you, isn't he?"

They both sat down on the bottom stair of LeComte's apartment house.

"Frederic has all my files from the KGB. He can leak a couple of pages and ruin Isaac. He and Monica are dreaming up headlines. 'The Spy without a Country and the Pink Commish.' I have to rat out Robert a little."

Barbarossa slept at Schiller's whenever he could. But he had to keep the same hours as Frederic LeComte. He discovered LeComte's favorite restaurant, a brasserie in SoHo called the New Moon, where LeComte liked to dine with Monica Bradstreet.

Barbarossa would look through the window and see Marilyn's face in the glass. He'd rub his eyes until Marilyn went away. He couldn't indulge himself on ghostly girlfriends. He had to clock the voyage of LeComte's dinners, from the first glass of red wine through the appetizer and the main course to the demitasse and dessert and the last little bowl of brandy. He grew feverish memorizing LeComte's meals. And after he clocked the cultural commissar three times, he broke into the New Moon just before brandy, when LeComte's eyes began to glaze and Monica's green hair dropped twenty degrees. Barbarossa arrived at the table and dug his Glock into the commissar's left ear. The restaurant grew alert. LeComte woke out of his delicious half sleep.

"You're crazy to come here, Joe."

"Nah," Barbarossa said. "I have to report to you, Frederic. I'm your snitch."

"You're not in our books," LeComte said. "You're a pennyante dealer who pretends to be a cop."

"But you shouldn't have pushed me into killing a man who was wearing one of your magic vests."

"Montezuma?" LeComte said. "That's water under the bridge. Don't make a fool of yourself, Joe. We're in a public place."

"It's perfect. Me, you, and the whore."

"Don't talk like that about Agent Bradstreet."

"Frederic, he's bluffing," Monica said, her green hair still at an angle. "I could blow him away."

"I'd love it," Barbarossa said. "Try me."

"No," LeComte said, seeing that mad steel in Barbarossa's blue eyes. "No . . . he's a lunatic. Vietnam Joe."

Barbarossa caught the bartender crouching over a telephone.

"Get the fuck away from that phone," he said, and with his free hand he took out his gold shield. "Don't be scared," he shouted at the restaurant. "I'm a police officer having a chat with the FBI."

Monica started to mumble. "He is a lunatic."

"I haven't recovered from my jet lag," Barbarossa said. "I have itchy fingers."

"What do you want?"

"Your life, Frederic. Only your life."

"A comedian," LeComte said, with a twitch between his eyes while Monica went for her gun. Barbarossa struck her temple with the flat of his hand. Her eyes wandered slowly and she fell off the chair and lay in her own darkness.

"I don't like ninjas," Barbarossa said.

"You'll suffer," LeComte said. "You'll suffer, I swear."

"Frederic, give me one reason why I shouldn't whack you."

"I'm with Justice," LeComte said. "I . . ."

"You're a rat handler . . . you don't do drugs, but you live off the profits of your dealers. Frederic, count to three."

"I won't," LeComte said.

"Count to three."

LeComte's nose started to leak.

"Frederic, I'm your personal demon. Montezuma's Man. I'll crawl into bed with you. I'll put out your lights. Wherever you go, I'll be there with my Glock . . . are you gonna do your demon one small favor?"

"Yes," he said. "Yes."

"You'll let go of Margaret, you'll give her up."

"Yes."

"And if you lie, Frederic, I'll be there every fucking day of the week. You'll have blood shooting out of your ears."

Barbarossa walked out of the Half Moon while the customers sat like stone, their eyes fixed on Barbarossa's disappearing back. His hand trembled under the white glove. He rode uptown to Schiller's, sat behind his pingpong table, like Chief Joseph in his tent, another narrowed warrior. His pager began to sing. He tossed it into Schiller's back room. He sat.

Two figures floated toward him. The boss and a blondie with curls in her hair, Marilyn the Wild. Barbarossa felt bumps all over his body, like a rash of love.

"Joey, where you been?" Isaac asked.

He muttered a single word. *Marilyn.*

37

S idel was father of the bride. He could have hired a hall, but
Her Honor would have felt slighted. She'd risen out of her
rocking chair for the prospect of a wedding in the Green Room
at Gracie Mansion. She had all the powers of a magistrate, a
justice of the peace. Cardinal Jim couldn't marry the bride and
groom. Marilyn had a Catholic mom, the Countess Kathleen,
but the girl was a bit of an atheist. Jim would only come as a
guest. Rebecca had to preside over the ceremony. Her staff had
prepared a lavender gown for her. She'd begun to exercise in
the attic. The Party chiefs were a little worried about this new
robustness. She'd lost her gray complexion. She might enter the
primaries and collect all the sympathy of an abandoned mayor.
They were careful around Rebecca Karp. She'd become a person,
not a shadow on a porch.

"Your Honor," said Saturnino Gomez, Manhattan Party boss.
"We'll all bow to your wishes. Isaac can still step aside."

"You cocksuckers," she said, "You buried me months ago.
Sidel is my candidate."

And the chiefs suddenly had someone to fear: their own un-
electable mayor. She seemed much more independent of Mario.

She would caucus privately with Sidel. An hour before the wedding, they were seen together, Sidel and Becky Karp. "They're vipers," she said. "Those Party people."

"Means nothing," Isaac said. "I'll have you at Gracie as a permanent guest."

But he was troubled. Sweets had arrived with Barbarossa's fucking nemesis, Wig, who couldn't stop grinning. Isaac had to pull Sweets into a corner.

"I didn't invite Wig to my daughter's wedding. What's he doing here? I suspended him."

"I put Wig back on the payroll," Sweets said. "He's a terrific cop."

"And a member of the Purple Gang."

"That's a myth," Sweets said. "I haven't seen one Purple in Harlem, and neither have you."

"But I didn't invite him," Isaac had to say again.

"He's my driver," Sweets said. "We can both disappear if you like."

"Come on," Isaac said. "You're the Commish."

"Acting Commish."

But Isaac was shoved into a sea of guests. He was the patriarch, the king. Reporters had crashed the ceremony. They curled up to Isaac, who had to bang at them with his elbows. He was mournful on Marilyn's wedding day. Margaret had fled Isaac's apartment without a note. She hadn't left the simplest sign of herself, not a single bracelet. And he was spooked by the apparition of Barbarossa's death. He could imagine Joe lying in a box, like Blue Eyes . . . and Sweets had to bring Wig to the wedding party.

Isaac delivered club sodas to his guests. The cardinal nudged him from underneath his cape.

"You're no politician, boyo. I'll eat you alive."

Jim's Manhattan Knights had destroyed the Delancey Giants, and the cardinal reigned in his powerhouse, St. Patrick's Cathedral. He gathered strength year after year. No mayor could compete with a cardinal's flock.

"Sonny, I'll give you my list."

"What list?" Isaac asked, like a boy inside the confessional.

"Of Catholics in your administration."

"Jim, I'm not going to appoint by race or religion."

"Jaysus," Jim said. "I won't have to eat you up. You'll fall like Humpty Dumpty. Are you deaf, dumb, and blind? New York *is* race and religion. I won't have an antichrist at Gracie Mansion."

"You're bullying me, Jim."

"Indeed. And you'll learn to live with it . . . but she's a lovely girl, that daughter of yours. Even if she was raised by the antichrist."

"I didn't raise her," Isaac said. "She raised herself."

But the cardinal had already gone off to politick with some clan. Isaac discovered two teenaged boys. They were wearing ragged suits that could have come out of a barrel on the Lower East Side. God, they were his very own nephews. What were their names? Michael . . . Michael and Davey. He was growing sly as a candidate. He fed them ham and cheese and the enormous hill of a rye bread. He'd forgotten all about their mom, Selma Sidel, who'd dragged Isaac's own little brother Leo through alimony court and sat him down in civil jail.

The king was a very distant uncle. He should have been kinder to Michael and Davey, more attentive. But he was falling into the land of amnesia. It wasn't a good omen. The town would have a king who'd disremember his own deputies the minute after he appointed them.

The chatelaine, Aurora Dove, flirted with Isaac. He growled at her. "Dove, you don't have to perform . . . I'm not gonna fire you."

He had an awful premonition that Barbarossa wouldn't survive his own wedding. Isaac would have to single out every fucking character with a gun. But the house was full of policemen. He couldn't frisk them all. His shoulders began to shake. He'd start to blubber soon. The king was a crybaby.

He bumped into Leo Sidel.

"Isaac, what's wrong?"

"Ah, Leo. I'm thinking about short pants."

"Whose?" Leo asked. "Yours or mine?"

"I didn't take care of you, Leo. I turned you into a hood."

"Isaac, control yourself. You'll embarrass your own daughter . . . I wasn't a hood. Did I hurt anyone? I hopped across a line of policemen with ration stamps in my pocket."

"Stolen stamps," Isaac had to say, defending his own crimes.

"Isaac, it was two or three wars ago. Think about something else."

But Isaac couldn't. And then a bald woman arrived at the wedding party. No, she wasn't bald. She had gray hair cropped close to her skull. It was Margaret Tolstoy without the camouflage of a wig. The whole congregation of guests turned to look. There was a mosaic of silence in the Green Room. She had the startling beauty of a woman who'd just stepped out of her own crystalline world.

And now Leo was blubbering. "Anastasia," he said. He'd been in love with the schoolgirl all his life. Isaac shouldn't have mentioned short pants. Hadn't he followed Anastasia home from school, adored her furtively while Isaac squeezed her hand? Whatever women he'd had were only reflections of Anastasia, pale counterparts. He'd go to sleep with images of Anastasia, yet he hadn't pronounced her name in forty years. It wasn't fair. Her absence had defined Leo Sidel.

"Anastasia, do you remember me?"

"Little Leo," she said. "Mr. Short Pants."

"The same. I never quite outgrew my knickers."

"You're monopolizing her," Isaac said, leading Anastasia away from little Leo. He wanted to stop the party, chase out all the guests.

"I won't move into this mansion without you . . . I'll live in the streets."

"The voters will love their vagabond king."

"I'm not a king," he said.

She kissed him, and Isaac was quiet. A door opened. Barbarossa, Marilyn, and Roz emerged from a conference room with that justice of the peace, Rebecca Karp. The bride wore earthly colors, red and brown. She wouldn't wear white at her tenth wedding. Marilyn had spent the morning doing Roz's hair. Roz had never seen her brother get married.

Larry Quinn, chief of the mayor's detail, whispered in Isaac's ear, and Isaac had to leave the wedding party. He climbed up the stairs to Montezuma's bedroom, knocked on the door, and announced himself. Two members of the detail let him in. The Sicilian Aztec was furious. He was sitting in his pajamas, like a rat under house arrest.

"I'm not supposed to be a prisoner, Signore Sidel."

"I can't invite you to my daughter's wedding. That would be obscene. You've been trying to get Barbarosaa killed. And don't bother calling LeComte. All of the mayor's lines are bugged. Cavaliere, you have no future outside this room."

And Isaac strode downstairs to the wedding. He panicked. Anastasia was gone. He looked all over for that closely cropped head of gray hair. His fucking heart sank. But her skull emerged from a trinity of people. She was standing with Marilyn and Joe and Joe's suicidal sister. Roz.

A ghost in pajamas whisked around him with its own brute force. Montezuma had gotten past his guards. He was clutching a black object. God, Isaac groaned in his confusion and screamed at Joe. "Blue Eyes, watch out."

And he jumped on top of Montezuma, wrestled with him on the mayor's carpeted floor. The mansion grew into a forest of guns. Wig and Sweets and Margaret Tolstoy and Barbarossa and

Larry Quinn were aiming their Glocks at Montezuma's eyes. The cardinal was clutching a lamp.

"Mamma," Montezuma said, "I just wanted to give something to the bride."

He'd carved a little wooden dog for Marilyn, painted it with black shoe polish. Now Isaac had to let that son of a bitch into the party. Montezuma was one more wedding guest.

But the wedding had stalled until Rebecca Karp strolled across the Green Room in her lavender gown, a mayor without her rocking chair, and glowered at the Glocks. It was *her* mansion. "Put the guns away . . . you cocksuckers, I have a girl to marry," she said to the cardinal and all the other guests.